CLARA

CLARA

an historical novel of an Ontario town 1879-1930

by

PAT MATTAINI MESTERN

Back Door Press

Second Printing, 1982

Published by The Backdoor Press,
P.O. Box 182, Guelph, Ontario N1H 6J9

Designed and printed at Ampersand Printing, Guelph, Ontario.
Typesetting is by Erin Graphics Inc., Erin, Ontario.

Some photographs in this book have been provided by
The Wellington County Museum, R.R.1, Fergus, Ontario.

The front cover drawing, "Memories", is by Brian Lowry of Guelph.

ISBN 0-88939-000-2

Dedicated to my Mother, Edith Scott Mattaini,
and to my Husband, Ted Mestern.

T his is the story of my town, my family and my home. It is also the story of Clara Isabella Young, her family and her home. I firmly believe people leave something of themselves in the homes they have loved and lived in. Now both Clara and I share the house she loved. I in the present and Clara in the past. Clara's home is only one of many links we share. The friendship between my grandparents and Clara spanned four decades and only diminished with Clara's death in 1930. My grandmother, Marie Mattaini and Clara Young were both sensitive, warm-hearted women. When we purchased Clara's 'Stonehome' in 1965 we completed an intricate chain of events linking the past to the present. With every day we live in the town, Fergus seems to draw nourishment from its strong Scottish roots buried deep in the limestone ridge it sits on, and we add other links to the chain, thus ensuring our children of stepping stones to the future.

Clara's 'Stonehome' has proved to be a gentle master for us, as it was for her. It surrounds us with security, its thick walls silencing the winter wind and cooling the summer sun. Sometimes in the dead of a cold winter's night 'Stonehome' snaps and cracks her beams in defiance of the temperature outside and if you listen carefully you can sometimes imagine voices are moaning around the eaves. My Grandmother, knowing Clara, used to say "It's her coming back for a visit".

As I searched through old newspapers and letters and listened to the stories of the older residents of the Town, the personalities of the people in my book became very tangible and three dimensional to me. My wish to you is that these people become far more than names on a page for you. As you read through the vignettes I am sure you will feel the pride, the pain and the pleasure they experienced during their lives. They are really all very special people.

Thank you to my husband Ted and to my mother Edith (Scott) Mattaini for their support, patience and encouragement.

If any mistakes in dates and events have been made, I apologize. I have tried to make the book as historically factual as possible but history is obscured by time and records are only as accurate as the mind of the person keeping them.

1. 'Stonehome' (built 1879)
2. Young's home from 1851 to 1879.
3. Templin Carriage Works (built 1868)
4. Dr. Groves Block
5. Royal Alexandra Hospital
6. Beatty Bros. Lower Shop (Original factory)
7. Charlie Mattaini's home and lumberyard (built 1906)
8. Old Melville Presbyterian Church
9. Town Hall (Drill Shed) and jail (built 1868)
10. Post Office (original site of Thomas Young's Store)
11. The Commercial Hotel
12. St. Andrew's Presbyterian Church
13. Catholic Church (built 1857)
14. Old Anglican Church site
15. Ruins of 'Westwood'
16. CNR Station
17. The road to Sootie's shanty through the Beaver Meadow
18. Miss McQueen's (Fessenden's) home (built 1870)
19. Miss Unsworth's Girls School (built 1842)
20. Dr. Groves' home (built 1890's)
21. A.D. Fordyce Jr. Library and home
22. Temperance Hall (built 1852)
23. George D. Fergusson's home
24. Anglican Church (built in 1895)
25. Tobin residence

A. Dam
B. Whirlpool
C. Washing Green and old curling area
D. Natural Bridge
E. Cave
F. Blair Street Quarry
G. Swinging Bridge
H. Gow's Kiln and Quarry
I. Stagnant Pond (known as the acid pond)
J. Club House (known as the C.P.R. cave)

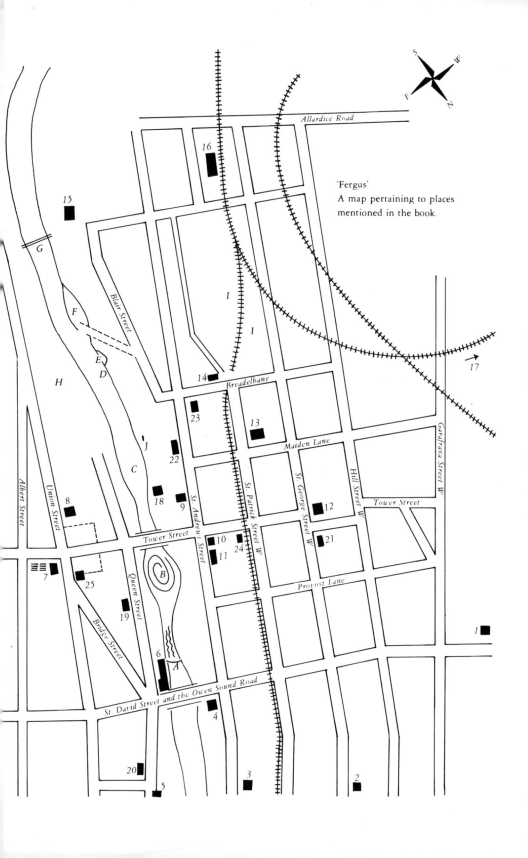

'Fergus'
A map pertaining to places
mentioned in the book.

"Stonehome"

'STONEHOME' — NOVEMBER 1879

Thomas let himself in the front doors of the house. A shaft of light from the late afternoon sun shone down the stairwell and lit the hall he stepped into. The smell of fresh paint and varnish pervaded the air and the silence was broken only by his own footsteps on the bare floor. Tomorrow when the drays would arrive with the furniture from St. George Street, he, Georgina and Clara would move in. But today he wanted to come to the empty house to be alone for awhile with his memories.

The parlour was to the left of the front door, as Mary would have wished it; the dining room to the right and the kitchen in front of him to the rear of the house. He ignored the parlour and dining room and went directly to the kitchen as though he expected Mary to be standing in front of the black iron cookstove awaiting his return from work. The kitchen had always been the heart of the home on St. George Street. Standing in this kitchen, he seemed confused and looked around the room bewildered at the sight. This was not Mary's kitchen, this riot of colour! Clara had chosen a pale yellow paint for the walls and brightly coloured rag rugs for the floor and the room reminded him of a bright summer day. It was very much like Clara! She was incorrigible and completely immune to feeling sorrow or depression. Thomas had never seen her cry, not even as a child.

He placed his coat and hat on one of the deep windowsills of the kitchen and sat on the sill of the other, looking out over the property to the rear of the house. His dream was finally a reality. He had promised Mary a home of her own thirty-seven years before, long before he lost his money on bad land investments in Luther. She'd been so understanding during those years they'd eked out an existence in Arthur and Brantford where he had been Land Agent, first for James Webster in his fledgling settlement and then working privately, finding homes and land for people coming into the community of Brantford. When they did finally return to Fergus in 1851 Mary was quite content to live in the rented quarters on St. George Street but he'd never given up his dream of a home for her. Every penny he could save went toward a home of their own. That didn't amount to much. He had four girls to raise, Georgina, Elizabeth, Louise and Clara but he managed occasionally to put 50¢ or $1.00 aside. He was a master of many occupations; school teacher, bookkeeper, artist. Always he had a dream: a house in the village he came to as a young man in 1835.

Mary was part of his dream. She'd been his fiancee for eight years before they married in 1842 but she was dead now. She was dead but his dream lived on. Georgina and Clara had helped him make it become a reality, encouraging him and contributing as much money as they could towards it. They said he deserved a home and that he needed to move from St. George Street and the memories of Mary. They said they needed a home also . . . a home that belonged to them, not one that someone else controlled.

Thomas rose from the windowsill and walked to the stairway. The dark brown oak felt smooth and cool on his hands. Mary liked oak and would have liked the stairway. Seventeen steps . . . he counted them as he walked to the second floor. The hallway was quite open and the bannister swept around the open stairwell to allow maximum light to enter from the front windows over the entryway. When Robt. Scott first proposed an enclosed stairwell, Thomas thought it a good idea. A door at the head of the stairs could then be closed to allow the upstairs to be self contained in the winter. But Clara fought tooth and nail to have the stairwell left open to allow the warm air from the lower floor to rise when the stoves were on during the cold weather. Two stoves and a fireplace heated the house in the wintertime but they were located on the main floor. Robt. Scott admitted to Thomas that Clara had a good point and the stairwell remained open.

There were four rooms on the second floor, three bed chambers and the fourth room, a sewing room for Georgina and Clara. Thomas looked into each room as he passed it. His room was painted blue. Georgina's was papered in a small patterned grey and pink paper. Clara's room and the sewing room were again a riot of colour. Reds and yellows leapt at him from both areas. They were the ultimate intrusion of his privacy. Clara's touch was everywhere in the home. He couldn't turn around that he wasn't reminded of her. It was Mary the house was to remind him of, his wife; not Clara his daughter.

Such a woman! He had absolutely no control over her actions and yet, she was devoted to him and had never done anything deliberately that would hurt him. She was like a raucous, impetuous child but she was twenty-three years of age!

He walked to the front windows. Again he had asked Robt. Scott for one large window overlooking the front walk but Clara had persuaded the contractor to add two small windows, one on either side of the hall. Her thought was that Thomas could use the hall as a library. With a small table and comfortable chair in the alcove he could sit and watch everything which took place up and down the street. Thomas himself had to admit the windows were a good idea. He stood at the larger window. Across the road and to the east a large stone building dominated the landscape. It had been a flax storage shed but recently a coffin manufacturer purchased the property and it became both his residence and business premises. To the north and beside his new house stood the stone cottage of Mrs. MacIntyre. To the south, other than the coffin manufacturer, the block was undeveloped. Below Garafraxa Street several homes and the Queen's Arms Hotel dominated the scene. If he looked out the small window facing east he could actually see right down the Owen Sound Road to the Argo Block on St. Andrews Street.

He'd purchased one quarter acre of land in the James Perry Survey in his daughter's names. Most building lots in the village proper were already taken up as new people came to the area but Clara, in her walks, had noticed these lots four streets north of St. Andrews. They were close enough to the main area that it didn't mean a long walk but far enough away they had privacy. Back of the lot a hardwood bush stretched to the Beaver Meadow. The bush was part of the James Perry Property. Possibly the only mature trees left standing near the village were in that area. Up to fifteen years ago Indians camped in the bush trading game and baskets for vegetables and trinkets. But they, like the beavers in the meadows, now shunned the larger populated areas.

By the fading light of the sun he stood back to survey the alcove. Ah yes! True Scott masonry! Robt. Scott Sr. would have been proud of his son. Neither worked from a formal diagram or plan. Thomas told Robt. Jr. what he, and his daughters had finally decided on incorporating into the house, how large he wanted it and exactly where he wanted it placed on the property. Robt. asked if a cellar was needed, measured the area and began digging. He did everything by eye. If the measurements were off a little, it made no difference to Robt. Jr. or Robt. Sr., for that matter. The building would stand solid! The wall to the right of the alcove was four inches wider than the one to the left!

Thomas chuckled and shook his head. Too bad Robt. Sr. died two years ago. He'd have been proud his son held up the family tradition! Robt. Sr. built the first log cabin in the settlement in December of 1833 for Mr. Buist (the Provost) and the first landowner in the Fergusson, Webster Model Community. He also built the first bridge over the Grand at Tower Street. Robt. Scott, Webster, the Provost, Walker, the Baker, Ferrier, Fordyce, Allan, Gartshore, the Miller, Hugh Black, Thomas Allardice and he had many a raring good time together in the early 30's. They survived fire, wheat smut and other crop failures, and fierce winters only to succumb to old age and heart failure. Of the early settlers, very few indeed would help him celebrate the achievement of his dream, his own home.

'Father. Are you here?' A voice interrupted his thoughts. 'Father?'

'I'm here child, upstairs.'

There were light footsteps on the stairs and Clara's unruly head of hair appeared on the stairwell to be followed by a slender body wrapped in a large blue cloak.

'I've been out . . . .'

'Not at that man Sootie's shanty, I hope. It's indecent for a young woman your age to go alone to a man's home!'

'No father. Let me finish.' She touched his arm gently. 'I've been out looking for you. You didn't come home for the evening meal and it's getting very late. I thought perhaps you were here and didn't want to disturb you but it is late now. I was concerned.'

'I am perfectly capable of taking care of myself!'

'Of course you are. I just thought perhaps you'd like company on the walk home. I'm sorry if I interrupted you. "Stonehome" does give one a sense of peace and security, doesn't it?'

'What did you call the house?'

' "Stonehome", father. An appropriate name for a house in a Scottish village, built by Scottish masons, wouldn't you think?'

'I'd thought perhaps a name with a connection to mother's ancestral home might be appropriate but she and you have been in Canada many years longer than in Scotland and England and she is buried in Canadian soil. She would have liked the name and she would have liked the house.'

'It should have been larger Clara. I wanted to build her a grand mansion on Union Street or Garafraxa.'

'This is what she would have wanted father. This would have been large enough for her children and granchildren. She would have told you — "a mansion is not necessarily a home". Many a log cabin where love prevailed were mansions in her eyes.'

It was difficult to see now that the sun had set so she took his arm to descend the stairs, talking all the while.

'Did you see father? They hung the oil lamp in the sewing room and I finished your curtains this morning and did you notice they have laid the carpet in the parlour?'

'I hadn't taken particular notice Clara.'

'Where might your hat and coat be father? The November wind is cold tonight.'

'On the windowsill, Clara, in the kitchen.' She went to retrieve the articles.

'Did you notice in the yard? I transplanted a rooting from the white lilac on St. George Street. A small rooting came from the tree in England where you courted mother and she brought it with her on the boat when she came to Canada to marry you. That was forty-five years ago . . . so long now. If it doesn't live I'll plant another in the spring.'

"He looked at Clara in the deep dusk of the lower hall. She was a small woman, fair of hair with a freckled countenance, so unlike his other three girls who were all tall and had the dark hair of the Barkers. It was a compassionate woman indeed who would remember to do such a small but generous deed. But he knew before a week had passed he'd be apologizing to someone for her antics! She and that man Sootie were a disgrace! The two of them with their practical jokes were the bane of his life. Was she not realizing her reputation was being ruined by her association with a thirty-four year old man? Did Sootie not realize he was ruining Clara's position in the community? He'd personally tried talking to her but his words fell on deaf ears. She might behave herself for a week or two but sooner or later she'd be in trouble again. If only Mary were here to talk to her....

'Your coat father. Shall I hold it for you?' He took the coat from her. He was no old man yet and didn't need help in dressing. Clara pulled the ample collar on her cloak up around her ears.

'Did you not wear a bonnet Clara? No self respecting woman would be seen without a bonnet!'

'I'm quite warm enough. The wind would only take my bonnet and throw it to Elora.' She had resigned herself long ago to Georgina and Thomas complaining about her dress. They'd already berated her for wearing the long voluptuous cloak. They'd said "It was so barbaric looking and not at all refined".

Thomas locked the doors behind them.

'Trees . . . Clara! We need spruce trees across the front of the property and there, along the east side to break the wind.'

'And a white picket fence father, with a gate. "Stonehome" needs a picket fence and apple trees in the back yard. It's excellent soil for a garden and they found good water quite close to the surface, when they dug the well. Tomorrow when we finally move our furniture it will be a proper home.'

The two walked along the side of the Owen Sound Road to Hill Street where they took a footpath along the manse property to St. George Street.

'You are happy, aren't you Clara? This house has . . . affected you in a very positive way.'

'I am happy father. I'm devoting myself to "Stonehome". Taking care of it, Georgina and you will be my "cause in life". I can care for "Stonehome" and carry on with dressmaking and millinery at the same time because we were farsighted enough to provide a sewing room. The house has affected you in a very positive way too father. You seem happier than you have been in some time. You are talking to me . . . nicely.'

Thomas glanced at the woman walking beside him. He could not help the way he felt towards her. She irritated him. Mary would have been so excited about her home too, if she'd lived to see it but it was now Clara's 'Stonehome'. She had stepped in where Mary should have been and he found it very annoying, although he had to grudgingly admit she was a proper housekeeper and an excellent cook.

* * *

On the same day the Youngs were moving into 'Stonehome' a solitary figure in a wagon travelled up and down the concessions and lines in West Garafraxa. Occasionally he would tether the horse, take a shovel from the wagon and dig in the brush and unplowed fields. He would crush the soil in his hands and crumble it between his fingers, repeating the procedure with each stop he made. He wasn't interested in the farmland to the south of Garafraxa. His travels had taken him through the marginal lands as far north as Luther and west to Arthur. Many long time residents of the areas shook their heads at the stranger. If he was looking for good soil he was too far north and into a heavy clay belt where the land was flat with a covering of tamarack and elm. It broke a man's will before it produced a living.

Luigi Landoni knew exactly what he wanted. He was a patient man and had searched five years already for clay of the right consistency and quantity to make a quality brick. Over those years he'd narrowed the choice of area to West Garafraxa. He'd come from Italy in 1874 to work on the Canadian Railways but was a brickmaker and builder by trade. His family in Canada, for he married a girl from Orton, and his relatives in Italy, especially Faustino, were awaiting word that a property had been purchased.

He could tell simply by the feel of the clay, what quality of brick would be produced on a large scale.

On this mild day in November with Indian summer lying softly on the land, he knew he was close to the right location. He tethered his horse to a shrub on land belonging to a Mr. J. Strong, on the 6th line. On the two one-hundred acre lots to the south of Strong's the soil yielded promising results but the quantity of the clay in proportion to loam was low. He lifted the shovel from the wagon and took a sampling of soil just inside the fence row. He walked ten feet and took another sampling; went ten feet north again and repeated the procedure. He turned east and walked twenty paces where he dug again. Each new shovelful told the story . . . rich reddish clay which, when squeezed together gently, fell in small clumps from between his fingers. He walked the entire property taking samples from all parts of the land. The 100 acre parcel met with his complete approval. Good clay deposits were right next to the 6th line where his horse was tethered but towards the back of the acreage the clay was wide spread and deep. Other areas of the farmland contained some loam and would support mixed crops for animals. He noticed a small barn and a log dwelling close to the road but no significant amount of acreage was under cultivation. As he planned on living at the site, a new larger home would have to be built, a house big enough for all his relatives.

J. Strong was just a mite curious about the stranger walking around his land, digging small holes in the ground. He'd been watching the progress of the fellow from the back window of the cabin. He finally dressed himself and went out to meet the man who was walking towards the building. The stranger extended his hand to Strong and in a thickly accented voice introduced himself.

'Luigi Landoni of Orton, Mr. Strong. I've been looking for land in the area. My apologies if I've intruded. By the look of your land you are a farmer by trade and a hard worker by nature.'

'A hard worker I might be but no man can call himself a farmer on this land. Even the acreage I've cleared doesn't support a decent crop. The winters stay too late and the frost comes early in the northern part of West Garafraxa. The land lies too close to the swamps of Luther to be productive.'

'Have you ever thought of selling? I've not enough money saved to invest in a farm to the south but I'm interested in your land. I shall be honest with you. I am no farmer but a builder by trade.'

'Come up to the cabin and we'll talk. My wife will say you're an angel sent from heaven. She's been wanting out of this God forsaken area for years. I can't say I'd miss the place either if I sold.'

Luigi took a last look over the fields before he ducked his head to enter the cabin door. All he could envision were men making quantities of deep red brick which would be sold to the farmers in the area. They would soon be prosperous enough to replace their log and frame houses with brick structures. The closest workable limestone ridge was just outside of Fergus on the river opposite Blackburn's, twelve miles away and no one would consider hauling stone that far for building purposes. They couldn't afford the cost. Brick, on the other hand, would sell cheaply, perhaps 1,000 for $6.00.

The sun was setting when Luigi walked to his rig, guarantee of sale in his hand. A price was agreed upon and a deal was made. As soon as the money and papers were properly handled the property was his.

Mr. & Mrs. Strong stood by their window watching the wagon retreat down the road.

'The poor man. You tried to warn him the soil was useless for farming but he wouldn't listen. I feel I've cheated him in some way. We've never been able to sustain ourselves here. How can he possibly? He doesn't even understand English properly.'

'Aye wife. He's not a farmer. He's thinking of more than farming for this land and he's welcome to it. Nothing we could do here would pay for itself. He might have luck on his side. Let's not worry about it. Tomorrow we'll hitch the horse and look for a house in the village of Douglas.'

'SOOTIE' — NOVEMBER 1879

To the west of 'Stonehome' and on the northern edge of the beaver meadow a small shanty nestled into the tall cedars. Several large maple trees, saved by some miraculous feat from the settlers' axes, gave shelter from the heat of the summer. A clump of large white birch stood by the door supporting a number of nails where tools, washbasins and odd pieces of clothing could be found hanging. In the winter they were replaced with snowshoes and traps. Away from the shanty and to the left a forlorn building stood which once served as chicken coop and stable.

The tall figure with his load of wood, bending to avoid the frame of the door, needed no horse. He walked everywhere. Neither did he need to raise chickens. The ladies in the village were only too eager to trade butter, eggs and cheese for fresh killed rabbit, partridge and goose. For an exceptionally fleshy rabbit, the butcher could easily be persuaded to part with a rasher of bacon or a small roast of mutton. He worked hard, when in the village, at any job he was asked to do. Often he walked the roads and paths of the counties to the north and west of Wellington and everywhere he went people knew and respected him. He never lacked a place to lay his head and never went hungry. He asked few questions and expected few to be directed at him.

With a backward kick to the door, it shut, catching on its latch. He walked to the cookstove and rolled the wood off his arms into a box behind it. The light from a single oil lamp on a table penetrated to the four corners of the small dwelling, which despite its ramshackle appearance outside, was quite homely and clean inside. The walls were whitewashed and spotless. A rough pine cupboard dominated one wall to the right of the door, holding pots, pans, crocks, bags of food, extra dishes and books. In fact one section of the shelving held nothing but books, periodicals and newspapers. Considering the man was a bachelor the cupboard and shelves were remarkably tidy. A table and three chairs dominated the main area of the shanty and were directly in front of the cookstove. Rugs covered the rough plank floor. A waist high plank bench held wash basin, pitchers and personal effects. A window and mirror shared the wall above the bench and towels hung underneath from a small rope line. A comfortable rocking chair was pulled up next to the stove with a small table beside it. A heavy, brilliantly coloured curtain discreetly hid a bed built into the opposite wall of the shanty to the cupboard. An oak washstand stood by this sleeping area holding more books, writing supplies, and tucked into a prominent corner facing the bed, a picture of Clara Isabella Young. Pegs in the wall held pieces of clothing and, a large wooden chest, under a second window, held extra blankets and good clothing.

The man himself was as tidy and clean looking as his residence. He fed the stove small pieces of kindling and pulled a fry pan to the front, over the heat. Walking to the cupboard he lifted the lid of a crock and extracted a large slab of fatted pork. He scraped the fat from an end of the slab, cut a thick slice and threw it into the hot pan where it sizzled and spattered until he added a splash of water. He turned the pork steak once, clamped a lid on the pan and pushed it to the rear of the stove where it would simmer slowly until he'd finished the rest of his meal. He busied himself with mixing a batch of scones, reaching between shelves and table. A griddle was pulled to the front of the stove, fatted and the unbaked scones were placed on the hot iron utensil. Within fifteen minutes he was seated at the table, fork in hand, having his noonday meal, his back to the door and windows.

Long before the knock came at the door, he knew Thomas Cruzon Allardice was approaching the shanty.

'Come in Cruz,' he shouted.

A figure burst through the door. 'Sootie, for the life of me, I don't know how you know I'm approaching your door if your back's to it. I've even tried to sneak up on you and you catch me every time.'

'It's your peculiar walk, Cruz. But you're in a rush today. Where's the problem?'

'One of the brindle milk cows has gotten herself into the quickmire. You're the only one that knows the swamp. We're all afraid to step in for fear we sink with her. If we can get ropes around her, the oxen might pull her free. Can you come?'

Sootie was up off his chair long before Thomas C. Allardice had finished his breathless speech. The quickmire was merciless, sucking its victim to a suffocating death in its oozing grasp. He was shouting to Thomas to bring a wide plank from his pile as he himself grabbed one and ran down the forest path outdistancing the older man in short order.

Thomas Cruz Allardice grabbed a plank and puffed along the path in the wake of the fleet-footed Sootie. There was no one he'd rather have as a neighbour but this versatile young man who seemed to be able to handle any situation. If Sootie couldn't save the cow, no one could.

James Anderson and Cruz's hired man Sam Woods were standing back from the edge of the quickmire with Sam at the head of the yoke of oxen. The cow was up to her belly in the black ooze and bawling pathetically.

'She's really in this time Sootie.'

"How'd she get across the concession road?'

'The dogs snapped at her heels and she took off. We all figured she'd hightail it back to the barn come milking time but James here heard her bawling and found her in the mire. He ran for us and Sam hitched the oxen while I ran for you.'

'Well we haven't much time, especially if she starts to toss her head around.'

Sootie circled the large area of quickmire testing the ground cautiously as he placed each foot down. The rise and fall of the water table changed the consistency and area of the mire from month to month.

'It couldn't be a worse time for her to be in there with all the rain we've had.'

He continued his slow and deliberate cat-step, feeling the soft earth through his mocassins. On the north side of the mire he retraced his steps several times, each time moving a little closer to the oozing mass.

'Over here! Quick bring the planks and ropes. Take the oxen in a wide circle around the mire and come in behind me. Be careful or we'll have three animals mired! Lead them up behind me slowly and stop when you feel the ground move under your feet. Cruz. You command the oxen. Make them heed! No wandering left or right. Bring them straight in.'

Anderson and Woods gave the quickmire wide berth and came up beside Sootie with the planks and ropes. Cruz and the oxen moved carefully and methodically around trees and stumps, brush crashing before them as the team manouevred itself behind Sootie.

'I'm going to have to work fast and rely on you men to be quick of action once I get the rope around her body. We'll choke her if we try pulling her out of the ooze with the rope around her neck at the moment. It would have been easier for me if you hadn't dehorned her Cruz.'

By now Cruz had brought the oxen around but had stopped fifteen feet behind Sootie.

'How'd I know she would mire herself. I can't come any closer. The ground's moving like calves' foot jelly!'

'Can you turn the oxen and back them off a bit? They're going to have to pull steadily once they're tied onto the rope. Don't let them stop because she'll only settle in deeper. Once she's moving her feet should begin to feel more solid ground and she can help herself. This area of the mire has the least water saturation and there's a heavy clay bank a couple of feet below the surface. It should hold until we get her free. Once I'm lying on the planks we have a matter of minutes until they begin to sink and me with them. James! You hold my feet. When I've thrown the rope pull me back quickly. I'm not about to end my life face down in this mire! Sam. You be ready to grab the rope when I throw it to you. Don't miss and don't walk forward to get it or you'll be up to your knees in seconds. Take the rope back to Cruz. Are you all ready? Cruz? Have you got the oxen turned?'

'I'm ready.'

Tension showed on the faces of James and Sam as Sootie moved quickly laying the long planks side by side on top of the black ooze. He bent to his haunches, grabbed the long coiled rope and deftly lowered himself until he was stretched full length on his belly on the boards. He spread his weight as evenly as possible over the two planks, having several feet to work with. James grabbed Sootie's ankles. The added weight on the planks caused them to sink slowly into the mire. Sootie raised himself using his powerful trunk muscles to hold his chest off the planks and free his arms. He adjusted the rope and swung it in a circle once above his head. With a flick of his wrist the rope then sailed in a carefully executed move over the body encircling her from rump to head. He pulled tight on the rope snugging the loop and knot up on her shoulders.

'Now Sam!' He tossed his end of the rope back to Sam and James hauled him mightily by the ankles up the planks to safety. Sam caught the rope and Cruz was already attaching it to the yoke of the oxen. Sootie and James raced up to the pair.

'This rope had better be heavy enough or you can wish your brindle cow a fond farewell. Are the oxen ready?'

The brindle cow was bawling continuously but not threshing around.

'As soon as she's close enough to the edge to feel the clay under her feet we'll throw the other rope around her neck and give a pull there too. Remember! Keep the oxen moving!'

Thomas C. spoke quietly to the two huge animals and they leaned into their neck yoke. The rope tightened as they moved ahead slowly. As soon as the slack was taken up the actual stress on the rope became apparent.

'Keep them moving Cruz.'

Cruz whistled and chucked to the beasts who inched their way forward, their hooves slipping in the soft earth.

'Is she moving?'

The rope resembled a tightly drawn violin string.

'Not yet. Pray the rope holds and keep those beasts leaning into the yoke.'

A sucking sound came from the quickmire as the rope put pressure against the rump end of the cow and she began to move slowly, like a heavily laden ship, through the ooze.

'Keep talking Cruz! She's coming!'

Inch by inch the cow was dragged through the mire as the obedient oxen threw their brute strength into the task, Cruz encouraging them in gentle whistles and words.

'She's nearly at the clay. Give me the second rope.'

Sootie walked to the edge of the mire, swinging the rope above his head. He arched it beautifully out over the ooze where it fell over the head of the cow and slid down her neck. Sensing a more solid base under the feet, the cow began to heave herself around. Sootie ran to the oxen with the end of the second rope pulling it taut and tying it into the yoke.

'Don't let them lax up now or we'll lose the first rope. She's threshing around. Give it one good pull.'

The sucking grasping ooze reluctantly gave up its victim as the stick came sharply down on the backs of the oxen.

'I don't like hitting them Sootie.'

'I understand Cruz.'

The closer to the edge she was dragged the firmer the footing under the quickmire became, the clay holding just enough to give her a solid footing. The ooze was like thick pea soup at the edge of the pit. The stick came down on the back of the oxen again and they gave a final heave against the yoke.

'Don't hit them again Cruz! She's free!' The cow staggered to a firm area by some elder bushes and Cruz commanded the oxen to ease off the ropes. Sam let off an ear piercing whoop and James slapped Sootie on the back.

'She's going to have a mighty sore rump and neck for the next week but if she gets a good warm wash it would ease the pain from the rope burns and remove the muck. Why don't you lead her back to the shanty and I'll tend to her? I've some sulphur salve for the burns. Come on up to the shanty all of you, the coffee won't take a moment to heat up and I think we all need a drink.'

Cruz and James fell behind to lead the plodding oxen and the weak cow. Sam had been hired man at Allardice's for only a short time and he cautiously followed behind Sootie down the path imagining he would be swallowed in seconds if he deviated from the beaten track.

'You live in a dangerous area!'

'Only if you don't watch where you're going. It sure eliminates intruders round my shanty.'

'Is there much of this quickmire around the area?'

'Yep. That pit is the only one I know that's bottomless. It's continually being fed by ground water making it a slurry of clay and sand. It probably does have a bottom but I'm not about to find it. There must be a spring down there somewhere too that keeps the mire in a continuous liquid state. You saw how fast the planks sank and you couldn't begin to remove them. They were like a fly in molasses. The harder you pulled the faster they sank. I lose a lot of good planks! Take heed! If you ever visit me come in by a beaten path.'

'Why do you live out here anyway?'

'I like my privacy. It's a challenge. First year I moved out I buried a pork barrel by the shanty for the winter figuring my meat supply would keep for the duration in the coolness of the earth. Went out to fill it with a haunch of venison one day and couldn't find hide nor hair of the barrel. I dug all around the area figuring I'd forgotten exactly where I buried it. Darn pork barrel hasn't shown up yet and that was nearly fifteen years ago. Probably someone on the other side of the earth is wondering right this very moment what is coming up through their hut. I learned my lesson about burying things! A farmer friend up the Allardice road further has been filling a "mire pit" since he came in 35. He tossed everything in it including rocks, stumps, brush, dead animals and some of the neighbours odds and ends too. His son is still heaving garbage into the darn pit! And, you know what, nary a dent has been made to fill it.'

'If the land is so sour why did any of the settlers choose to buy in this part of Upper Nichol?'

'It's good loam soil except for the swampy areas. Actually the best farm land there is. Someday they'll find a way to drain the swamps and you'll see crops will grow right where that darn brindle cow nearly did herself in today.'

'Well, I've never seen such a swamp before.'

'I have! The Beverley in Puslinch. We don't have the rattlesnakes up here that live in the Beverley. A few years ago three men robbed a store in Puslinch and took off into the Beverley with what money the storekeeper had. Obviously they weren't from the area and the locals just sat back and waited. The farmers round the swamp set up a 'swamp watch'. Two days later one of the fellows staggered out the west end swollen crazy with bites. The other two just disappeared into the ooze. Nine months after the robbery some locals were out in a flat boat duck hunting and found the bag of money hanging in a tree.

'Another fellow figured he committed the perfect murder. He hit his wife over the head just to stun her and put her body in a grain sack. It was the dead of night so he loaded the unconscious woman into the back of a farm wagon and took the road to the Beverley figuring he would dump her into the swamp and no one would find her. He wasn't too smart! The horses were spooked by an owl that swooped down over their heads and they bolted. The wife had regained consciousness and managed to roll herself out the back of the wagon, still in the bag. Next morning farmers on their way into Galt found the woman still in the sack and bruised but alive. They followed the wagon tracks which led helter skelter off the road and right into the middle of the green slime and muck. The woman's still alive and quite well off. She married a banker second time around.'

There's been nothing like that happened around here surely?'

'Nothing serious. Young wags moved Wallace's outhouse one night around the end of October. Wallace didn't see anything wrong with the new location when he went looking for it at three in the morning. It was only fifteen feet due north of its former location and over a bit of a sink hole. He was sitting in the privy only a matter of minutes when he experienced a definite sinking feeling. He vacated the premises immediately and when he went out next morning to inspect the 'damage' found 2/3's of the privy sunk out of sight in the hole. If you look over there you'll see a privy roof sitting on the ground but still attached to the rest of the building. The bottom of the privy is resting on the bottom of the sink pit.

'Lucky Wallace didn't fall asleep in the outhouse! The man I worked for a year ago had a habit of falling asleep in his. He went out one night and didn't return to bed but his wife didn't worry too much as she figured he was asleep. She knew eventually he would wake up and find his way back to bed. Next morning when she woke up and realized he hadn't come back she investigated and found him dead as a doornail sitting up in his two holer.'

'Sam, you're going to fit in well around here. It's a good sense of humour you've got! There's the shanty. Cruz and James aren't far behind us so let's wash up quickly and get the coffee on.'

'You'll need a change of clothes. I'll wash up while you attend to yourself.'

Sam stopped at the pump just outside the door while Sootie went in for a change of clothing. He quickly went to the sleeping area and placed the picture of Clara face down on his washstand. He figured there was no need to cause talk in the village about an eligible bachelor having a picture of a charming lass right next to his bed.'

THE VISIT, FEBRUARY 1880

Thomas had settled in to read his newspaper. The wind was howling around the house but he was reasonably warm by the kitchen stove. The door to the hall was open and he had secured the doors to the parlour and dining rooms to allow the heat from the stove in the front hall to circulate through the lower floor. The bedrooms had only the benefit of the stove pipes to warm them and a cold breeze slipped down the stairwell. Georgina and Clara had long since gone to bed as was their habit on the evening of the 'local news'.

The Fergus News Record was published every Thursday. Thomas looked forward to the paper's arrival as it was really the only link he had with the 'outside world'. He was unable to travel and he read avidly every book and newspaper that came through the door. He had his daughters bring him a selection of books from the Mechanic's Institute each week. He could sit for hours on a cold winter's day reading but when the paper arrived all books were put aside. Because he wanted to read uninterrupted by any distractions the girls would retire to their rooms so that Thomas could have the kitchen table to spread his paper on and a good oil lamp to read by.

He'd just gotten into the gruesome details of the slaughter of the Donnelly's when the back door opened and Sootie came in, the snow and wind swirling in with him. Thomas looked up in surprise. He was a little annoyed as he didn't expect Sootie, but Sootie always turned up when least expected. Thomas invited him to unwrap and sit down. He knew Sootie had come down from Peel Township and would have news. Sootie pulled his boots off casually and hung his outerwear by the back door.

'Bad night Thomas. it's not fit for anyone to be out and not knowing where they're going. When I started this morning from Alma it wasn't bad but the snow closed in quickly at Cumnock. I stopped in at the British Hotel and came on down when the storm let up a bit. The last four miles I went by the fence lines.'

Sootie pulled Clara's rocking chair up to the stove, opened the oven and promptly propped his feet on the open door. He leaned back in the rocker and didn't speak for several minutes as he absorbed the warmth of the fire, his toes stinging from the cold. 'Winter's worse this year than it has been. There's a drift up the back of my shanty as high as the roof. Cutters are going right over the fences on the concession roads. Some drifts are fifteen feet high.'

'You've never felt a winter like the one of 1841,' Thomas said. 'It was nothing to be shut in the cabin for three to four days at a time. Three people froze to death ten feet from their cabin door not a mile from here. You're a fool to be out tonight Sootie.'

'I won't deny that Thomas.'

The fire crackled in the stove and the two men lapsed into silence again. Sootie closed his eyes and stretched even further into the heat.

Thomas sat quietly also, observing the man. Sootie's fine chiselled features had only made him more handsome as the years progressed. Thomas still knew very little of the man. When Sootie arrived in 1860 and presented Mary with a letter she had immediately welcomed him into their midst and destroyed the paper. She had explained to Thomas privately that her family owed Sootie a tremendous debt and she was repaying it by allowing the young man into her home. She wasn't even going to ask Thomas' permission! Sootie had certainly fit in well, picking up the manners and speech of a middle class family quickly. He was quick about everything that he did and he did everything well. Thomas viewed the boy as he might a son, for he never had a son that lived. He taught him bookkeeping and other manly pursuits. Sootie repaid the Youngs with hard work and absolute loyalty and was a companion to the four girls. Clara especially took to the charms of the stranger. Sootie spent most of his time with her filling the need in the child's life for adult companionship and instilling in the child the love of a practical joke! At first there was nothing wrong with the friendship, but gradually Clara grew away from Thomas' influence, and under Sootie's. Thomas became quite jealous of Clara's attentions to Sootie and showed his jealousy in anger to the girl. She repaid his anger with love and never complained about his outbursts. Sootie was a fun loving, mischievious character and unfortunately, in Thomas' eyes, Clara developed his love for life. They were both always in trouble and he was forever making excuses for his daughter but he never apologized for Sootie. He was fully convinced that Sootie had become 'father' to Clara and had replaced him in her affections. He finally made it quite plain that Sootie should find accomodation of his own. Sootie moved to the shanty on the north edge of the beaver meadow but he still arrived at Young's unannounced whenever he felt like it.

Watching the man beside him, Thomas had to admit that the dark haired, dusky skinned man, who had a silver tongue in his head and a knack for making money, certainly was above reproach in character. The women of the village were especially charmed by the man and had been ever since the day he arrived. Sootie's conduct was always exemplary as far as the women were concerned.

When Clara settled into 'Stonehome' and began devoting herself to the house and her dressmaking Thomas' opinion of Sootie changed a little. Perhaps he had been a bit too harsh with the man.

When Sootie began to speak he did so carefully. He knew Thomas was of volatile nature and chose his words wisely. He knew Thomas had been watching him as he relaxed and did not want to upset the man tonight. He had been in Peel Township checking the plight of the negro family which had been driven out of Fergus some fifteen years before. They took no possessions with them in their night flight from the village when their shack had been pulled down around their heads by drunken Scotsmen. They had gone to Sootie's and he took them to settle on land in Peel, giving them the money to buy their claim. They were just managing to eke a living from their land. Only three members of the original family were left as the others succumbed to scarlet fever and were buried in a separate unmarked negro cemetery in the Township. They were viewed with suspicion in Peel also. Sootie didn't mention the visit but asked instead about the curling match between Fergus and Elora.

'Ah! The curling match! It was a roaring affair from what I have heard. Elora was the winner this time. D'you remember the match seven years ago Sootie? Such a match I've never witnessed before or since. It was enough to make Webster and Allan roll over in their graves!'

Both men knew the game of November 1873 well and they settled back to reminisce.

It was the insults about Webster and Allan that started the grudge matches in the first place. It's a pity that both men died without resolving the feud. They are still remembered fondly in the villages, each to his own. Webster for Fergus and Allan for Elora.'

'It's healthy rivalry that keeps the matches alive today. That and the sharp cut of a good insult.'

'Well I remember the insults. Henderson started the fight in '73 by yelling that the curling stones belonging to Elora were made of the same material they carried around in their heads — lead. One thing led to another and a few bloody noses ensued.'

'Webster would have enjoyed the whole affair Sootie but Chas. Allan could never take a joke.'

When the feud came to such a head again it was decided the only way to settle the matter forever was to have a curling match to prove which was the better of the two communities. It was as though the integrity of the villages rested on the stones in the match. People took the game very seriously indeed, almost as seriously as their drinking.

'Word spread quickly about the match and all eyes were on the beaver meadow, the official curling rink of the village. The match would take place when the meadow froze. Fergus was chosen as the site, the villagers of Elora thinking of all the free whiskey flowing that they didn't personally have to dispense. When the beaver population moved out years before, the villagers constructed a dam to hold back enough water to make a decent rink. The washing green was now unsuitable because in past years waste from the mills had fouled the river to the point where it often didn't freeze until January. With settlement on the upper Grand taking place rapidly the river water began showing signs of overuse and misuse.

'When the word went out that the ice had been tested and was safe, the match was called for the next Saturday, being the last Saturday in November.

'Because this day was not to be taken lightly, the village began to fill early as supporters from neighbouring communities began to arrive. Everyone from Elora who could walk must have come. The stores and taverns on St. Andrews Street did a roaring business. Local taverns hauled barrels of whiskey to the meadow and several hours before the match the ladies began to arrive with chairs which they set around small fires built on the ice to warm their feet. At the appropriate time all the team members and anyone else who wanted to join in were led by the skirl of the pipes to the meadow. The whiskey having flowed freely on St. Andrews Street made the twist to the kilts just a little more pronounced. None of the competitors, being true Scots, would be caught without a kilt! It might be the dead of winter but tradition had to be upheld.

'The lines were drawn up and stones were placed to the side of the rink area. The curling stones of the 1830's were wooden, but these were the best granite rocks that could be had! Rounds of toasts were proposed and the first throw was given to Elora, as a gesture of goodwill. Fergus was favoured but both villages had an equal number of supporters, each to cheer his own team, of course.'

'Do you remember, Thomas, when Fergus was winning, Elora took over the whiskey barrels and vice versa.'

'It wasn't the whiskey as much as the bets that were being made among the blades and the flirting of the women; shameful!'

Sootie remembered the flirting as he'd had his share. It did something to a man's ego to have a woman flirt with him. All men enjoyed it. Looking at Thomas tonight sitting beside him, Sootie revised that. Most men enjoyed a woman's flirtations.

'It was the crowd. They were too loud. You couldn't hear a thing over the shouting. D'you remember the final throw, Sootie?'

'Aye, Stewart's!'

As Stewart of Fergus stepped up for his throw, the crowd of spectators moved closer to get a better look at the play. The game had been see-sawing back and forth between the villages and the final outcome would rest on Stewart's rock. Stewart backed off several paces, hestitated, moved forward with the grace of a ballet dancer, kilt swirling round his knees and threw his stone. He bent into the throw gracefully and held his position long after the stone left his hand. There was a sustained silence, then a steady murmur getting louder as the rock manouevred down the ice. The sweeps leapt to the fore flailing the air with their brooms, slithering down the ice with the stone. The crowd hushed again as the stone flew right and true to its target. A roar of approval went up from the Fergus supporters.

The second before the hit, a cracking sound rent the air. Curlers, spectators, stones and whiskey barrels sank slowly into two and one-half feet of cold icy water. Stewart, still in his stance, felt cold icy water creeping past his bare knees. 'Ye Gods' says he, probably thinking like a good Scotsman about what was under his kilt! He leapt a good two feet into the air aiming for dry land. Wm. Black just stood there, a pained look on his face as the water reached for his belly button.

The Washing Green and Curling Flat on the Grand River west of the Tower Street Bridge.

Curling on the 'Washing Green', Fergus.

The ladies made their own way to shore with their sodden skirts pulled well above their knees, showing a good bit of underwear and leg. In a situation like this there was no chivalry. It was every man for himself. They had more to protect! Someone yelled to save the whiskey. A number of hardy souls who couldn't feel the cold anyway for the amount of alcohol in their blood rolled the barrels through the water to shore.

'Did you see the look on Stewart's face as the icy water crept past his knees, true Scotsman that he was?"

'No, I was helping Georgina and Clara out of the water. They were drenched to the skin. Their clothing acted as a wick and by the time they got back here water was up to their waists.'

'No harm was done. Remember, they all went back to the Wellington and the fight started all over again when some fool made the remark that the Elora stones sank pretty fast, proving they were indeed made of lead.'

Sootie got up to feed the fire and pulled the tea kettle to the front of the stove. He asked Thomas' permission to make a pot of tea for them and, having gotten an affirmative answer, set about looking for tea , sugar, milk and cups. Thomas directed him to a tin with some scones and jam. While the kettle was boiling Sootie pulled some papers from his pocket. He had carried out some business transactions for Thomas while in Drayton and Glen Allan. Thomas trusted Sootie with money matters as the man certainly had a nose for moneymaking ventures and never invested unless he was sure of success.

Business wasn't on Sootie's mind tonight. He had not come to talk financial matters to Thomas. Over the cup of tea he got down to the gist of his visit.

'Thomas, I did not come tonight to talk sport or finance. I have a question to ask you which is of profound importance to me. I have been a loner now for thirty five years. I am not a lonely man but think it time I shared my life with a woman. I wish to marry Clara.'

There was absolute silence. Thomas neither spoke nor moved. The wind moaned through the cracks around the back door. It and the fire crackling in the stove were the only sounds audible in the house.

Sootie continued, 'I'm asking you for your daughter Clara's hand in marriage. I love her Thomas. I have since October 1870. I realize there is an age difference. I am thirty five and Clara is twenty four but I love her. Age makes no difference when love is involved and I'm sure Clara likes me. I've not told her of my feeling towards her. I knew it right that I ask your permission first.'

Thomas rose and firmly shut the door between kitchen and lower hall, his knuckles white with rage on the doorknob. He turned, crossed to the table and smashed his fist against the boards, causing the china to dance on the surface.

'No! I tell you no! . . . You will never marry Clara . . . .'

* * *

Clara lay in bed, listening to the wind howling around the eaves of 'Stonehome'. She shivered and shrank further under the quilts. She had thought she heard Sootie's voice below but dared not venture downstairs in her nightclothes. He had been away for some time and she dearly wanted to see him but her father would not have approved. As the wind rose and fell it seemed to play tricks on her ears for she thought she heard Thomas' and Sootie's voices rising and falling also. It was impossible, for sound does not carry far in the house and Sootie was surely still in Peel. She fell asleep with the moaning of the wind in her ears.

* * *

The snow swirled and engulfed the figure as he fought his way through the beaver meadow to his shanty. The tears froze to his face. He was crying for the first time in anger and frustration over what Thomas had verbally thrown at him. If he chose to marry Clara he would do it without Thomas' permission and Clara, if she accepted, would be thrown out of 'Stonehome' and would never receive a welcome there again as long as Thomas lived. In all of Sootie's years he never knew a man to be so vindictive and nasty. He had serious thinking to do and he couldn't think properly near the woman he loved. Once at the shanty he packed quickly, taking only a few necessary items. With great difficulty he penned a note to Clara asking that she care for the shanty while he was away. He dearly wanted to write on the bottom that he loved her but he stifled the urge. He slammed the door firmly and walked into the blizzard again. He was leaving Fergus and didn't know if he would ever return. He felt so much anger that he didn't trust his actions or emotions if he stayed in the village. He knew not where he was going nor did he much care.

* * *

Thomas methodically banked the fires in the kitchen and hall stoves. He bundled himself against the wind and checked the chicken coop behind the woodshed to make sure the latch was on the door and that the chickens were safe from the fox. He looked into the storm and thought that any fool out in the blizzard on this night deserved to freeze to death. He locked all the outside doors to the house, lit a small finger lamp, blew out the kitchen lamp and retired to his room. His conscience would not let him sleep and in the early morning he unleashed so much anger on Clara that she ran to her room in tears, not knowing what she had done wrong.

CLARA ISABELLA YOUNG — 1881

Clara would be considered a beauty by anyone's standards. She was a small boned woman. Her delicate features were enhanced by a flawless complexion, a liberal sprinkling of freckles and a halo of light brown hair. She never wore the restricting corsets of her Victorian counterparts as she had no need to. Her waist was a tiny twenty inches.

She prided herself on being properly schooled in all the genteel pursuits of the time. She read avidly and was an expert needlewoman and housekeeper. Her size belied the energy she possessed. Aunt Bella Smith, who was at 'Stonehome' for a visit, constantly implored the woman to slow down.

'You're going to work yourself to death before you're thirty.'

'It's a waste of energy to sit and do nothing.'

'A woman must remember her health at all times. You should be resting each afternoon as I do. There's no need in this day and age to turn yourself into a "washerwoman". There are plenty of young immigrants and farm girls who hire themselves out to do housework. You don't have to do heavy lifting. You're a lady Clara! Look at yourself. Five years ago, I'd have said it wasn't possible. You were a scrawny girl, not even beginning to show your womanhood. But you're not going to keep yourself a desirable woman long if you insist on doing this laundry. You're ruining your hands and you'll have the build of a blacksmith if you continue to carry those heavy buckets around.'

Clara glanced at her Aunt sitting in the shade of the back kitchen.

'Bella. I have never been used to having work done for me. You married a man with money and can afford to rest while your work is being done for you. I've never held to the idea that women are fragile and must guard their health. Some women are perhaps less sturdy that others but I've not been ill a day in my life and I'm not about to hire some poor farm girl to do this for me.' She indicated the pile of clothing on the old kitchen table.

Bella, fanning herself to keep the flies away, sniffed. 'Well don't expect me to lift a finger to help you. I came for a visit and rest, not to indulge in heavy labour.'

'You sit there and tell me all the news. I'll do the work.'

Clara disappeared into the back kitchen and reappeared with a steaming bucket of water. She filled one of the copper tubs on the table and began grating soap into the hot water. Another thing her Aunt didn't approve of was Clara making her own soap.

'Tell me about Toronto! I've never been there.'

'It's not that you haven't been invited.'

'I don't like to leave father.'

'You'd fit in beautifully with the young women in the city. You have the looks to attract many a beau. There's theatre to attend and beautiful parks to enjoy. The city is an exciting place for an attractive, well mannered woman. You'd not have to lift a finger. All those in our circle of friends can afford help.'

'There must be many who can't!'

'Of course there are but not in our area of the city.'

Clara had no desire to live in Toronto and the thought of underpaid, overworked help rankled her. She changed the subject. 'Aunt Louise is well? She didn't come with you this time.'

'Fergus holds painful memories for Louise. She prefers not to come anymore.'

'I haven't heard from your children, Elizabeth and Louise either. How are they?'

'They're well. I've had so much heartache Clara. Just two of my seven children are alive. It is tragic . . . to bear children and to see them die in infancy or childbirth. I accepted the first two deaths but began to question my faith after the third and fourth. Why does He give and take away so quickly? James was so upset with me for questioning my faith he threatened to go to the minister and denounce me. The whole affair has left me with a "nervous" problem.'

'Uncle James himself hasn't been well has he?'

'He works much too hard. He says he should never have sold "Glen Lamond" to Mr. Wilson. But if he hadn't we wouldn't have moved to East Toronto and he wouldn't be so successful in brokerage and real estate.'

'If you had remained here at 'Glen Lamond' you would be doing your own laundry instead of having a servant do it for you, Auntie.'

'I sometimes wish we were still living close to the village. For all Toronto is an exciting, bustling city I miss the neighbourliness of a smaller community. That's a concession to you Clara! But I'd still not be doing my own wash.'

Clara was busy transferring buckets of rain water from the pump to the copper wash tub and two wooden rinse tubs. The legs of the old kitchen table had been cut down to make using the scrub board more comfortable for her. In the winter the laundry was done in the kitchen but as soon as the first sign of spring arrived everything was moved out to the table.

'Have you ever thought that restricting yourself by dieting and trying to achieve the fashionable look by corsetting might have had something to do with the loss of your babies?'

'Clara Isabella Young. That is not a subject to be discussed with your father sitting within earshot in the kitchen. I don't think that even warrants thought. Women wouldn't do it if they thought there was harm in it!'

'Why do you think I'm not wearing a corset Auntie. They are a danger to a woman's health. It is unnatural to pull yourself into a shape you were not meant to be! This isn't my theory, although its perfectly true. Dr. Grove insists that's what causes the deaths of some women in childbirth or the death of the baby itself, because it can't develop properly!'

'You can comment, being the size you are. It's a different matter for a larger woman to be "flattering" to men.'

'Have you ever asked the men what they like? Perhaps corsets are as revolting to men as they are to me. You don't see farm women tying themselves in every morning and they have seven or more healthy children.'

'Enough said young lady or you'll have Thomas to contend with. I'm sure he's listening.'

Clara let the subject drop. She placed white cottons in the hot tub and began to scrub each piece methodically against the washboard. When cleaned to her satisfaction she wrung the article out and put it in the first rinse tub.

'I've heard a lot about Dr. Groves recently. He doesn't seem to have the support of many of his colleagues for some of his theories. Do I know the man? Did he live in the village when I was here?'

'You left in '60. His family moved to West Garafraxa in '56 so you wouldn't remember him. He finished school in the Old Temperance Hall in '65. You will remember Matthew Anderson and George Stewart though. Matthew chose to come to the Fergus settlement in '41. He had an opportunity to explore Africa with his school chum, David Livingstone but he chose to marry and raise his family here.'

'George Stewart lived just down the street on the property he owned at the corner of St. David and St. Patrick Streets. Did you realize that Livingstone's wife Mary Moffat was a cousin to your grandmother Mary Moffat Young! That branch of the Moffat family went to Kuruman, Africa in 1810.'

'Africa has always been a fascinating country for me. I read all I can about it. The country is full of superstitions and black magic. It's frightening.'

'Surely you don't believe in such blather.'

'I certainly do! There are strange happenings, even around here, ghosts and the like.'

'Now you're talking nonsense Clara. There's no such thing as ghosts.'

'You surely remember Piper James Campbell don't you? He was a piper at the Battle of Waterloo and a friend of the George Muirs of Upper Nichol. He decided to come out to their homestead and walked all the way from Montreal, playing his pipes. He settled in the area of Cumnock after going back to Montreal for his trunks by horse and cart. When the Muirs both died he decided to go back to "Argyleshire".'

'He was a bit of an eccentric wasn't he? He believed he had to die in Scotland. He didn't trust steam locomotion and insisted on a ticket to the homeland on a sailing vessel. I recall he sold his home and moved in with Lillies at Cumnock until he could obtain a ticket on a sailing ship. But, if my memory serves me right, he died very suddenly.'

'Yes and instead of Lillies taking the passage money and shipping his body home they buried him in Belsyde Cemetery and erected a large monument over his grave. On a quiet evening you can hear bagpipes coming from Belsyde! Everyone says it started in April of '69 when Campbell was interred. They say he's piping his way to Montreal to catch the ship.'

'Have you heard the pipes?'

'Some nights they're as clear as a bell.'

'They must be coming over the hill from somewhere in Nichol. Sounds travel on a clear night.'

'That may be Bella but you can't explain the wailings heard from the old Gerrie house on Tower Street as noises coming from Nichol. He was a cooper and died in his sleep. It was in '60. There were seven children left, the oldest only 10. His wife died several years before him with the birth of the last child. The children spent a day with their dead father before they realized something was wrong. There were no relatives and the children were split up among the villagers. While they were together they were a close knit family but they all died young. They say you can hear wailing in the house every year on February 2nd. They come back to the house to mourn their father on the date of his death.'

'I suppose you've heard the wailings too.'

'I've not heard the wailing but I've seen a ghost!'

'There are no ghosts Clara.'

'As sure as I'm doing this laundry I've seen a ghost. Remember Mr. McIntyre, the soapmaker?'

'His clothing caught fire. A cauldron of fat boiled over into the fire and he was horribly burned. He died a day or two after it happened and no one could help the poor man.'

'That's right. His huge soap cauldron lay at the back of his house since '63. The people who eventually bought the house wouldn't go near it. They talked of ghosts and seeing apparitions and let the weeds grow up around the black kettle. I went by rather late one night, walking with a friend. We'd been by many times before and saw nothing. But on this particular night as plain as day in the light of the moon, there's a man, a strange grey figure, leaning over the kettle. His features weren't distinguishable but he was dressed in homespun workclothes, just like McIntyre used to wear. I can remember McIntyre because I used to watch him work. This figure just stood there bent over the kettle and as soon as we walked towards it, it vanished!'

By now Bella was at the tubs, sleeves rolled up, soiled apron around her waist, helping Clara rinse the cottons. She never could resist a good story.

'You were only five or six at the time McIntyre lived down the street from you. How can you remember him?'

'But I do. Mother got very upset when she found me over there because she knew the danger. I could only go if Sootie was with me.'

'What about this "Sootie"? Your father refuses to discuss the man.'

'We shouldn't be talking about him so close to the kitchen where father can hear us. It is a touchy subject. Bring the basket. We'll talk at the line.'

Bella lifted the heavy basket and carried it around to the side of the back kitchen. A clothesline ran the length of the property. Clara smiled to herself as she walked along empty handed.

'You hand me the laundry. I'll do the pinning. Your corsets won't allow you to reach above your head.'

'They're not that tight young lady! Now what about this fellow? We were in Toronto when he moved in with you. He seems a nice enough man. Is he still in the area?'

'He's been gone for a year and one half. I'm used to him leaving but he's never been away so long before. It was strange how he left. He would normally come to tell me he was going to be away but he didn't this time. He left a note at his shanty. I thought I heard him one night but father said he hadn't been here. There was a fierce snow storm raging that made father irritable for days.'

'Mary wrote that you and Sootie were like brother and sister. Anytime we visited he put himself out to be polite and friendly. I rather liked the fellow.'

'Our relationship is hard to explain. Father had no time for me and Sootie assumed his role. He isn't old enough to be my father and is more like an attentive brother. That's the best I can explain it Aunt Bella. I do miss him.'

'That explains a lot. Thomas stepped in as a surrogate father for us when we arrived with your mother. Sootie stepped into your life at a time when you needed a father's attentions. Possibly Thomas had had enough of raising children, what with raising we five Barkers and another four of his own. You were the last of the line. You shouldn't set your hopes on the man returning after this length of time.'

'That's the strange part Bella. I know he'll be back. He's never written to me but I know he'll come back. I've no idea where he went or why he left. I will see him again.'

'You were always full of optimism as a child and you've not changed as an adult.'

'That's the way to be Auntie. Always look to the bright side.'

'Well there must be a bright side to this laundry!'

'There is. We're finished. Let's change and go visit Steeles.'

MEMBERS OF THE '35' — 1881

Thirteen men sat around the table in the private dining room of the Wellington Hotel. From James McQueen at the head of the table they sat in order of Robt. Mitchell of Arthur, James Duguid of Upper Nichol, Alex D. Ferrier of Fergus, Thos. Young of Fergus, Thos. Valentine of London, Ontario, Alex D. Fordyce Jr. of Fergus, Thos. Allardice of Upper Nichol, David Henderson of London, Ontario, James Smith of Toronto, David Smith of Upper Nichol, "Sandy" Hutchinson of West Garafraxa and Geo. D. Fergusson of Fergus.

When James McQueen stood everyone ceased talking amongst themselves.

'Gentlemen and friends, I welcome you, the surviving members of the '35' to our 46th dinner. I am pleased to see everyone could attend and have taken the liberty of ordering brandy and glasses to be placed on the table. For those who do not partake there are pitchers of water. I have noticed with regret that we are down to twelve members.'

'Don't sound so morbid McQueen. It was entirely predictable in December of '35 that our numbers would dwindle! No one lives forever.'

McQueen nodded his head solemnly.

'True David. When we all met at Buist's on that blustery December evening we were 34 in number, all those men who came to Fergus between '33 and '35. Since 1862 we have had the pleasure of Geo. D. Fergusson's company representing his father, the man who co-founded the village and gave it his name. Welcome tonight Sir.'

Geo. D. acknowledged Mr. McQueen. 'I am only here to represent my father. I have no right to sit with such an honoured group for I did not personally settle in Fergus until 1852.'

Mr. McQueen continued, "Unfortunately there is no representation for James Webster the co-founder of the village. There are several daughters still alive but we have never allowed women to attend our dinners before and shall make this one no exception.'

'That's a pity McQueen for women do liven up the festivities.'

'Do they Davie? Do you recall the party at Todd's when Webster, Rev. Patrick Bell and Thomas Young, sitting in our midst tonight, were leaving for Scotland in '37. It was a restrained party indeed until the good Reverend removed the ladies! I recall I personally didn't arrive back home for several days.'

'It would not have hurt to have had representation from the women of the village for they stood beside us as we carved a living from the bush.' Thomas C. Allardice spoke quietly to the assembly. 'Many of us would have given up and gone back to Scotland if our womenfolk hadn't given us support and encouragement.'

Thomas Young nodded agreement.

'You speak the truth Cruz. But we are old men now and few of us have a wife left to stand by our side. Few women from '35 have survived to join us tonight either.'

Mr. McQueen broke into the discussion. 'At this time we usually "call the roll" to remember those who have gone before us. I think we should carry on with this tradition. Does everyone agree?' He looked over his glasses around the table. The twelve men nodded an agreement.

'I read now the names of the original members of the '35' and hope that as I mention their names, you will remember them in a favourable way and, if comments are to be made, they will be in keeping with the solemnity of the occasion."

'We'll try, Mr. McQueen, to restrain ourselves.'

Postmaster McQueen held a book in front of him and proceeded to read the names written therein.

'Geo. Skene, died Douglas 1864.'

"Robert Mitchell, present and in our company.'

'From Arthur and a long way to come with the wind howling the way it is. I'll be staying at the hotel for the night.'

'Are you still surveying land Robert?'

'It's a job for a younger man Thomas. The swamp in Luther finally defeated me.'

'James Duguid, present and in our company.'

A frail old man raised his glass and acknowledged his name. He had been brought to the dinner by his son and could not get around without the assistance of a sturdy arm.

'Francis Anderson, died 1875.'

'Alex Fordyce, Sr, died 1852.'

'Alex Fordyce Jr, present and in our company.'

'I am here McQueen but partaking of water only.'

'It's your preference Alex. Leaves more for those who do partake and they won't let a drop go to waste!'

'Andrew Grant, deceased.'

' "Baker" James Walker, died 1866.'

'Such a grand old man he was, a real credit to humanity.'

'He was the gentlest of gentlemen.'

'Alex D. Ferrier, present and in our company.'

'But not for long gentlemen. I'm leaving for Scotland where I'll spend my remaining years.'

'Did the winters finally beat you Alex?' James Duguid was always complaining about the winters.

'No James. I could still walk from Guelph to Fergus and back on a weekend and in the dead of winter but I'm lonesome for the homeland and I want my bones to lie in the Highland soil.'

Most of the assembled gathering knew how Alex felt.

'The old Provost, Mr. Buist, died in Scotland.'

'Jas. McLaren? Has anyone heard from Mr. McLaren?'

There was no comment from the men.

'We will presume he is deceased unless we hear otherwise.'

'James Perry, died 1860, Fergus.'

'Geo. Wilson, died Scotland, 1867.'

'Thomas Young, present and in our company.'

'I'm here McQueen, alert and well.'

'Looks like the young ladies are keeping you well fed Thomas.'

'I cannot complain.'

'Thos. Valentine, present and in our company.'

'My pleasure to be here gentlemen. It is a long train trip from London to Fergus but I wouldn't miss this dinner and the time passed pleasantly for I had companionship.'

'Do you still sail Tom?'

'Yes and I've charted some of the Lake Huron shoreline this past summer that hadn't yet been done by the Government. I sailed out of Owen Sound north to Manitoulin.'

'Living on a "yacht" is a far cry from the old bach hall at "Irvineside" of "35".'

'If I had a choice, I'd go back to "bach hall". We had some good times, all of us, at old "Irvineside". Robt. Do you recall trying to make cheese. The pigs wouldn't eat the first finished wheel. But we persisted and put the second wheel under the planks of the cabin floor to age.'

'To ripen! And ripen it did. When we lifted the plank and unwrapped the cheese it nearly walked away by itself!'

'It was the bugs in it and not the smell that caused that Robert.'

'Gentlemen, we must persist with the list.'

'Hugh Black, our old friend the Proprietor of St. Andrew's Inn, died Fergus 1855.'

'Twas not the vituals inside the Inn as much as the free barrel of whiskey Hugh would sit on the stump outside that kept men returning to the Inn.'

'He and his good wife ran a first rate Inn and were among the first in the village to build themselves a snug stone cottage, "Craigshead". In his later years he always allowed that farming was preferable to innkeeping and he also maintained pigs ate cleaner than humans.'

'Not having eaten with pigs I couldn't comment on that.'

'Thos. C. Allardice, present and in our company.'

But I'm thinking of going back to Scotland to die gentlemen, and soon.'

'You've twenty good years left in your tough hide Cruz. You'll not go back for awhile.'

'Alex Drysdale, died in Scotland.'

'Geo. Hamilton, died 1879.'

'David Henderson, present and in our company.'

'I'm here in the flesh and came up on the train from London with Thomas Valentine.'

'James Lamond Smith, present and in our company.'

'Unlike my brother-in-law David, I came by carriage from Toronto and am staying with Thomas Young. I'm pleased to have health enough to come.'

'With all three of you marrying a Barker sister; you, James and Thomas will have a good deal of reminiscing to do in the next few days.'

'Aye! When Thomas' wife Mary brought her three unmarried sisters with her to Arthur it surely played havoc with the bachelors around the Fergus setllement.'

'Geo. McHardy, deceased unless any of the gathering has heard otherwise.'

No one spoke.

'Andrew Burns, considered deceased unless he notifies us otherwise. Does anyone know where the gentleman moved to in the last year?'

All heads shook a negative answer.

'John Davidson, died 1860.'

'James Davidson, died 1860.'

'Davie Blair Fergusson, died 1855.'

'My brother was the only one of the Fergusson family to continuously live in the settlement from 1834. I represent him also on this auspicious occasion.'

'David Smith, present and in our company.'

A small man who frequently sat on a pillow to bring himself a little higher at the table raised his brandy glass in a toast to the assembly.

'I'm here. You couldn't keep me away.'

'Brandy hasn't done your size any good Davie. You haven't grown an inch since last year.'

'Height has nothing to do with quality my laddie. Smaller might be better. Consider the case of the elephant and the mouse, afore you open your mouth to speak about a man's size. The mouse can run rings around the elephant.'

'Ah but consider the consequences of the elephant eventually catching the mouse by stepping on it!'

'Eventually! The key word is eventually.'

James McQueen interrupted the conversation to change the subject. Everyone liked to tease Davie about his height.

'I can see the conversation over dinner will be a lively one tonight. Davie, does your daughter Mary still write poetry?'

Davie's eye's brightened immediately at the sound of his daughter's name.

'She does and sells it too. It now has been in newspapers from Ottawa to Toronto and has appeared in Ladies journals too in Canada and England.'

'I've read some of the poetry Davie. She's an excellent poetress. Please tell her James Lamond Smith appreciates her work.'

'Thank you Lamond, I will.'

'John Gartshore, died 1873.'

'Do you recall the cabin Gartshore housed his mill workers in. It was one large room with an immense fireplace at one end and the other end was strewn with sheets and blankets of some of the workmen. There was a loft also strewn with blankets but no table and chairs. When the workers ate they just lifted a plank in the floor and everyone sat with their legs dangling in the dugout beneath the cabin using the floor for a table.'

'It was better than Todd's cabin. He had a centre hearth with a hole in the roof to let the smoke escape. You'd sit round his hearth in the middle of his cabin and the snow would be coming down through the hole. Rain was worse! It nearly always smothered his fire. He used to keep a roaring fire on through every rainstorm, even in the hottest of weather because he hated to light a fire fresh.'

'His cabin was like the crofters' and farmers' in Scotland. They always had a central hearth with sleeping quarters built round the edge of the home.'

'Todd used to call himself a "smoked ham". I would say pickled suited him better, a "pickled ham.'

'Gentlemen, we are deviating from our list.'

'Rev. Patrick Bell, died Scotland 1869.'

'Alex Hutchinson, present and in our company.'

'James McQueen, present.'

'That is the list gentlemen with the exception of Charles Allan who wished his name stricken from our records after his defeat to James Webster for Representative on District of Wellington Council in 1842.'

'He removed himself from Fergus to live in Elora and removed himself from our records at the same time. A sore loser he was and he never relented even though we sent him an invitation every year until his death in 1859 to join our group.'

'Do we have enough brandy to proceed with the toasts and shall I order the meal to be served?'

'Another glass of brandy won't do us any harm but food in front of me now would be most welcome. My stomach is telling me I've been smelling our dinner cooking in the kitchen for the past hour. I move we proceed with our meal.'

'You were always one to enjoy food Robert. Tough scones, venison, tea and sugar were not a diet for you were they?'

'Not when I had to live on them for a winter. Bring on the victuals!'

'One more question gentlemen before we proceed with the toasts and dinner. With two of our present members seriously considering retiring to Scotland and another two having to journey from London is it worth holding a 47th dinner in '82? We are thirteen tired old men, some of us barely able to make the trip to the hotel!'

'Speak for yourself McQueen!'

'As long as there are two members to gather , we must hold the dinner. That was the pledge made at the Buists in December of '35 and all of us will vote to honour that pledge tonight. Already some of our comrades on the list have been forgotten by the villagers and we have a duty to keep their names alive. We must never forget the contribution they and we made to the Fergus settlement. It is up to us, the surviving members of the "35" to remember, until the last of us is in our grave.'

'Well said Thomas Young! It is the answer I wished to hear. But the pain of seeing our numbers dwindle drastically over the last while has been difficult to bear. We have all been the best and closest of friends.'

'Let's raise our glasses in a toast to "the members of the 35". But don't ask us to rise to the occasion. I'm being truthful when I say most of us couldn't!'

'Gentlemen! A toast and I shall not ask you to rise. I raise my glass to those "members of the 35" who have gone before us and who are reserving a place for us to join them in their new settlement.'

All glasses were raised. Davie Smith rose with great difficulty and, pulling his small frame up to its fullest height, said, "A toast gentlemen to those "members of the 35" that are present tonight to celebrate . . . that we continue to lead healthy, God fearing lives so that we will eventually join our fellow members and not travel in the opposite direction to where we assume they are not residing! To put it in layman's terms. Let us assume when the time comes we'll be off on a ship for Scotland and not end up in Australia!'

Everyone raised their glasses to Davie Smith's humorous toast. He had always been a witty, charming man.

David Henderson rose. 'A toast gentlemen! To the founders of Fergus: Adam Fergusson and James Webster, who by their dedication and courage saw a dream come true, that of establishing a settlement in Upper Canada.'

He tipped his glass to Geo. D. Fergusson who stood to acknowledge the toast.

'I accept the toast on behalf of my father and James Webster. Thank you. And now may I propose a toast?'

'To the Village of Fergus, a little bit of Scotland transplanted to Canada, so dear to the hearts of us all!'

The twelve old men rose from their seats as a body and raised their glasses high. There may have been a tear or two in an eye of the members but no one would ever admit to it.

"To Fergus!"

AUTHOR'S NOTE

Adam Fergusson was born on March 4th, 1781 at Woodhill in Perthshire Scotland. His father, being a prosperous landowner could afford to give his son an excellent education in the best institutions. During his early academic years Fergusson studied history seriously and was impressed with the manuscripts of the French Jesuit priests who travelled the wilds of Canada in the 1600's. Ultimately he chose law and was called to the Scottish Bar. He never practised law seriously as he inherited the family estate and turned his interests towards farming. Through extensive reading he set about learning all there was to know about agricultural practices. He was a founding member of the Highlands and Agricultural Society whose aim was to reform archaic farming methods. His own estate became a model of what could be achieved by the new techniques of farming.

Fergusson could never quite forget his love of history and the diary of one Father Daillon who described in detail fertile lands along a water course in Upper Canada. Fergusson believed that if he could choose the land and his settlers he could carve a successful settlement in the wilderness of Upper Canada and, by instilling in them good agricultural practises, could have them self sufficient in a short period of time. Having both the time and the money for travel he journeyed through the Upper United States and part of Canada in 1831. During his travels he was much impressed by the fertile soil of Upper Canada but didn't locate the 'Grand River' written about by Father Daillon. In 1832, back in Scotland, Fergusson published several booklets, one being called "Practical Notes Made During a Tour of Canada and a Portion of the United States". This booklet was useful in giving prospective emigrants accurate and useful information about conditions in Upper Canada.

A young man by the name of James Webster, born at Balruddery, County of Forfar, Scotland on May 28th, 1808 was quite impressed with the booklet and immediately corresponded with Adam Fergusson. A friendship developed between the two although there was a difference of 25 years in their ages. Fergusson had sons as old as Webster.

After his return to Scotland, Fergusson found his thoughts turning increasingly towards Upper Canada with the spaciousness and opportunities it offered. In early 1833 he sold his ancestral home 'Woodhill' and sailed on the 'Eagle' for Canada with his second wife and seven children. His good friend James Webster and the children's tutor, Rev. Patrick Bell, inventor of the first reaping machine, had preceded Fergusson and were already established in Niagara awaiting his arrival.

Webster had been making enquiries as to land available in Western Upper Canada and was directed to various people including Thomas Clark who at one time owned all of Nichol Township. When Fergusson had settled his large family in Niagara he and Webster travelled throughout the western part of Upper Canada looking for suitable settlement acreage. From Clark's description of Nichol, Fergusson realized he was possibly close to finding Father Daillon's 'Grand River'.

On October 5th, 1833, a party from Niagara including Webster and Fergusson made their way to Guelph by way of Dundas and the Beverley Swamp. The next evening the party reached the Gilkinson settlement of Elora. Fergusson knew when he sighted the gorge in Elora he had found the 'Grand River'. After an overnight stay in the 'Manor house' at Elora, Fergusson's party made their way along the south bank of the river to the lesser falls, three miles north-east of Elora. The soil proved to be of excellent quality and the limestone rock was close enough to the surface to provide building materials. The fall in the river was more than adequate to run mills and the forest cover would provide wood for cabins and fuel. By the end of October Fergusson and Webster had purchased approximately 7,400 acres spread along both sides of the river.

On December 20th, 1833 the first log cabin was erected and the Fergusson settlement was begun.

Adam Fergusson himself purchased 100 acres at Waterdown and had a spacious home built which he named after his ancestral home, 'Woodhill'. He only resided in Fergus one summer but he always took a great interest in the settlement. Several of his sons built in the Fergus settlement but the actual choosing of settlers, erecting of mills and directing the clearing of the land was left up to Webster who lived in Fergus until 1852 when he moved to Guelph. His death occurred on February 6th, 1869 at Guelph.

Adam Fergusson died at 'Woodhill' Waterdown on September 26, 1862.

AUGUST 1882

The front door slammed and a small body propelled itself up the stairs towards the sewing room.

'Aunt Clara! You must come quickly!'

'Adam Fordyce Barr! If you don't slow down you'll hurt yourself. What is so important that I should follow you now. So far this fine day I've rushed to see butterflies, ants and a large lumber wagon. I've got to finish this braid.'

'There's a man outside with an oxen team who wants to talk to you. He says it's important.'

'Why didn't you say so in the first place Adam. It's Thomas Allardice!' Clara put the ribbon aside quickly and flew down the stairs almost as fast as the excited child who was taking two steps at a time.

Thomas was standing at the head of the team, a patient old man who loved his prize team enough to use them long after oxen had been replaced by horse power. He was a familiar sight in Upper Nichol perched high on the seat of the ox cart.

'You're a fine sight for an old man's eyes! Has the boy been keeping you busy?'

'Adam and I are getting on nicely. He loves the fields as much as I but I have several dresses to complete before the fair so we've not been out for several days.'

'That's what I've come about. Sootie is back! He's been at his shanty for the past day. He knew I'd be coming through the village and sent a message for you.'

'I knew it Thomas! As soon as Adam said an ox cart I knew what you'd come about! Why hasn't Sootie come to the village? Is he alright?'

'The man is well. He's travelled a long way. Did you know he was in the West? He's tanned and fit as a fiddle but says he has no time to run after a woman. He told me to tell you he'll be at the shanty until Sunday then he's heading up to Minto for several days. He said you'd understand.'

'I do understand. Thanks Thomas.'

'Does the boy want a ride in the cart? I'll not be back this road today but tomorrow I'll come get him and we'll ride around the village.'

'Could I Aunt Clara?'

'Of course. It'll be an experience to tell your mother and Aunt Louise. They both know Mr. Allardice.'

The kindly old gentleman tipped his hat to Clara and laboriously climbed into the high cart.

'I'm going to have to perfect a lower cart.'

'Or you're going to have to grow longer legs.'

'There's no chance of that at my age. Until tomorrow Laddie.'

A gentle word and a touch of the stick put the oxen into motion and the cart began its slow trip up the Owen Sound Road towards home.

'I won't fall off that cart and hurt myself will I? Mother won't let me ride the mill wagons.'

'There's a big difference between a lumber dray and an oxen cart. I'm sure your mother wouldn't mind you riding with Mr. Allardice. Come along. I need an extra hand with the braid.'

The two entered the coolness of the house letting the wooden screen door slam behind them.

'Clara! Can't you keep that child quiet? I'm trying to balance the books. With all the noise I cannot begin to concentrate.'

Thomas sat at the kitchen table, his back to the front door.

'Sorry father.'

Clara put her finger to her lips and the pair ascended the stairs in absolute silence. Three layers of carpeting did help! Clara had long ago made sure no one would hear her leaving on her midnight jaunts. Once inside the sewing room Clara closed the door.

'Now we can talk?'

'Yes, Grandpa has a difficult time concentrating with noise around him. He must have absolute silence when he's doing books and he doesn't have a study or office to work in. Sometimes he uses this room but I've got these dresses to finish so he's working at the kitchen table.'

'He wasn't mad at me was he?'

'Of course not! He shares his bedroom with you doesn't he? And tells you stories. He's just concentrating on his work to-day.'

She gave Adam the roll of braid.

'You hold tight to this while I plait the ribbon. Never let the tension go. Always wind the ball slowly as I feed it to you.'

She held six ribbons, three in each hand. Deftly she formed the intricate braid, folding each ribbon over the other in a definite sequence. Adam kept the tension on the finished ball of braid.

'You're doing well.'

'I hold the skeins of wool for mother when she winds it into balls. Will you tell me a story?'

'Certainly. What will it be today. Knights and witches or Princesses and plowmen?'

'Will you tell me about grandmother?'

Clara looked at the serious expression on Adam's face.

'Why do you look so serious? And why do you wish to know about your grandmother?'

'Everytime I ask Grandpa he doesn't say anything. Mother only tells me a little and then she must run off to the baby.'

'Your grandmother wouldn't like to see such a serious expression on a young child's face. She loved to see children happy.'

'Was she a nice lady?'

'Your grandmother was an exceptional woman and a lady indeed. She was sincere, intelligent and far too generous for her own good.'

'Aunt Louise says she came to Canada on a ship many years ago because Grandpa made her promise she would marry him.'

'Grandpa didn't force her to promise anything. Grandmother Barker was a very young girl, only fifteen when grandfather came to Fergus. Before he left Scotland in 1835 they became engaged to be married. That means each promised the other they would wait to be married until Grandmother Barker could come to Canada. Her father was a fairly important artist in England but was ill. Her mother died leaving six children. Grandmother being the eldest daughter felt she must care for her father, brothers and sisters. Grandpa waited until 1842 before grandmother could join him in Canada and when she came she brought her brothers and sisters with her because her father died. Grandpa inherited a ready made family!'

'Grandpa went a long way to meet her.'

'He travelled all the way to Montreal to meet the "Souter Johnnie" on October 16, 1842. On October 18th they were married at Trinity Church, Montreal. Grandma was so tired from the voyage she could barely walk the first day on land. But other passengers were worse off than the Barker family. Cholera was rampant on board ships, on Grose Isle and on shore. All the way across the Atlantic Grandma nursed sick steerage passengers. She knew a lot about medicines and brought medicinal herbs with her, both dried and cuttings to grow in Canada. She also brought the lilac root. No one brought much with them to Canada. Many had only the clothing on their backs and a small trunk of possessions; remembrances of home, an heirloom piece of plate or silver, a heavy coat, several pair of shoes, a woven shawl, or a clock. They tried to bring some tangible reminder of the land they were leaving, trusting to God they would find security, generosity and food in their new home. When Grandpa came he brought books and art supplies for he was a scholar and not cut out for farming. That's why he opened a store and does books now for a living.'

'That's why he taught school. That's what he told me.'

'What else did he tell you?'

'He said he lived for awhile in a swamp and then in a large city before he came back to Fergus.'

'That's right. After they were married they lived in a large frame house in Arthur called "the mansion". When Arthur went into decline Father moved his family to Luther Township and he tried to farm a swamp! Of course, no one could make a living in the marsh so he moved everyone to Brantford where he sold property and worked as bookkeeper.'

'Mother, your grandmother, never complained during those moves even though she had small children. She lived in a floorless cabin in Luther where the table and chairs sank into the mud of the floor. In 1851 when father was restless again mother declared Fergus to be their final and last home. Your grandmother could be very stubborn when she wanted to be! Father didn't mind. It was to Fergus he'd come 26 years before from Scotland. He had a soft spot in his heart for the village. After they moved to Fergus mother had three more children, six in all. I was the last. The two youngest died at an early age for lack of a proper doctor in the bush.

'Mother said she lived in a large log house on St. George Street and that she left from there with my father for Lindsay after her marriage in 1871.'

'Your grandpa rented a log home on St. George Street and had an addition put on at his own expense. There were certainly happy times in that home. Your grandmother was a "doer". She could never stand by when work was to be done and she was always in demand as a midwife and nurse. Dr. Mutch used to rely on her for nursing a seriously ill patient or helping to set a fracture. I suppose her great interest in medicine stemmed from the fact she did lose her two first born children through genuine lack of medical knowledge. Mother feared nothing and could take the sight of blood better than most men. She stood a head above the other women in the village, always collecting a blanket or food for some destitute family. She had no time for frivolous societies.'

'Grandpa didn't mind her doing all this?'

'Your grandpa was proud of her. He viewed her as being equal to him in intellect and stamina and he treated her well. She lacked nothing in attention or affection. She was happy, surrounded by her family. She needed nothing more and considered herself lucky to have a husband who supported and encouraged her.'

'Why did she have to die?'

'That's a very grown up question for a young boy to be asking.'

'I want to know.'

'She died because she was so busy looking after us and trying to help everyone else in the village she didn't take care of herself. When a person works very hard they wear themselves out just like your clothing wears out if you climb too many fences in it. Her heart wore out and she died. There is nothing you can do for a worn out heart. Clothing you can mend but a human heart you cannot. Mind you, Dr. Groves claims someday, somewhere, a person will find a way to mend a heart but that has to be years into the future and we're talking about the past.'

'Can you wear yourself out holding a roll of braid?'

'I suppose a young boy could. Let's walk down to the river and just happen to stop by Mrs. Kemp's for an ice cream soda. Your Aunt Louise will be taking you back to Lindsay on Sunday and we must make sure you're well fed.'

'A capital idea Auntie.'

'Where would you hear a phrase like that?'

'From the lady next door. She uses a lot of strange words.'

'Well you shouldn't use strange words until you know what they mean. Remember, not a sound going down the stairs and we mustn't slam the front door going out. Grandpa might not approve of an ice cream soda just before dinner.'

THE HOMECOMING

Long after Adam, Thomas and Georgina were asleep Clara slipped out the front doors and walked quickly to Garafraxa Street. There was always the possibility some latecomer would see her on the Owen Sound Road but few people lived on Garafraxa Street West of St. David. She walked quickly, excited with the prospect of seeing Sootie again. Darkness held no fear for her and she walked silently as though she were part of the night. When she reached the brook she stood a moment looking east towards Hill Street. The Steele House stood where the village women used to do their wash on a bright spring day. In the moonlight Clara imagined she still heard the voices of the women and children as they soaked the heavy homespun coverlets and clothing, rank with the odours of a winter's use, in the clear fast flowing waters. The 'washing bee' took most of the day as the articles were stretched on the grassy bank of the stream to dry. Occasionally they would be turned and reshaped. Hampers of food appeared at the noon hour and everyone shared in the repast. The menfolk came just before supper to help with the task of carrying the sweet smelling wash home. One of the jobs of the children was to chase any stray dogs away from the clean, drying clothing.

She stepped across the large stones in the stream bed and began walking west, following its course to the beaver meadow. The night peepers silenced themselves as she passed close by them, only to begin again when she was safely out of their way. Her mocassined feet covered the ground quickly and gave her the ability to feel the earth beneath her feet. Sootie had given her the mocassins and taught her the feel of the swamp. Her feet were as sensitive as his to the changes in the texture of the soil.

Beyond the meadow she avoided the Allardice road but walked a narrow foot path running parallel to it through the cedar bush. Always her feet did her thinking for her and she deviated twice around small mud pits in the pathway. She stopped occasionally to listen to the night sounds around her. Cattle or deer cracked dry twigs as they grazed, an owl hooted from a tall dead pine tree and the smells of the warm summer night surrounded her. She felt sorry for the 'day people' who would never shares these senses with her.

A light shining through the forest cover caused her to pause and reflect on the situation. Sootie had obiously hung the lantern knowing she would come. How would she greet him after two and one half years? Was a handshake too formal? Yes. She decided a handshake in the middle of the night was not only too formal but quite funny. An embrace was out of the question! One did not embrace a brother unless a death had occurred in the family. She would merely say hello as though he'd been gone several days. But she certainly was curious as to where he'd been and why he hadn't ever written. She would never ask for an explanation. It was Sootie's way that he'd explain everything if he thought it necessary.

A movement in the bush drew her eyes to the right. Sootie stepped from the darkness and stood beside her.

'I thought you'd like to be walked the last few rods. It's good to see you again.'

Clara glanced quickly at the man by her side. He was as lean as ever but had a moustache and beard obscuring his features and long hair falling over his shirt collar.

'Goodness! If father saw you now he'd have a proper fit! You're looking well.'

That was it. There was no need for her to have wondered how to greet the man. He'd taken care of the situation quite tactfully by greeting her on the path.

'How long have you been watching my progress?'

'A long time Clara . . . a very long time indeed.'

One of Clara's favourite walks, Belsyde Ave., Fergus.

The high gorge cliffs below Sentinel Rock on the Grand River.

Grand River, Fergus, Ont.

"The Whirlpool" on the Grand River, Fergus.

A DROWNING — APRIL 1883

Constable Alpaugh stood on the washing green and watched as the boat made its way into the current and the men began pulling upriver to the whirlpool. When the word raced along St. Andrews Street everyone congregated on the bridge and along the bank to watch. The Constable looked with disgust on the crowd of men, women and children all waiting for the gruesome spectacle of a body being hauled to the surface. They never gave thought to what might have caused the young man's anguish in the first place that he would jump off the cliff into the whirlpool. Perhaps one of them was to blame.

Because Sootie knew the whirlpool and its currents well, the job of recovering a body from them always fell to him and he had arrived as soon as he'd been found.

'River's running high. I'll need three strong men to help. Two to oar and steady and two for the grappling hooks. The current will push the body under the cliff face if we leave it too long.'

Alpaugh's voice bounced off the cliffs as he shouted to the spectators on the bridge. "Roberts, Anderson, Henry! Down here! You've just been deputized. The rest of you, move along. It'll be no sight for children to see.'

The pool now caught the bow of the boat and it began to turn left, being gently pulled into the centre where it could spin forever with the bits and pieces of wood and other debris brought down by the April rains. There was no danger to the boat and the oarsmen corrected the turn. The spring runoff made the pool more vicious than it usually was. Sootie and Henry threw the grappling hooks over the side and the long, slow process of dragging the bottom began. The boat made its way up and above the pool, across towards the bank and as the current caught it, it was pulled back down through the pool, the oarsmen pulling out and away from the cliff before the boat hit the rockface. The circles became larger with each swing. Sootie and Henry knelt in the boat working the grappling hooks. It would have been more satisfactory to have stood but no one, save Sootie, could have survived a swim through the pool if the boat capsized.

Alpaugh sat on the bank watching the progress of the boat. He and Sootie worked well together, one complimenting the other; not so much 'the brawn and the brain' as equals. The Constable needed Sootie's intimate knowledge of the village, its inhabitants and the river. Alpaugh commanded authority in the village but Sootie seemed to command respect. He was the eyes and ears of the people. Nothing escaped his attention but he was always discreet in his dealing with the villagers and the Constable. The Constable's first real encounter with Sootie had been under entirely different circumstances. The Alpaugh family was well known in the village in the early years as they were hunters and trappers from the Grand Valley and Luther area who used to come down to sell their venison and fur. So he applied for the job of Constable when Lingwood gave it up. He had heard of Sootie but had never laid eyes on him. From all reports the young man was quite an addition to the village! Alpaugh looked forward to his first meeting and chuckled as he recalled exactly how it came about.

It was in June and the naked bodies clung to the supports under the bridge. It had been a hot day and the young blades had gathered at the 'washing green' for a swim. One suggested they strip and swim upstream to the privacy of the Tower Street Bridge. The water was deeper under the bridge and the fellows could dive from the supports to the pool below without too many people watching them. They were close enough to the whirlpool to feel the pull on their legs but they knew enough to give it wide berth. Sootie had the strength to swim into the pool and he had twice in the past several years pulled young men to safety. It was illegal to swim in the river nude within the confines of the village and the Constable strictly enforced the rule, if he caught the culprits. He usually made no real effort to catch them. A lookout stayed on the bridge and shouted a warning when the Constable hove into sight. The fatal mistake was that all were enjoying the cool water and no one stayed on the bridge.

Alpaugh was not stupid. He had been to the sawmill and had seen the flash of naked skin under the bridge. He tried to ignore them because it was such a hot day but Mrs. Johnstone had to complain. She had a good view of the boys under the bridge from her home on the south side of the river and probably watched for a good while before she stomped across the bridge to find him.

'They're at it again! Sinful I call it that I can't sit at my window without seeing naked flesh!' she'd said.

"What window, Mrs. Johnstone?'

'The storeroom window, on the lower floor.' She realized she had been caught peeking and stomped back across the bridge to watch the proceedings.

He gave some thought to his plan of action. If he went down the river and waded across at Blair Street he could sneak up the bank to the 'washing green' and accost them as they got out to claim their clothing. They all had to come out sooner or later. He'd give them a good lecture but he wasn't a vicious man. He had been young once too and did his share of naked bathing. Of course, the young ladies in the village were truly embarassed if they happened on the boys. The mothers complained bitterly about their daughters being subjected to such vulgarity so the village fathers instructed him to deal with the situation.

It took him some time to make his way down, then back up river, but the look on the young lads faces was worth the effort. He was quite an imposing figure standing amidst their clothing. He sat down and waited patiently as one after the other got tired of clinging to the supports, dove into the water and sheepishly claimed their belongings. Alpaugh knew they wouldn't escape through the whirlpool upriver so he would eventually have all of them. As the sun went down there was one pile of clothing left being guarded by a slightly hungry constable. For the life of him, he could not see a body in the supports under the bridge and he began to suspect the culprit had braved the whirlpool. He would have to be a fool! The clothing gave no clue to the owner's identity. He bundled everything together and made his way home, quite worried that he had perhaps caused the drowning of a young man.

The one pile of clothing left behind belonged to Sootie. He said afterward he had never been so embarassed in his lifetime. He had come close to it when he joined Thomas Young's evening classes to learn writing, mathematics and 'the classics' and found he was the only male among fifteen 'genteel' women. He was also the only person in the class who couldn't hold his pen properly. Sootie had been so eager to learn he endured the classes as long as Thomas held them, paying his own tuition rather than take Thomas' charity.

Sootie recalled this embarassment as he sneaked through the streets of the village, stark naked, with a full moon overhead. He had several miles to go to reach the shanty and his path lay alongside the beaver meadow. The mosquitoes were severe enough for a person fully clothed! He couldn't afford to lose the clothing and boots but he wanted to face Alpaugh as an equal, with clothes on. His pride wouldn't let him give himself up in the afternoon. His main worry had been that someone would leave Kehelers or the Wellington Hotel, spot him and sound the alarm. He had streaked up Tower Street, past the St. Andrew's Church, along the stone fence in the graveyard where he found some privacy and out into the mosquito infested meadow.

The Constable was ensconsed at the table, making himself at home by pouring a cup of tea when Sootie opened the door to the shanty. 'Sootie, I've been waiting for you. Come on in. I don't think we've been formally introduced. Alpaugh here.' The Constable held out his hand without getting up from the table. 'Sit down. Have a cup of tea. Not a bad night for a wee walk is it?' Alpaugh remembered the conversation as though it was only yesterday. The naked body covered in red welts sat down opposite him at the table, crossed his legs and proceeded to sip tea as though it was an everyday occurrence to do so naked, never flicking an eyebrow, or anything else!

'I got to thinking over my supper just who owned the clothing and about the whirlpool. Then it struck! It's that Sootie fellow I've heard about but never seen. I didn't see anyone swim the pool today. You didn't did you? You clung to the rafters of the bridge, blending in with the wood!'

'Yes Sir.'

'I just strolled on out here to have a little chat. You weren't home so I made a spot of tea knowing you'd appreciate one when you arrived from . . . wherever.'

'Kind of you, Alpaugh.'

'Not at all Sootie. Moquitoes were bad tonight coming through the swamp. They got me on the face and neck something fierce.'

'You're lucky. With me they usually aim lower.'

'You should wear clothes then laddie. Do you do this often?'

'Only when I know there's a cup of tea waiting for me after my jaunt, but its usually a woman serving it.'

Yes, the man surely had a way with words. . . .

Shouting disturbed his train of thought.

'Alpaugh! He's here on a ledge under the cliff face. We'll pull the body under the bridge before we bring it into the boat. Clear the bridge will you. It's not a pleasant sight.'

The Constable bellowed to the crowd on the bridge to move along again, knowing full well they'd not move an inch.

'Bloodthirsty ghouls! You're all bloodthirsty ghouls; the lot of you!'

He made his way to the edge of the green to catch the rope Anderson threw from the boat. The Grand River in April was an unpredictable enemy ready to catch the unwary or unwise traveller in its watery grasp and Anderson pulled hard on the oars to beach the craft. Alpaugh looked at the body.

'What're your thoughts Sootie?'

'Well dressed, not a local. Doesn't look like he lacked money. There's a good looking horse up by the smithies, probably belongs to him.'

Alpaugh turned away from the boat. If it wasn't financial problems that drove him to jump into the whirlpool, it had to be a woman! Two women probably; one wondering where her son might be and the other not caring where her scorned suitor might have gotten to.

The Constable viewed women as necessary evils. He married one, a pretty good woman too who did his bidding and kept a tidy house and full larder. Take the case of George Clephane though. The fellow had been sent over from England by his father, the Sherrif of Fifeshire because he was a bit of a rascal. He had come aboard the 'Souter Johnnie' and had been smitten with the charms of Louise Barker who was on the same ship, she being the sister of Mary Barker Young, late wife of Thomas. Clephane had followed Louise to Fergus and settled down to drinking and wooing. Louise would have no part of the fellow. She couldn't tolerate his drinking and living off his father's monthly remittance. She finally moved to Toronto to live with her sister who married the Smith from Monklands. Clephane met his death by falling off a horse and hitting his head on a culvert. That was thirty-one years ago. Alpaugh was reminded of the story every time he walked through the 'Auld Kirk Yard' at St. Andrews and saw Clephane's headstone or stood in church and sang 'There were Ninety and Nine'. Clephane's sister, mourning her brother's untimely demise wrote the hymn in honour of his memory. Louise Barker? Alpaugh figured she probably didn't bat an eye when told. It was nothing to her. She'd scorned him which only caused him to imbibe more and he was certainly drunk when he hit his head.

'Will you get on home now and let a man cross the bridge? Can you not find something better to do?' He pushed the crowd along ahead of him as he crossed the bridge and made his way to the blacksmith shop. A chestnut mare stood docilely at the side of the shop. He gently patted her flank as he examined the saddle pouches. It was just like Sootie to notice the horse. The note he found in the pouch told the story. It was definitely a suicide and definitely a woman.

A SUMMER AFTERNOON'S ENTERTAINMENT
1884

MacDonald and Moore came onto the fight long after it had started. Miller from Fergus and Flanagan from Arthur were clenched together rolling in the mud and manure of the cattle pens below St. Patrick Street. The fences were ringed with spectators. MacDonald and Moore joined them.

'Who's fighting?'

'Fergus and Arthur.'

'Who's winning?'

'Flanagan was. Can't see too much now. They're covered in mud but Miller's nose was bleeding.'

The fighters were on their feet again. Miller shook Flanagan off his back and planted a good left to the Irishman's jaw. Some of the spectators mock punched along with Miller.

'How'd it start?'

'Sootie, over there. He asked Flanagan if it was true a good Irish girl by the name of "Betsy" was in the family way and had to get married. Flanagan said she didn't and asked who might have spread such a lie. Sootie pointed to Miller. Flanagan walked over and said to Miller, "The girl did not have to get married!"

' "What girl?"

' "Betsy."

' "Is she Irish?"

' "Yes."

' "Then she had to get married! All the little Irish wenches do, you know. Their mothers can't control them!" '

Flanagan took a swipe at Miller saying something about Irish honour and Miller took a swipe at Flanagan saying something about Scottish purity and the fight was on.

The more they shoved each other around the enclosure the muddier they became. Both were heavy set, muscular men but Flanagan had a weight edge over Miller. Miller fought dirty, aiming low. Flanagan threw punches that, if they ever connected, would have put Miller through the fence. The spectators were enjoying every minute of the scuffle.

'Flanagan! Your mother was born in a potato field!' That was Smith on the sidelines. Flanagan leapt to the fence, grabbed Smith by the legs and threw him into the mud with the retort. "You didn't know who your mother was!'

Wilson went to Smith's aid and O'Hagan jumped in to assist. Before you could say 'Tam-O-Shanter' the fence had cleared save Sootie, MacDonald and Moore and everyone was rolling in the manure mud and swiping at each other.

'Some donnybrook, MacDonald!'

'Move your feet Moore or they'll have you in there too!' Moore threw his feet over the fence where the brawlers couldn't reach them.

'Alpaugh!'

'Miller, Flanagan! Break it up. The Constable's coming!'

All fighting came to an immediate stop and the scrappers ran in all directions, looking like a pack of two legged pigs and smelling the same. Sootie, MacDonald and Moore found themselves racing through the same alleyway.

'Well, does she have to get married Sootie?'

'If Flanagan had of stopped long enough to think he'd have realized there wasn't a "Betsy" that I know of! Doesn't take much to irk an Irishman does it? I figured we needed some good entertainment on a dull afternoon.'

MacDonald and Moore stopped dead in their tracks. Sootie turned left on St. Andrews Street and quickly walked toward St. David Street and Templin Carriage Works where he could play checkers and keep low for several hours.

'Do you believe that man! He started the fight on purpose!'

A large hand grasped each man by a shoulder. 'You laddies look pretty clean. Did you have anything to do with starting the brawl?'

'You might ask Sootie here . . .' But Sootie had long left and if anyone asked him where he had been during the past hour all the checker players at Templins would have sworn he was playing all afternoon.

WALTER ELY — MARCH 1885

It was now the late spring of 1885. The winter had been generous to the residents of the village and spring came early. By late March the snows had turned to rain and the streets of the village had turned to mud.

'You'll have to go yourself today. I've got the woman's complaint and I'm staying in bed. You know right well I don't like Walter Ely either and he'd rather deal with you. He has an eye for you Clara and you mind how you lead him on! We need laces and an assortment of beads, some good linen yardage and a bolt of soft grey, lightweight wool fabric. Watch the price of the fabric closely. It might be cheaper in the long run to buy from Wm. Patterson in the village.'

'Are you sure you don't want to walk with me? You've been in bed two days now. Surely the fresh air will help you.'

'You're no authority on what will help me Clara! If you'll be good enough to stop at Phillips Drug Store to purchase a bottle of "Dr. Ambroses' Nerve Bitters" I'd appreciate it. The bottle will give more relief than any tongue lashing you can give.'

Clara resigned herself to the fact Georgina was in one of her 'moods' and wouldn't budge from her bed.

'Is there anything else you might like?'

'Check Pattisons "Grand Millinery Opening" to see what creations the other milliners in the village expect women to wear this spring and take careful note Clara. I know you detest hats but other women wear them. And ask that Mr. Ely about collars this spring.'

'Are you sure you don't want me to speak to Dr. Groves about visiting you? Perhaps he can suggest a proper tonic for you. The nerve bitters contain a goodly amount of alcohol. It's not out of my way to his office.'

'Don't you dare approach Dr. Groves regarding my health. It is not in your place to speak to him. He's too busy a man to have you bother him about something which is none of your business!'

Clara backed out of Georgina's bedroom. When she was this moody it was best to face her all the time otherwise a book or brush might be aimed at her back. She dressed warmly and when ready to leave went to the kitchen.

'Father, it was the "Poetical Works of A.C. Swinburne" you asked me to purchase at Phillips and you also wanted your shoe repaired. I have it here in my coat. Can you think of anything else we might need.' Thomas sat by the fire, his tartan shawl around his shoulders.

'Nothing else Clara.' He hesitated a moment. 'I heard the conversation a moment ago between Georgina and yourself. Do you feel you should talk to Dr. Groves? She has been unwell recently, hasn't she.'

'She's not talking to you either, is she? She's bitter, father, because she never had a chance to be anything but a mother to her sisters. She went directly from school to raising us.'

'It's a first born's responsibility to step in when a mother dies. A woman has no place other than in a home. What would she have done if she hadn't kept house for us after Mary died?'

Clara had been through this argument many times before.

'She gave up her young adulthood for us, for me. She never had a beau, father. She might have been a teacher or a doctor.'

'You're speaking nonsense Clara. A woman in the 60's would never be chosen for medical school.'

'But she could have nursed or taught. She spent the best years of her life behind the door at St. George Street . . . I'll go now. I've got to give some thought to speaking to Dr. Groves.'

Thomas called after Clara as she let herself out the door.

'I approve of Mr. Ely. He's the type of man you should associate with . . . far more appropriate than that scoundrel in the swamp.'

Clara smiled to herself and called back down the hall. 'I approve of him also.'

The fresh spring air put a bounce in her step as she negotiated the puddles and mud on the footpath people laughingly called a 'sidewalk'. She greeted everyone with a smile, a word or a nod of her head. The ferrier raised his tongs in salute as she passed the shop just above St. George Street.

The smells issuing from the ovens of the Victoria Bakery lured her to the display of delicacies in the window. The ovens had been on since four o'clock this morning baking the day's supply of bread. She turned from the window and glanced towards the corner of St. David Street and St. Andrews Street where the Groves Block, the Argo Block, the Marshall Block, the Wellington Hotel and the Tecumseh House/Murphy House dominated the scene. The main streets of the village had certainly changed since the early 60's. As she rounded the corner onto St. Andrews Street proper, the whole of the main area seemed lined with solid stone structures. Here and there a wooden building still survived but each year fire took its toll and a stone building rose from the ashes. The Groves Block and the Marshall Block boasted a facade of red Credit Valley Sandstone but Clara personally liked the rough, grey look of the local limestone.

The street was a sea of mud. Wagons had been exchanged for sleighs but even then the horses found it hard pulling their loads through the mire. Planks were laid across the street to enable the ladies to cross and the men lounged nearby hoping to see a flash of ankle or calf as the women hoisted their skirts to get them out of the mud. She crisscrossed the street from one side to the other leapfrogging around the worst of the mire.

John Tindale had a display in his window of two articles he'd found in the walls of an old tenement building he demolished over on Tower Street. One was a wooden mold for making plaster of paris casts of silver and gold coins. The other was an elaborate metal device used for the final molding of the metal coins from the plaster of paris molds. The local constabulary thought the pieces dated from the early '40's. Imagine! A counterfeiter in the village and it must have been someone everyone knew for there were few strangers in the area in the early '40's. Because Tindale had a sale on staples she entered the store.

'Mr. Tindale, good day to you.'

'Miss Young. You're out early this morning braving the mud. Can I be of service to you?'

'50 lbs of your finest bread flour and 15 lbs of a good quality white sugar please . . . to be delivered to "Stonehome". Do you have any of the early run of maple sugar left?'

'There's a supply coming in today, Miss Young, if they can get through the mud. Can I put your name down for a gallon?'

'Of course, Mr. Tindale.' She checked the price of the imported figs then bade him a pleasant day and left. She was munching a fig when Robert Kerr stepped out of his doorway to watch the progress of a dray stuck in the mud.

'Mr. Kerr. Just the man I was coming to see. Could you see to mending this shoe?' She pulled the shoe from her coat.

'A strange place to have an extra foot Miss Young, I'd say. Most people only have two and walk on both.' Mr. Kerr loved a practical joke as much as Clara.

'I'll drop it around to the house tomorrow if your father'll be in. I would like to visit with him.'

'Make it this afternoon Mr. Kerr. Father's hopping around the house on one foot and it's most annoying.' Both laughed at the obvious humour in the thoughts of a very staid Thomas leaping around the house on one foot.

'Miss Young, Miss Young!' Mr. Sherwood was calling from his door. 'The seeds and herb packets are in stock now. Perhaps you would like to browse. They won't last long.' She went immediately to choose her seeds for forcing on the windowsills of 'Stonehome'. She chose tomatoes and peppers, lemon balm and summer savory.

'I'll have to consult my last year's supply to see what else I shall need, Mr. Sherwood,' she said as she paid cash for the seeds. Most of her purchases were made with cash although the merchants were used to trade or barter. Because she lived in the village, she had no butter, eggs or cheese to trade, although she did often trade her dressmaking services for a large item of clothing or furniture.

'Do you wish these delivered?'

Heavens no! They are four small packages. I'll carry them along with me.' Most of the merchants were only too glad to give delivery of purchases as part of their customer services.

'If your new wallpapers come in Mr. Sherwood, please inform me immediately. I wish to have the dining room repapered. It will keep your man Donald Small busy for a day at least.' Mr. Sherwood held the door for her and as she stepped into the street she nearly walked over J.R. Craig who was the owner of the Fergus Music Store.

'Mr. Craig! Would you come tune the piano? I should say, would you send one of your employees to tune the piano for us.'

'Of course, Miss Young. This time I shall make sure your father is out walking before I do and I shall finish before he returns!'

'He did give you a bit of a rough time two years ago didn't he. He doesn't believe the piano should be played at all but don't worry. The day you come, I'll personally take him for a long walk.'

J.R. Craig raised his hat to her and continued on his way down the street. She lifted her skirts high enough to allow a good deal of calf to show and walked across the planks, bowing to the 'gawkers' when she reached their side of the street. Mrs. Kemp's Variety Shop was her next stop and practically next to the plank walkway.

'Clara, I do declare girl! You are a flirt!'

'You may as well give them what they want, Mrs. Kemp. Did you notice some of them actually blushed when I bowed!'

'Tisn't ladylike Clara, not at all.'

'When have you known me to act the part of a lady when buffoonery is called for? Tell me quickly. Did Sootie leave a message for me?'

'He did. He's back in the village but won't be at the shanty until late tonight. I saw him heading for Dr. Groves not half an hour ago, so he must be needed. Clara why don't you marry the man?'

'He's a brother to me. I have never considered marriage as the outcome of our relationship. He's told me marriage is not in his plans now or forever more. I have a beau anyway, Mrs. Kemp.'

'Who might he be?'

'Walter Ely, the sewing notions salesman who comes to the Commercial every month. He has two showrooms set up with fabric, sewing aids and trims.'

'And he's asked you to marry him?'

'He hasn't yet mentioned marriage, but father approves of him.'

'Your father's blind to the facts,' Mrs. Kemp snorted.

'My father's an old man but blind he's not!' Clara leapt to her father's defence.

'He's a respected member of the community Clara. But your mother's death affected him greatly and you know as well as I he's not himself these days. It's a stranger in your father's shell that walks down the street on occasion and sometimes I wonder! With your antics it's a wonder you haven't been to blame for his behaviour too.'

'Mrs. Kemp, you've an Irish tongue in your head but you speak the absolute truth. Will you tell Sootie I'll see him later and if he has time, to come around to the house. Father is in a mellow mood today.'

'Get away with you Clara. I'll tell the man.' Mrs. Kemp watched the girl leave the shop. It was a naive girl that she was if she didn't realize Sootie was in love with her but possibly there were problems and Thomas was certainly one of the biggest.

Clara decided her next stop should be the Commercial. The Doctor would be out anyway. All the hotels in the village provided showrooms for travelling salesmen but Walter came back to the Commercial each month on the second Tuesday to Friday because he thought the rooms were well appointed and the service first class. His showrooms were always on the second floor and Clara nodded to the attendant as she climbed the stairs. Walter met her at the door of his suite.

'Clara, my dear Clara. How have you been? What have you been doing since I last saw you? You've certainly not changed for the worse in a month. You're lovelier than ever.'

Clara blushed. 'Mr. Ely, you do carry on. I've been well and what I've been up to since your last visit is really not your business! Have you brought any new bits of trim with you? Do let me pass and look.'

Mr. Ely realized he'd been standing directly in her path and slipped aside to allow her into his showrooms. She sorted carefully through his stock of beads. 'You seem to have a large supply of these grayish, blue beads Walter. Are you overstocked or are they the latest spring colour for decorative touches to blouses?'

'They're a new colour out and I brought them to Fergus especially for you. They match the colour of your eyes perfectly.'

'I'll take a box Walter . . . and your laces . . . they're so soft . . . they're machine manufactured, but wool, aren't they. I've not seen anything so beautiful nor felt such softness!'

'They are imported from Britain and the first in wool that I've carried. They are soft but nothing can match the softness of your voice Clara.'

She giggled and looked at him somewhat amused.

'I am serious Clara.'

'You are very bold, Mr. Ely. What might you suggest in the way of fabric for spring wedding gowns this year? What are fashionable brides wearing in Montreal and Toronto?'

'Wool, light weighted woollens and soft cashmeres until June, then white linen or fine cotton. Your gown should be light blue wool, to compliment your complexion. I'll provide the orange blossoms.'

'Is this a proposal Walter?'

'Just a query Clara. I was interested in knowing if there are any other . . . suitors . . . interested in your charms . . . or am I the only one?'

'There are no other suitors Walter. I do find you most attentive and rather charming. If I purchased several bolts of your blue woollen fabric would you deliver them to "Stonehome" and consider staying for supper?'

'Nothing would give me more pleasure my dear Clara!'

'Then, I shall expect you for supper at 7:00 pm.' She offered her hand which he, like a gallant gentleman, kissed.

'Until 7:00 pm Clara.' He walked her to the front door of the hotel. She stepped out into the sunshine to find Sootie standing to the side of the door waiting for her.

'Sootie. I thought you were with Dr. Groves! It is good to see you. Tell me everything about your trip. Have you time to walk me home?' She took his arm and they walked toward Tower Stret, Sootie in obvious animated conversation with her.

Walter Ely, who had watched Clara leave, saw and heard her comments to Sootie. He turned from the door. If he was the only suitor Clara had, who the devil was the handsome man escorting her down the street and, by the looks he gave her, quite obviously taken by her charms also? Women can never be trusted to tell the absolute truth! He walked over to the desk.

'Mr. Couse. Who is this . . . Sootie fellow I hear about?'

'The one who was waiting for Miss Young?'

'The one and the same!'

'A relative I think, perhaps a cousin.'

Walter climbed the stairs to his second floor showrooms again. 'First cousins? I hope with a sincere prayer that her father doesn't hold to close cousins marrying!'

'Were you talking to me, Mr. Ely?'

'It's nothing Mr. Couse. I'll handle the situation.'

THE IMMIGRANTS — MAY 1886

W alter couldn't help notice the woman in the seat opposite him. She was young and had the most delicate features of any woman he had ever seen and she was dressed in black garments from head to toe. Perhaps she was in mourning? She travelled with a young man of eighteen or nineteen and a small child and spent most of her time glancing out the windows of the coach watching the landscape rush by. When she spoke to the boy and child it was in a low voice and in a language foreign to his ears. He surmised it was Spanish or Italian as she had a Mediterranean caste to her features. The child eventually left her seat and came over to stand beside him. He had been re-arranging one of his sample cases and the bright ribbons must have attracted her attention. He gave her a length of brilliant blue ribbon and she sat quietly beside him playing with it. The woman glanced over and smiled but made no move to retrieve her child. The little girl was around the age of two and knew some English words, articulating them well when she spoke.

'Rope?' She looked at Walter with sparkling dark eyes.

'Ribbon. It's blue ribbon.' He repeated ribbon, pronouncing it slowly.

'Ribbon.' The girl was quick to pick up his pronunciation. He rummaged in another bag he had on the seat beside him and produced a brown paper bag full of molasses drops. He always carried candy with him. Quite often his customers would bring young children to his display rooms and he was always prepared to treat them. He held the open bag to the child.

'Do you want a candy? Here. Take a candy.' She looked into the bag. He took one of the hard pieces and put it in his mouth.

'Food ... Mama ... food!' She eagerly took one of the pieces. He offered the bag to the boy and woman across the aisle. Hesitantly she took the bag and extracted a piece of candy, passing it to the boy who took a piece and handed the bag back to Walter.

'Grazia.'

'Do you want another piece of candy little girl?' He again held the bag to her.

'Food . . . Marie?'

'Marie.' The child looked at him immediately.

'Your name is Marie, isn't it?'

'Marie ... Mama ... Romeo.' She pointed at each one as she mentioned their names.

'Mr. Walter Ely, at your services child.' He pulled a dark curl on her head.

'Weelly?'

'No, Walter,' again he pronounced the word slowly. 'Walter Ely.'

The conductor strode through the car.

'Belwood . . . Belwood . . . five minutes to Belwood.'

That word sent Romeo and the woman into action. They began gathering their personal effects together. Obviously they were disembarking the train at Belwood. Walter was travelling through to Fergus. He set his case aside and helped the boy lift the bags and boxes down from the rack. Such a quantity of luggage they had between them! Marie sat with the ribbon in her hand watching the activity. When the train came to a full stop he assisted the boy off the train with the luggage. Marie followed her mother obediently and stood off to one side of the platform, the pile of luggage growing with the addition of trunks from the baggage car. There was not another soul on the platform except for a farmer loading seed sacks into his wagon on the far side of the tracks. What were they doing in Belwood standing on the platform with no one to meet them? Walter sat by the window watching, as the train pulled away from the station. Marie waved to him and he returned the gesture, wishing he could have been of more assistance.

Smellie stopped work to watch the train's arrival then went back to loading his sacks of seed. The next time he stopped to mop his brow he noticed three people standing amidst trunks and luggage on the platform. A young boy was earnestly talking to a woman and a child sat on one of the larger trunks. Both glanced anxiously and frequently over the Grand River towards the village of Belwood. They were obviously expecting someone to meet them. He carried on with his loading but kept an eye on the group. He was almost finished when he noticed the woman approaching him, lifting her skirts as she negotiated the

North Broadway, west side, Belwood.

tracks. He leaned against his rig and removed his hat while watching her progress. There was nothing shy about the woman as her walk was one of a determined, self assured person. As soon as she was within talking distance she spoke, quickly and quietly. Not a word made any sense to him except 'Landoni'. As she talked she watched him closely for recognition of a word.

'Landoni?' he repeated the one word he recognized.

'Landoni, Landoni!' she repeated the word over and over again, beckoning the boy to come to help her communicate.

'You know the Landoni's?'

The young man gestured wildly in a northerly direction.

'Dracon . . . Landoni . . . Louis!'

'If you're looking for Louie Landoni's brickyard above Dracon, it's over there.' He pointed in a westerly direction. 'Louie was to have met you here. Is that right?'

Arms began to wave frantically in all directions and words tumbled out. Heavens, these Italians could talk! Smellie'd never heard language spoken so quickly. He'd read somewhere they spoke with their hands too but he had to see it to believe it! He finally threw up his hands in a gesture of silence.

'I'll take you.' He walked to the head of his team and led them over the rough track to the pile of luggage. The young boy immediately sprang into action helping rearrange the seed sacks to make room for the trunks. When all was loaded, Romeo settled himself among the seed bags. There was nothing to do but lift the woman up onto the seat beside him. She was as light as a feather. Grain sacks weighed more than she did! The child put out her arms to him.

'Marie, I Marie.' He picked her up and put her on the seat beside her mother.

'You speak better English than the rest of them. I . . . Smellie.' He pointed at himself.

'Welly?'

'That's close enough.' The drive to Louie's was out of his way but he was willing to make a detour. He didn't mind helping a woman in distress. Smellie flicked the reins and the horses settled into their harness. The hill in Belwood would be their only heavy pull. He glanced at the woman beside him. She was quietly crying into her handkerchief. Heaven save him from a crying woman! The best place a man could be when a woman was crying was as far away from her as possible! The child seemed perfectly content resting against him playing with a blue ribbon. Even if he could speak the woman's language, he wouldn't interrupt her. He never did know how to stem a woman's tears. He chose to pretend he hadn't seen her tears and concentrated on the road ahead.

Carolina swayed gently with the bumps and surveyed the land she would call home. She missed the mountains of northern Italy but she would learn to love Canada. Where was Faustino? Why was he not at the station to meet her? She had not seen her husband in two and one-half years. He was almost a stranger to her. Marie was two years old and her father hadn't seen her yet. She was so emotionally tired that tears came easily to her eyes. She didn't like to cry in front of the stranger but the tears came suddenly and she couldn't stem their flow.

Soon after she and Faustino had married in their small village church in Vergiate, Italy, he had left to work on the tunnels being built through the Alps between Italy and Switzerland. He had left her in the home of his parents where she tried to be an obedient and dutiful daughter-in-law. She always felt uncomfortable in the crowded stucco house clinging to the steep hillside. Faustino came home once after their marriage to visit and to tell her he was going to France to work on the great iron tower for the Exposition, the Eiffel. Nine months after his visit she gave birth to Maria. When she asked for paper to write to Faustino her mother-in-law replied, 'Why write! It is only a girl child.' Carolina treasured Maria as the only possession which truly belonged to her and Faustino. Perhaps her in-laws were angered by the fact that her marriage had not been arranged to Faustino as was the custom but that their marriage was one of love and trust. They were childhood sweethearts and always knew they would marry regardless of what arrangements their parents would want to make and it caused problems on both sides. She was poorly treated by her in-laws and never given enough to feed the child. She coaxed a hen to nest under her bed by leaving the shutters of the bedchamber open. The egg which the grateful hen laid was kept a secret and fed to the child. When Faustino wrote that he was sailing for Canada she became despondent and only Maria could make her smile.

A day came when a cousin, Romeo, arrived from Canada with the money for her passage. Romeo was to chaperone her and the child on the voyage. When it became apparent that Carolina and Maria were leaving Vergiate, the relatives plied her with articles of clothing and linen. It would not be right for Carolina to arrive in Canada without a dowry chest. Faustino would expect generosity from his family and Carolina's relatives were to be impressed.

Carolina was so pleased to be away from Vergiate and on her way to Canada she gave no thought to the journey ahead of her and to the fact Romeo was not used to children. He was only a lad of eighteen and it was quite an endeavour for him to have come back to Italy in the first place to chaperone her. Their route went through France where her cousins enriched her dowry even more with new bobbins for lace making and linen cloth as she had been an acomplished lace maker, weaver and dressmaker in the village before she married. In Calais they bought passage on the first ship sailing for New York. As they had to be frugal because money was scarce, they purchased steerage passage so there would be money for land passage from New York to Ontario, Canada.

The voyage was a nightmare. Romeo was so ill he climbed into his bunk and Carolina never saw him leave it again until the ship docked in New York. She, herself, lay in agony in her bunk, unable to keep food and drink down and growing weaker by the day. When the sailors heard Maria cry from neglect and hunger they cared for her throughout the voyage across the Atlantic. Carolina didn't see her for days at a time. These men who didn't speak her language taught Maria the language of her new home, English. They anglicized her name . . . Marie.

After resting and recuperating in New York where they found a rooming house run by a huge, sympathetic countrywoman, they arranged overland passage from New York to Niagara Falls, Toronto, and Belwood.

She took her handkerchief and dried the last of the tears. She must show strength to Marie. She had to shake herself of the sadness she felt. The stranger had been generous enough to give them a ride and she didn't like to embarass him further with her tears. She found all the men in the new country courteous. The stranger on the train was another example. She glanced at the man in the seat beside her who was a big, broadshouldered labourer, used to hard work; a good man. He quickly glanced her way and she smiled at him.

Smellie breathed a sigh of relief. She was smiling! Perhaps she sensed they were nearing Louie's property. He gave a holler to the men working the clay close to the road. Marie jumped on the seat beside him with fright.

'Hey! One of you run get Louie. I've got some passengers he forgot to pick up.'

'Who are they?'

'Tell him a child by the name Marie is one of them. That's all I know.'

Men ran down the fence row from the brickyard. By the time the wagon manouevred the lane a large gathering of people had assembled and the woman was lifted bodily from the wagon. There was much crying and kissing and more crying. He sat high on the seat of the wagon taking no chances. The child pressed closer to him and he put his arm around her. With all the excitement she'd been forgotten.

'I don't blame you child. I'm afraid to step down into the middle of it too.'

Whoever she was, the woman was the centre of attraction. She suddenly drew apart from the gathering and approached his wagon holding the hand of a dark haired, solidly built man.

'Faustino Landoni.' She indicated to the man that he should shake hands. Smellie put his hand down to the fellow.

'Smellie, at your service.'

'Marie,' the woman called softly to the child and raised her arms. Smellie gently lifted the little girl out of the wagon to the woman. She, in turn, gave the child to Faustino, who gently, as though he was entrusted with the most precious gem in the world, cradled her in his arms. Tears ran down his cheeks.

'Maria . . . Maria . . . bambino, Maria.' He whispered softly to the child.

The young boy began unloading the luggage and many hands helped him this time. Smellie stayed on the wagon seat. When all was unloaded Louie indicated he should step down and join in the celebrations.

'No thank you Louie. I'm late enough as it is and the missus will be asking all sorts of questions. News travels fast around here and I'll have some explaining to do. Who is she?'

'Carolina Landoni, the wife of Faustino. They have not spoken to each other in many months. Thank you!'

Smellie turned his team and set off towards home. In some cases he knew a long absence from a marriage might just be the thing! But is this case he was glad to be a part of seeing the two people reunited.

THE GOOD DOCTOR — APRIL 1888

'Son. You've got to go quickly and get my driver. Bring him back immediately. Go up the highway to Garafraxa and west to Allardice Road, turn north and go nearly a mile up. There's a path into the swamp on the right hand side of the road. You'll find him there. Tell him the doctor sent you. Your father's life depends on it. Go quickly!'

While waiting for Sootie to arrive he checked his medical bag and rummaged through his cupboard for several instruments he thought he would need. It sounded to him, from the description of the illness in the note Billy brought with him, James Lowney had suffered a rupture. Time was of the utmost importance and the Lowney farm was miles up country over some pretty rough roads. He hadn't gotten much sleep last night but, if Sootie remembered the blankets, he could sleep soundly on the trip. Bumpy roads only served as his lullaby. Familiar steps came down the hall.

'Buggy's ready, Dr. Groves. I hitched the heavier horse. The roads'll sure test his strength today.'

'Did you remember blankets?'

'Blankets and hot coffee . . . the blankets for you . . . the coffee for me.'

Doc checked his instrument bag again and followed Sootie down the hall.

'How long before we get there? Speed's important today. It doesn't look good.'

'Three hours if we don't put the wagon in the mire on the Alma road. The rain has made the road impassable in some place. The horse is fresh though and raring to go.'

Billy had followed Sootie back to Queen Street and was standing hat in hand by his horse. Doc put his hand gently on the lad's shoulder.

'You go in the house and tell the housekeeper I said you are to have a hot meal and a comfortable bed. Don't try the ride home before you've had a sleep. I don't want you as a patient next.'

Sootie gave the Doc a hand into the buggy, put his bags under the seat and threw a blanket in his general direction.

'You'll not close an eye after we get to Salem. The roads are good that far.'

Doc put the blanket around his legs. That would be the most he would probably hear from Sootie on the entire trip. He was not one to waste idle words. He looked at the craggy features of the man next to him. He was quite attached to this forty-three year old mystery! Sootie had arrived at his door one night shortly after he set up practise in the village in '71 asking for help. He had his left hand wrapped in strips of his shirt. When he unwrapped the hand he found two fingers badly mangled. It seemed Sootie had injured himself on his trapline and had walked eight miles to the village for help. He had lost a lot of blood and Doc didn't know how the man made it the eight miles. As he worked on the fingers he realized Sootie had not flinched with the pain nor complained although it must have been unbearable.

'Doesn't it hurt?' he asked.

'Sure as hell does Doc, but I'm not complaining. Just save the fingers.'

He'd immediately recruited the man as his driver and helper. He needed a person that could stomach blood. When he asked in the village about Sootie's background no one could help him. The young man was well thought of and only close to one person, Clara Young. Most people felt it strictly a platonic relationship because Sootie and she had been raised together for awhile. Once he questioned Georgina about Sootie and got a very negative response, although when pressed she did admit he was a highly principled man.

He settled down on the buggy seat, pulling another blanket around him. He knew he was in very capable hands. The jostling of the wagon was music to his ears.

Sootie drove with an experienced eye to the road ahead while the man in the seat beside him snored gently. He adjusted the blanket around Doc's knees almost reverently. He glanced at the fingers on his left hand flexing on the reins. Doc had saved the fingers and deserved absolute loyalty. This small man with the brilliantly clear eyes had his admiration and support. He was a clever human who stepped into the boundaries of medicine few people chose to cross. He railed against practises he saw as outdated and invented new methods and treatments for ailments which, for too long had gone unchecked and taken lives. Doc boiled his surgical instruments, flushed out impurities with warm water and insisted on absolute cleanliness in an operating area. He wasn't afraid to look for the uncommon, to question the diagnoses of other doctors and to deviate from normal procedure if he deemed it necessary to save a life. He was a rebel among men of his profession but most doctors eventually had to admit he was right. Sootie admired the rebel with a cause. With an eye to the road and a heavy hand on the reins they finally reached their destination.

'Doc.' He shook the man carefully. 'We're nearly there. You might want to gather your wits about you before we arrive.' Doc shook himself awake and breathed deeply several times.

'Fast trip Sootie?'

'You've been asleep 2½ hours. The road's been pretty rough. I nearly mired it in the long swamp. You never noticed.'

Lowney was lying in the main bedroom of the frame house in obvious pain. Doc went to work immediately prodding, questioning and checking all vital signs. He turned to Sootie and beckoned him outside where he paced up and down the porch.

'Sootie, without an operation he stands no chance of surviving the rupture. With an operation he has a little more than 50% chance of surviving and he's not capable of making that decision.'

'His wife is level headed enough. If you approached her with the facts I'm sure she'll give her consent.'

'It won't be pleasant. I've only seen one other rupture similar to his and the patient did not live. The operation is a delicate one.'

'You tell the wife. I'll start to clean the kitchen. You'll want to use that room won't you?'

'Yes. We'll need clean sheets, boiling water, a door to carry him on, some strong men to get him to the kitchen and someone to assist me with the instruments, maybe the eldest daughter. He's a big man and you'll be needed at the feet. I'll find the Mrs.'

Sootie went immediately to the kitchen and began giving orders. The youngest son was sent to the neighbours for men to help lift Lowney. Another was instructed to remove the door to the parlour. The daughters were set to work with scrub brushes and buckets of hot soapy water. Once Doctor Groves came into the kitchen Sootie handed the situation to him and helped with the scrubbing of the door and kitchen table. The floor around the operating area was made spotless also. Everyone sensed that speed was essential and worked quickly.

'Carefully men. Lift him up onto the table and then leave. All you weak knee'd women leave also. Go to your mother in the parlour.' He turned to the eldest daughter. 'If you're going to faint, leave immediately. You'll be left on the floor to revive yourself if you don't. I've no time for you. Your father's life is my responsibility and is in my hands.'

The room was cleared except for the Doctor, the daughter and Sootie. Sootie knew what his job was. He took his boots off, helped Doc administer an anesthetic, and went to the foot of the table whereupon he climbed onto the table and sat on Lowney's legs. Normally he would have stood at the foot of the table and held the legs firmly. Lowney was nearly 250 lbs and weight was necessary on the legs to keep a man that size quiet. Sootie always watched the operation. He couldn't get over the delicate hands of the doctor groping around in the blood and tissue. His own hands were so large and rough compared to the good doctor's. Groves' hands saved lives. They knew exactly what to look for and where to find it in the incision area. Sootie always tried to hide his hands when Doc was operating. They looked so 'uncouth' in comparison.

'Are you alright girl? Doc was talking to the daughter who had been working beside him.

'I . . . I'll be O.K. It's the blood. I've never seen so much blood. I'm thinking of my father and I'll be alright.'

Spunky girl, Sootie thought. He'd seen many a tough man leave a room when blood began to spurt. The most agonizing operations were amputations. Even Sootie felt revolted at them.

The minutes slid by as the doctor performed the delicate work inside the abdominal cavity. The only sound was the ticking of a mantle clock on a sideboard.

'Sootie! Quick, the anesthetic!' Sootie quickly vacated Lowney's feet. The man had a tremendous tolerance for anesthetic! He delivered another several drops to the cloth he placed on the man's face and went back to the feet.

It seemed hours later when Doc stitched the last piece of flesh together and heaved a sigh of relief. The entire operation took less than an hour altogether.

'It's up to God and time now.'

The patient was left on the kitchen table with a light covering over him. Doc rubbed his neck and began the long vigil by the patient. Neighbours arrived with food and all ate hungrily. Sootie slept first, Doc taking first watch with the patient as this was the crucial time. He was never far from Doc, lying in a corner of the kitchen on a couch. They spelled each other off every three hours and eventually the daughter was instructed on what to look for and left to sit with her father.

Both men now slept fitfully on proper beds. When Doc awoke he went immediately to the kitchen where the patient still lay on the table.

'I've kept a careful watch on him Doctor Groves. I've checked everything you asked me to. He's not moved but he did waken and I administered the drops as you instructed.'

'Good girl.' Doc examined Lowney closely. He shook his head in approval. 'I think you'll have a father to walk you down the aisle. Go get your mom. Ask her to change the sheets on her bed and send your brother for the neighbours. We'll try moving him.'

Billy had arrived home again and with the help of a few neighbours, Lowney was transferred gently from the kitchen table to door to bed.

'Now, if you'll clean the kitchen, we'll all have a bit to eat.' That was an encouraging word from the doctor!

Forty-eight hours had passed since the operation and after leaving explicit instructions with Mrs. Lowney and her daughter the two men climbed into their wagon for the return trip to Fergus.

'I've lost no one to neglect after an operation yet, Sootie. I wouldn't leave here if I figured they were incapable of handling the situation. That daughter should consider nursing. She's very responsible.'

Doc wrapped himself in the blankets again and settled himself against the seat.

'Take the road as fast as you can. Let's try to beat our record on the return trip. I'm anxious to be home.'

Sootie gave the horse a crack with the reins and the wagon bounced to the main road. Doc liked fine horses and speed and Sootie was always up to a challenge.

'Wake up Doc. We're nearly home.'

'How long Sootie?'

'Two hours.'

'Let's try for 1½ next time boy. Give me a hand down. I'm a little stiff. Must have been a darn rough ride.'

THE TALK — AUGUST 1889

Walter stood to one side as Jake lifted the sample cases onto the wagon for the trip to the Commercial. It was one of those hot, hazy days when the cicada beetles kept up their constant drone as though doing a 'rain song' to hasten the thunder shower which would ultimately end the heatwave. Walter wiped his brow with a handkerchief. A hand fell heavily on his shoulder.

'I think you don't mind walking to the Commercial today.' The fingers tightened on the shoulder.

'Ready, Mr. Ely. You want to go on now?'

'He doesn't mind walking down today Jake.' The fingers tightened again.

'I don't mind walking today Jake. Put the cases in my rooms. It's such a nice... hot ... day for walking.'

Jake waved and pulled away from the railway station easing his team over the tracks and down St. George Street. The fingers relaxed on the shoulder.

'Who the devil do you think you are?' Walter wheeled around to face his assailant.

'Sootie, Mr. Ely. May I introduce myself properly and apologize for the "heavy handed" tactics?'

'Sootie who? You must have a last name. All I've heard is Sootie.'

'I could say Jones or Smith but it's Sootie, just Sootie. I have taken a last name for document purposes but its not common knowledge.'

'I've actually wanted to talk to you, Sootie.'

'And I to you Mr. Ely. Shall we walk.' They followed the path of the wagon, across the tracks to St. George Street and east along the street towards the main business area.

'I want to know your intentions regarding Clara ... Miss Young, Sootie.'

'And I, your intentions Mr. Ely. You are a travelling salesman and have been known to woo young women as far north as Palmerston.'

'How do you know my business? That is over. It was a frivolous flirtation, nothing more!'

'And Clara, is she a "frivolous flirtation". Be honest Mr. Ely. I can be a dangerous enemy.'

'Perhaps you should ask the same question of yourself Sootie. You've known her longer than I.'

'You do not possess all the facts Mr. Ely. You should find them out before you condemn a person's actions. Shall we sit down before we discuss anything further. I think I've made myself an adversary and that was not my intention. Indeed, if you are serious about Clara, I'm quite willing to do anything I can to assist you.'

Sootie led the way through the Catholic school yard to the front of the small stone church. He motioned for Walter to sit on the step. When he did so, Sootie sat beside him. Walter had been watching the man closely and spoke now quietly.

'Sootie. I think I should level; with you. I have known other women but I've never before met one that, in my estimation chalks up to Clara. She's intelligent, capable and beautiful. My intentions are completely above board as far as she's concerned. I plan to marry her . . . but you do also, don't you?'

'I did once. I should perhaps level with you also Walter. I approached Thomas Young asking for Clara's hand in marriage but was rebuked. You must understand Clara to know why I did not approach her directly but sought Thomas' approval first.'

'But you still love her. Does she not share your feelings? Would she not marry you without her father's permission?'

'Again you must understand the situation. I lived awhile with the Youngs and was regarded by Mrs. Young as one of the family. Clara accepted me on brotherly terms. I have never outwardly shown any serious affections towards her. After Thomas' rejection of me, I realized it would be useless to court her. I would only do her much emotional harm. There are several . . . circumstances now that cannot be resolved. I do still love her, very much. Perhaps in time I'll learn to love another, but it takes time.'

'Why are you willing to assist me? I'd be taking a vital part of your life from you.'

I want to see Clara happy. If you are the one she's ultimately to marry I will not stand in your way. I will do everything I can to help your cause. If I thought that you were being dishonest in any way with her emotions I would . . . I would not hesitate to destroy you, your reputation or your business.'

'Those are strong words, sir!'

'They are true words, Mr. Ely. You are not my enemy yet but I will not stand by and see Clara hurt.'

'I will never hurt Clara, Sootie. I have business interests in Bruce County that I'm hoping will flourish. As soon as I can assure Clara a home and financial security I will ask her hand in marriage.' Sootie was silent for a moment. Everything Walter had told him so far corresponded with the information he had been able to obtain on the man.

'It was imperative that I hear those words directly from you. I've resigned myself to the fact that you shall probably wed Clara and I will support your efforts.' Sootie stood, towering above Walter.

'I'll say no more. You have my word as a gentleman that what was discussed today will go no further.'

Walter stood and extended his hand to Sootie.

'I give my word also. You have no need to fear that this conversation will go any further than these steps.'

Sootie shook the hand offered. He applied just enough pressure to make Walter understand he was serious in his threat to destroy the man if he deceived either Clara or himself. He could easily have broken every bone in the man's hand!

'I'll not be bothering you again. If I can be of assistance leave word with Jake at the Commercial.'

Sootie walked around the side of the church leaving Walter standing by the step. He nursed the sore hand thinking the man could probably break every bone in his body! He certainly was a fair chap, offering to help persuade Clara into a marriage if it meant happiness for her! He must love her very much if he would go to the point of interviewing her prospective husband.

BRASS CANNON, FIREHOSE & PRIZE GEESE

There always was competition and rankling between Elora and Fergus. Over the years a number of incidents took place which caused a large wedge to be driven between the two villages, the first being that James Webster and Charles Allan ran for the same government office. Webster won and Allan moved bag and baggage from Fergus to Elora.

The first shots were fired shortly thereafter when the men in Elora cast a brass cannon for the Queen's Birthday and after a few drinks and a few random shots around the settlement of Elora, decided to take on the 'enemy'. They dragged the cannon three miles through the thick bush and, in the early morning hours set it up on the hill above St. James Square, right beside the Auld Kirk. They proceeded to fire at random and managed to knock down two chimneys and put three good sized holes in several walls before they were subdued.

Things were quiet for awhile with the occasional skirmish in a tavern but nothing serious happened until the day the Elora Fire Brigade was called out to a suspicious grass fire and found when they applied pressure to the hose, the water came out everywhere but where it should. On closer examination they found the hose was indeed not theirs at all. The Fergus Brigade had switched hoses!

The next time the Fergus Citizen's Band went to parade they found their uniforms, which were stored in one common depot, were without buttons on tunics and pants.

A truce was called by Fergus who invited the rival community to a 'Truce Dinner'. Congeniality and whiskey flowed freely all night. Old grudges were forgotten and the Elora residents went home well fed and content only to wake up in the morning to see, out their windows, a brilliant orange church spire!

The fighting now got down to a more personal level. There was always an agricultural fair where the two communities vied for top prizes in flowers, vegetables and livestock.

One Fergus gentleman raised geese and had one particular prize goose named Thadetasmus who took all the prizes in the local agricultural shows. Thadetasmus had never been beaten but an equally enthusiastic goose raiser in Elora came close to the blue ribbon on a number of occasions with his entry, Hero. One day Thadetasmus was put out in his own enclosed section of the verandah for his daily exercise. When the owner went to check on the bird he found a plate of half eaten yeast and a very large, grotesque Thadetasmus. The yeast was fermenting and expanding in the poor goose's stomach! When he reached down to pick up the massive bundle of feathers, Thadetasmus exploded! Fragments of goose flew everywhere and the former owner had to have a doctor remove a piece of Thadetasmus from his eye.

Of course, the man from Elora was immediately suspected of a 'foul act' and apprehended. He had a witness to prove he'd never been in Fergus on the day in question and demanded an apology. He got one and an invitation to dine on the following Sunday. He accepted as he was known to never turn down a dinner invitation and to come early and stay late hoping he might entice supper from the good hostess also. Dinner on the appointed day was excellent with the main course being roast stuffed goose. It was only when the man returned to Elora and couldn't find his goose, that he realized he had just devoured, with much relish, Hero!

Several nights later Thadetasmus' owner found himself nailed into his own outhouse in the middle of the Owen Sound Road, two miles north of the village and his home.

But all rivalry was forgotten when January rolled around each year and the invitations went out for the most prestigious Ball in Southern Ontario, The Bachelor's and Benedict's Ball at the Town Hall, in Fergus.

THE BACHELOR AND BENEDICT'S BALL
JANUARY 16, 1891

'A re you enjoying yourself Clara?'

'Yes. It's a splendid dance. With so many people from out of the community, it is exciting. Look, there is the Member to the Legislature of Ontario and his good wife. The ladies are all so exquisitely dressed!'

Walter swung her through the steps of the waltz with skill and ease. He cut a dashing figure in his suit. Clara was enjoying herself but not for reason of being in Walter's arms. She felt nothing exciting about being so close to him. That surprised her. From the novels she read she was supposed to feel 'breathless' and quite weak.

The Town Hall was disguised for the night with bunting, cedar boughs and furniture loaned from Thomson's warehouse. Doctor Groves' electric lights glowed dimly from the ceiling. It was normal practise for him to shut the plant down at 12:00 midnight but as he was enjoying the Ball also, the lights remained on.

'Have you heard the orchestra before?' Walter leaned into the music.

'I heard it is their first engagement in Fergus.' Clara leaned demurely away from Walter.

Marcicano's Italian Orchestra had arrived by train from Toronto especially for the occasion. They played well and the couples on the floor showed their appreciation after each number with applause. in total there were over 500 people in attendance at the ball and the floor was crowded with dashing men and beautifully coiffured women.

Clara had to put up with a lot of opposition when she announced she had accepted Walter's invitation to the Ball. Georgina declared she'd never heard anything so ridiculous as Clara's going to a dance. Thomas refused to discuss the issue. His silence spoke for itself.

'You can't dance Clara.' Georgina was at least truthful.

'I'll learn. We danced when mother was alive. I'll learn.'

And learn she did. Sootie manouevred her through the steps, playing his fiddle and directing her at the same time. She was never once in his arms.

'That's right Clara. Left foot forward, right across, left, together, back, together. . . .'

She held her arms out to an imaginary partner and waltzed around the shanty in the dark of the night when everyone else in the village was asleep. She saw nothing wrong with visiting the shanty, day or night. Most people in the village never knew and if some talked she could withstand their comments by telling them they were 'dirty minded people.'

'Clara?' She was brought back to the dance floor with her name being whispered in her ear. 'Would you consider sitting this dance out?'

She indicated an affirmative and Walter led her to one of the couches placed in a discreet corner of the hall. 'I've known you seven years Clara. I think we have a good relationship. I like you. I assume your feelings are mutual.'

She looked at Walter. 'Yes they are. You are a fascinating man.'

She knew this moment was coming. She suspected the invitation to the Ball also would include a proposal of marriage. She had prepared herself for the question but she had no answer for Walter. At one point she was ready to say yes. Walter was probably her last chance to have children but that was no reason for marriage. She believed there had to be love also. What was love? Clara was very confused. Was she not to feel some physical response to Walter when he touched her? Why was she hesitating. Was she being too selective?

'You'll have a fine home in Wiarton Clara. It won't be "Stonehome" but it will be comfortable.'

'Couldn't we live in Fergus? I have always known Fergus as home.'

'I'm afraid not. My business is now in Grey and Bruce counties and my home is Wiarton. I'm sure you'll adjust. Georgina will learn to take charge of the house.'

Why did he have to bring Georgina and Thomas into the discussion! 'You've taken me off guard Walter. I must think seriously of your proposal.'

'I think you've known of my intentions for some time Clara. I must have an answer tonight. I am not a young man. Thirty eight is rather late to begin a family.'

'We should perhaps dance Walter. We're being watched. I must be blushing. You're right. I've been unkind to you and you deserve an answer tonight.'

'Is there a chance Clara?' She looked at him and in all sincerity said, 'Walter, I don't know.'

Mercifully her card showed no partners for the next three dances. She had purposefully not accepted partners for the dances feeling she might need a rest. She put her cloak over her shoulders and went out into the cold night air. The wall of the Town Hall provided support for her as she gave serious thought to Walter's proposal. When she heard the announcement of partners for the quadrelle she went back inside to find Dr. Groves was down as her partner. The shrewd Doctor's only comment during the dance was a fatherly 'Don't do anything rash Clara!' She looked up in surprise at this amazing man.

'Is it that noticeable Abraham?'

'Only to one who knows you Clara.'

Walter had the last five dances indicated on her card and during one of them, she couldn't remember which, she broached the subject for the last time.

'Walter. I have thought seriously of your proposal. It was difficult, very difficult and you must understand my reasons for saying I am sorry, I cannot accept you marriage proposal.'

'You can't accept! It sounds as though someone's told you not to.'

'Perhaps they have. Can't wasn't the proper word was it? I've decided I can not marry you because I would be deceiving you. I find the words "I love you" hard to say. I'm confused Walter. I'd be deceiving you if I said "I love you". I don't think I know what love is.'

'You'll learn Clara. I'll be kind and gentle. You'll learn to love me. You'll learn what love is.'

'Will I, Walter? I'm thirty-five and perhaps too old to learn.'

'Clara, I love you!' He took her gently by the shoulders. 'Look at me, look me directly in the eyes. I love you and I will wait for you if you change your mind. Do you understand? I love you!'

She looked up then to his eyes, turned quickly from him and ran through the couples on the floor . . . .

When McVicar was in trouble he always ran for the jail. He even knew where to find the key so he could lock himself in if the Constable wasn't around. It was for his own good. His wife was always out for his blood with the rolling pin! Tonight he had spent the pig money and he was taking no chances. It was bad enough for a man to get a little sleep with all the stompings and carryings on above him at the ball and the cell beds were not too comfortable but to have a woman crying her eyes out right next to your cell . . . and for that woman to be Miss Clara Young, a woman who was old enough to know better was the last straw! He would have let himself out except that he remembered the look in his wife's eye the last time he spent the pig money!

THE SECRET — FEBRUARY 1891

Clara let herself quietly out the front door of the house. She simply had to go for a walk. The atmosphere in the house was smothering her. She was dressed warmly and made sure Georgina and Thomas were very much asleep before she opened the door and went out into the clear night air. A soft snow covered everything, purifying the filth of the January thaw. If it was difficult walking, Clara wasn't noticing and she took her frustrations out by walking quickly along the grooves cut into the streets by the sleighs. She was 35 years of age, sharing a home with a sister who spent her days swinging between despondency and normality and a father who never spent a day without complaining. She had, in the 70's, several half hearted proposals before Walter's but had turned both suitors down. She turned Walter down also but it had been the most difficult decision she had ever made. She thought she loved him but there had been that question mark. Tonight again, as she walked, she asked herself . . Why had she said no? She couldn't recall how many times she pondered that question in the past three weeks. It seemed she thought of nothing else. Was it concern over her father's failing health? Was it because of Georgina's health if she withdrew her support from the family? Was it because she did not want to burden Walter with her family? Was it really because she didn't know what love should be like?

Clara loved life. Sootie had taught her that and always said she had a gypsy soul that yearned to be free! She loved friends around her, good music, singing — but her father kept a firm hand on the doorlatch and "Stonehome", her home, remained a silent prison to her. She loved the house and its garden. The home was her first love until Walter had made an appearance and she saw personally to the decoration of the house. If she couldn't be gay outside the home she could surround herself with colour and gaiety inside. The rooms vibrated with colour, not at all Victorian. The windows remained undraped and open to the sky except for blinds. Thomas accused her of 'horrifying tastes' but didn't demand she redecorate. She would persuade Georgina to play the piano and the two would sing. Thomas would join in reluctantly and only if hymns were played.

Clara used to invite friends home but as Thomas became more quarrelsome she met them elsewhere. Seclusion didn't bother Georgina who demanded Clara give an explanation for every walk she took. That's when Clara began to take her walks in the dead of night when neither Georgina nor Thomas knew. She felt she was the mistress of the house and therefore never once thought of leaving the situation she found intolerable. She commandeered the kitchen, took charge of the garden and transacted many of the financial matters now that Thomas couldn't manage. 'Stonehome' was her gentle master and her purpose in life.

Georgina held a job as Tailoress and left every day for work leaving Clara with the house and Thomas. When Thomas' demands became unbearable Clara would shut herself in the sewing room where she would sit at her machine by the window working and watching the activity on the streets below. She took her anger out on the treadle of the machine. The room had a calming effect on her and she could never remain unhappy for long. She would soon be back downstairs, cooking, dusting or doing handsewing near the heat of the kitchen stove or out under the lilac tree. She realized that the day her father died she would have to find some work outside the home just as Georgina was doing now. She dreaded that day.

Clara found herself on the bridge at Monklands. She stood watching the brilliant moon lay shadows on the ice of the river. Perhaps she was blaming Georgina and Thomas unfairly for her negative answer to Walter Ely. Perhaps it was 'Stonehome' that held her in its grasp. The house stood solid and substantial, a testimony to its builders and the founders of the village. It represented security to Clara, a security which was always there. Even after Thomas and Georgina were no longer part of the village 'Stonehome' would stand. She was afraid to lose that security! For some reason security was love to her just as money is to others! She had always been afraid to reach out into the chasm of the world around her. She stood forever on the brink wanting to taste the wine but glued to the rim of the glass by insecurity! Somewhere in her life she had a taste of insecurity. Perhaps when her mother died some invisible strings had been severed and 'Stonehome' had cemented them together again.

Sootie caught up with her on Union Street. She knew enough to ask neither where he had been nor where he was going. He had a habit of disappearing for hours, days or weeks at a time without explanation but always reappearing when he was most needed. He was muffled against the cold and matched her light quick step in the ruts. Sootie had the uncanny ability to tell at a glance Clara's various moods and tonight he perceived it was not a good one. There was no way she could hide her problems from him.

'You're further away from home than usual tonight, aren't you?'

'I'm not asking where you've been but would you walk with me for awhile tonight Sootie?'

'My time will never be more well spent.'

'I feel trapped Sootie. I had a chance to leave "Stonehome" but I didn't take it. I turned Walter Ely down flatly.'

'I know. Why do you feel trapped Clara? Don't you possibly mean depressed?'

'Possibly. It's the situation at home. It's not the house but the atmosphere.'

'Clara. You always remind me of a captured swallow. You fly always against your bars to free yourself but you cling to the perch for security. 'Stonehome' is that security. The swallow's security was food. When the door was finally opened you stayed on the perch. You need security, and "Stonehome" rather than a man gives it to you. You were never meant to be a free spirit. You need your two feet firmly on solid ground. You devoted your life to "Stonehome" the day you moved in. I could see in your eyes your love for the home. If I asked to choose between house and man you would say "Stonehome".'

'Was I ever deceitful Sootie?'

'Delightful, but never deceitful. Why do you ask?'

'I feel I deceived Walter into believing I loved him. He wouldn't have pursued the marriage proposal if he didn't think I was giving him some encouragement.'

'Walter is old enough to have a mind of his own. You might be accused of being an outrageous flirt but you were never deceitful.'

'I could have had freedom Sootie. A freedom from my responsibilities.'

'Only to find more responsibilities. Freedom has different meanings for each individual. I had freedom once. I think I should tell you about it. I had as much freedom as I wanted but no security.'

They sat down on the steps of the Presbyterian Church looking over the quiet village. By instinct the pair sat in the shadow of the church building to avoid being seen. This was Clara's favourite vista. The streetlights were out as it was long after 12:00. Only one light shone from a window down on St. Patrick's Street. The moon softened the blackness of the night.

'You must promise me Clara that you will never speak to anyone about what I am going to tell you. This is no fairy tale. I've kept my past locked in my heart for many years.'

'I've never let you down Sootie. We've shared many secrets in our time.'

'I arrived in Fergus at Thomas' door in 1860, a pauper with a note for your mother.'

'I know Sootie. That's all I know!'

'I was homeless, ragged, unschooled and filthy. I never knew a proper home. I never had a home. I don't know where home is!'

'Sootie! Everyone in the village assumes you came from Scotland. You must have a home.'

'No. I came from England but there was no home. I don't know who my mother or father are.' He waved his hand toward the village. 'Of all the people in the village, I know of no other person who hasn't known a mother or father. I remember only a woman who raised me in London until I was nearly five. She turned me out when I interfered with her profession. She entertained men professionally. I went into the streets of the city and for the first little while had nothing to eat nor a place to sleep except under the bushes in the gardens and what food I could find in the trash. Then I noticed other children, like myself, even younger, with older children protecting them. They were begging on the street. Every one of them was filthy, ragged and homeless. I learned quickly and survived like the rest of them to steal and beg and lie. We ran in packs like dogs

[*Authors Note: In 1884 Fergus had nine street lamps run on coal oil. They were replaced on November 29, 1890 with electric street lights powered by Dr. Grove's electric plant. The lights came on at dusk and were shut off sharp at 12:00 midnight.*]

but dogs were treated better than we were. London was full of 'children of the streets'. They were almost a city within a city. Eventually I went back and found the woman who raised me. I demanded to know everything she knew about me.'

'Was she your mother? Did she accept you again? This surely must be a tale Sootie!'

'This is no tale Clara. I am serious. I have never in the past lied to you. You find it impossible to believe such a story because you have been raised a protected woman. There are many things you don't know about life Clara. In answer to your questions, she was not my mother and she did not accept me again. She was a bad character, just as bad as I had turned out to be. She did give me some information on my past. It seemed my father was a gypsy who roamed Europe in caravans. He came from Bellinzona, a small village on the Swiss/Italian border. My mother was a noblewoman who had no qualms about casual love affairs. She lived in central England and became quite smitten with the charms of the "gypsy prince" who happened by her door. Their affair was purely of a physical nature. By the time my mother realized she was pregnant, the "prince" was long gone out of the country. My mother wanted no part of me but for some reason decided to go through with my birth so she secluded herself until after my "arrival". She then gave me to the daughter of her groundskeeper and offered her money for my upkeep, to be sent to her every month as long as the girl moved as far away as possible from the estate.'

'Your mother at least gave you a name.'

'No. The midwife told my mother I was the colour of soot and so she bestowed "Sootie" on me. I have no last name. I do not know my mother's name or title. The woman could not be persuaded to tell even though the money for my upkeep was never sent as promised. She did well to raise me for five years. I do not blame her for my state. I am ashamed to tell you that by age thirteen, I saw and experienced more of life than most men in their seventies. Don't think less of me now Clara for that statement. I had to survive. There were many like me, bastards of titled persons turned out to fend for themselves. There still are.'

'You are no bastard Sootie.'

'In my fourteenth year a man by the name of George Barker befriended me.' Clara jumped visibly at the name.

'My uncle, the brother who left Canada a year after he came in 1842 and went back to paint in England!'

'One and the same man. He took me in and gave me a decent life for a year.'

'What was he like Sootie?'

'He was not a man you'd want to know. I did him a great favour Clara but I had to leave England quickly as a result. Before you ask, I don't think I should ever tell you. The details are far too sinister and complicated for you to hear or grasp.'

In fact Sootie knew the details would turn her forever against him. He had taken years to come to grips with them himself. 'Suffice to say, I took a great burden off George's shoulders and placed it on my own. I left the country with much haste and only the clothes on my back and a letter for your mother. I was accepted into your home and eventually into the community. When I saw your home I knew I wanted to be part of your lives. I accepted you as the family I never had. I also wanted to be an asset to the village rather than a liability so I worked hard, listened carefully and observed well. I studied with Thomas and still read every book I can find.'

'You found security and you're still a free agent.'

'You might say I have the best of two situations. I have even experienced love, true lasting love.'

'When Sootie? What was it like? I must know!'

'That's a different story Clara. It is very early in the morning. You had better be getting back home. You must not breathe a word of our conversation tonight. You know how the village would take my story.'

They walked together up Provost Lane to Garafraxa Street and up the road to the doors of 'Stonehome'. Sootie said good night and went on up the road. How could he possibly tell Clara the most anguishing part of his life story? She must be told but not when she herself was so distraught. He looked all of his 46 years as he disappeared into the night heading for his shanty.

Clara stood at the doors of 'Stonehome' watching the figure retreat from sight. It was as though she was seeing him for the first time. He was like a rough cut gem, always turning a different facet to her. He had always appealed to the child in her. Tonight he touched her as a woman. His secret would be safe with her.

ONE WOMAN IN A TUB — 1893

Long after Georgina and Thomas went to bed, Clara pulled the tin tub from its corner in the pantry. She did it carefully so that it made no noise scraping across the floor. The fire had been stoked and pots of water were heating on the stove. Everything was done quietly so as not to disturb the two upstairs. She was used to doing everything quietly at night!

It was a nuisance to fill the tub and more of a nuisance to empty it. The pantry was cold but she didn't dare pull the tub into the kitchen for fear Thomas might wander down the stairs.

Years ago she thought nothing of swimming in the river, until Thomas found out who she was swimming with and what she was swimming in! He had been right. She did not know of any other young woman in the village who swam in their underwear with a man eleven years older than herself. What that fact had to do with getting clean made no sense to her, but she gave up swimming. Her abolutions consisted of a thorough wash in her bedroom or kitchen with the shades drawn. The day she walked past Tindales and spied the large tin bathtub she knew it had to come to 'Stonehome'. It was a sloped backed tub, big enough for all of her to fit into if she sat with knees up and was made of sturdy metal with deep blue and yellow painted flowers on its exterior. Thomas would have no part of the tub when it arrived so she hid it from his sight in the pantry. Once a week, rain or shine, summer or winter, the tub came out.

She lugged heavy pots of water from the stove to the pantry and filled it by the light of a coal oil lamp. She pulled the shades and checked to make sure she had Pear's soap, towels and a dressing gown. It took some time to shed bodice, skirt, camisole, chemise, slips, pantaloons, cotton socks and shoes but finally she eased herself into the water. A ledge built into the tub held her soap and wash cloth. Ah, how she enjoyed the soak, hair pinned back from the nape of her neck. She surveyed her kingdom. Crocks, tinned goods, bags and kitchen utensils sat on shelves and hung from nails around the room. She was reminded of an old advertisement for the Victoria Bakery James Walker used to put in the News Record. She knew it by heart and could even sing it if she wanted to. She stifled that desire when she remembered Thomas sleeping above her.

> *Victoria store for bread and buns,*
> *Victoria teas have got the runs,*
> *Victoria cakes and crackers too,*
> *Victoria fruit the season new.*

Victoria candies and Xmas toys,
Victoria sleighs for girls and boys,
Victoria sugars to sample true,
Victoria syrups you can see through.

Victoria goods are cheap and real,
Victoria store for prize oatmeal,
Victoria for all knick knack
Victoria once and you'll come back.

She never asked any of her friends but she was sure no one else in the village was forced to bathe in a dark pantry. Tonight she had gathered a bundle of fresh lemon balm, tied it together and put it in the tub with her. The fragrance of fresh balm mingled with the spice smells of the room. Once, while she was bathing, a little mouse poked his head up through the hole he'd gnawed in the floor, looked around, scurried up to the shelves and threaded his quiet way among the tins of grapes, pie peaches and oysters. He seemed to know exactly where he was going and, sure enough, he stopped at the oatmeal sack to feed. Clara threw her soap at him and managed to knock the 'Pure Gold Baking Powder' tin into the tub with her. Fortunately it wasn't the mouse! The mouse retreated hastily to his hole and she decided to put the tub over the hole in the future or stuff it with newspaper.

She did a lot of thinking in the tub, mostly about how it was when the village was less sophisticated. She and Sootie managed to play some pretty good pranks in the 60's. Thomas never forgave them for the 'surprise' they sprang on the Hamiltons. Hamiltons had left on their honeymoon leaving a full house of new furniture behind. Sootie and she had climbed through the basement window armed with hammer and nails. They nailed every window in the house shut from the inside with the exception of one in the basement and piled all the heavy pieces of furniture against the outside doors before crawling back out the same window they entered by. When the newlyweds returned they couldn't budge doors or windows. Hamilton followed two sets of footprints through the mud to Thomas' back door, one large and the other small, a task not too dificult to do as the properties were back to back. Thomas went looking for Clara knowing Sootie would make himself scarce for several days and he was hopping mad! Clara was on the second floor of Boswell's store on her very first day of apprenticing to the milliner and sat at the window amidst hat forms, ribbons and lace watching the progress of her father up and down St. Andrews Street looking for her. At the time she couldn't even understand why she needed to learn a trade but she was glad to be out of Thomas' way. He did calm down by the time she arrive home to make his supper.

She was often unjustly accused of the pranks Sootie pulled. He and Crawford once took the wheels off all the democrats outside T.H. Cunningham's Carriage Shop and hid them in the Constable's stable. Cunningham advertised in the paper that 'whoever took the wheels off the Democrats had better return them promptly.' Imagine the Constable's chagrin when Cunningham pulled them out of his hay mow, after receiving an anonymous tip!

Sitting in the tub with her knees up reminded her of a story Dr. Groves told her yesterday.

'Horace Baldwin had been a tall man, 6' 7" at least, and when he died the family laid him out on two tables in the parlour. A nephew was sent to the city to purchase a coffin. When he and the coffin arrived it was found Horace didn't fit because of his size. The nephew took charge and decided to saw off the feet. Half way through the job he thought the body moved and he fainted dead away. Another relative had to carry on with the gruesome job, once it was started.'

Dr. Groves figured two holes in the end of the coffin would have sufficed. Clara would have liked another two feet at the end of her tub.

The water was cooling quickly so Clara soaped and rinsed just before she got out. As she dried herself briskly she thought her body hadn't deteriorated too much in her thirty six years.

Emptying the tub took stamina and ingenuity. In the summer she opened the window just enough to put a large funnel into the opening and proceeded to bail the tub out by the bucket full — pouring it out the funnel. She'd place a long piece of eavestroughing at the window ledge before she'd get the tub out. The water flowed out the funnel, through the eavestroughing and discharged onto the Dean's lawn where a large brown patch was developing from the soap. The Deans never caught on to Clara's trick and she was always very much concerned when they mentioned the dead patch. Tonight she would have to haul the water to the back door because a storm window had been put on the pantry window. For all the work she had to do, she considered the bath worth the effort.

APRIL 23, 1894

The soft morning sun fell across his bed but Thomas felt no compulsion to rise. He would be late for breakfast again but Clara would not complain. Even with two pillows he had difficulty breathing during the past night. Dr. Groves had been quite blunt with his last visit.

'You're an old man Thomas. You can't expect much now. It's a matter of time. Put your affairs in order.'

Thomas had been ahead of the good doctor in his thinking. In '89 he had paid John Thomson $15.76 towards his funeral expenses. He had chosen the coffin and the colour of the lining and had left a good morning coat with John to be put on his body when he died. Depending on what other details his daughters decided on, after his death which didn't concern Thomas, it should not cost them more than another $10.00 to bury him.

But he wasn't thinking of death this bright late spring day as he lay abed. He was thinking of Edinburgh, Scotland. So many of the early settlers of Fergus went home to Scotland to die. He knew there was no hope of a trip for himself as he was an old man but he often daydreamed of home. His mother Mary Moffat Young had wished for a girl when he had been born December 2nd, 1810 but he'd proven himself an asset to her by becoming a classical scholar at Edinburgh University and a tutor to one of the leading Scottish families. He found teaching dull and sought adventure in Canada where he opened a store in the fledgling Fergusson settlement in 1835, with a post office in 1836. In 1837 Webster engaged him to return to Scotland as a business agent for a period of two and one half years. He had accepted, returning to Mary in England, courting her and extracting a promise of marriage from her. He'd returned to Fergus in 1840 and immediately was drawn into Webster's new business ventures in Arthur and Luther.

'Father.' Clara was knocking at his door. 'Are you ill?'

'I am lying abed daughter. Can a body not rest in this house?'

'Do you wish breakfast in your bed?'

'I'll rise. If you give me a little time I will be down. Leave an old man be!'

He sat on the edge of his bed for awhile orienting himself to the upright position. The dressing went slowly as he was meticulous about his appearance. Descending the stairs took even longer. Each step was executed carefully. Clara busied herself in the kitchen. She knew enough not to assist him. He was viciously independent. Once in the kitchen breakfast was eaten in absolute silence. Georgina had long ago gone to work and Thomas had no desire to speak to Clara. Once his plate was pushed back, Clara spoke.

'What are your plans for this morning?'

'A walk . . . in the garden and down to Ross's.'

'Promise me you will not cross the main roads!'

Thomas rose and reached for his coat. The slight pain went down his arm again.

'Father . . . .'

'I promise. Give me my cane.'

He steadied himself with the cane as he made his way through the summer kitchen and out into the spring air. The soil gave up its rich earthy fragrances and the smells of warm rotting compost and fresh green grass excited him. He walked cautiously along the garden path.

'Good morning to you Mr. Young.' Mrs. MacIntyre was in her back yard. 'You are in high spirits this morning.'

'You might need glasses Mrs. MacIntyre. I do not feel "in high spirits".'

'The lilac has good bud again this spring.'

'It never fails me, my lilac tree.' He sat on the bench beneath the tree and closed his eyes letting the pain in his arm subside. Eventually he rose and walked to the front of 'Stonehome'. The spruce trees were a good size, providing some protection from the north and east winds. The gate through the picket fence was open to the street. Dray and light wagons continuously passed on the road going north toward Mount Forest and Owen Sound, and south to Hamilton. There was good reason for Clara not wanting him to cross the thoroughfare. He turned toward Garafraxa, walking slowly and painstakingly to the corner. The area was completely built up with fine stone and brick homes. He recognized no one on the street. The children were strangers to him and their mothers had little time to speak to an old man. Across Garafraxa Street, Georgina sat in the Ross Tailor Shop but he dare not cross the road to see her for the number of horse drawn vehicles using the road.

Last year when the village fathers had celebrated the 60th birthday of the settlement only Alex Fordyce, James McQueen and he were present to represent the members of the '35'. When Alex died in January of this year, James and he were alone, the last surviving settlers who came to the bush settlement as very young men between 1833 and 1835.

He turned and made his laborious way back to the house. This time he made sure the front gate was closed behind him. This massive stone structure before him had been his home for 15 years. It certainly wasn't showing its age as he was. Funny how times change. He remembered returning to Fergus in 1851 and finding Dr. Mutch's house at the corner of St. Patrick and St. David Streets the only home with a front door painted and it was startling bright blue. In 1864 that scoundrel Sootie had painted six doors in the village a brilliant orange in the early hours of July 12. In 1879, when it was considered very fashionable to let the beautiful wood grain show on the front doors of your home, Clara had painted the two massive front doors white! He affectionately patted the stone wall of the entry as he climbed the front steps.

'Is that you Father?'

'Were you expecting someone else?'

'I thought perhaps Sootie would stop in . . .'

'I don't want that man around here.' Thomas was fighting with his coat and Clara came to assist him.

'If there is one thing I would have done differently in my life, it would have been to have turned that man away from my door thirty-four years ago.'

'Yes father. Don't get yourself upset.'

'I'm not getting upset. I am stating a fact! I want to read.'

Once again he took the stairs one step at a time and made his way down the hall to the niche. A comfortable chair beckoned and he sat with photo album on his knees. Today with the sun streaming in on him, warming his face and hands he would insert pictures Louise had sent him of their nieces and nephews. He could see to write with the sun shining on the book.

Sometime later Clara came up the stairs, and not wanting to startle her father approached him quietly.

'Would you like some tea?' She touched his hand softly. 'Father?' His hand fell to the side of the chair. Thomas Adam Young was dead.

AUTHOR'S NOTE

In the mid 1850's, with much of the north American continent traversed and settled, the attentions of the European countries turned towards the huge continent to the south of them, Africa. Their interest was two-fold. They needed raw materials to fuel the industrial revolution and they had a missionary desire to bring Christianity to the savages. Along with England, France, Germany and Holland, Portugal and Italy were active in claiming rights to parts of the continent for their respective countries. Italy's interest in East Africa began in the fourth century A.D. when Greco-Roman traders brought goods and religion to the port towns along the Red Sea. For Italy, a country overcrowded with people, East Africa also offered thousands of acres of land for colonization. The main thrust of the Italian occupation was in the Horn of Africa and Red Sea areas. By 1884, encouraged by the British, the Italian government proclaimed a protectorate over the Eritrean coast on the Red Sea and shiploads of prospective immigrants were sent from the homeland to settle the area. Between 1885 and 1889 various Italian entrepreneurs managed to establish claims to the area on the Horn of Africa known as Somaliland. The one country holding up the connection of the two protectorates was Ethiopia, caught in the middle. With the treaty of Accialli in 1889 the Italians were led to believe they had successfully made Ethiopia into their protectorate also and began an inland thrust to unite the Eritrean Coast and Somaliland. They were met with fierce resistance on the part of the Ethiopians who were ruthless warriors under the leadership of Emperor Menelik II, aided by French advisors. The Italians, desperately needing manpower and reinforcements, recruited every available boy and man in their homeland who could carry a rifle. In some of the poorer sections of Italy where illiteracy was prominent the young men were led to believe they were signing colonization agreements for land in Africa, but found themselves instead thrust into the bloodiest, most inhumane war of the late 1800's, ill equipped to handle the Ethiopian tribesmen who were a ferocious and formidable enemy.

Carlo Mattaini was a young man recruited from a village in Northern Italy, thinking he was going to Eritrea to build houses and bridges for his fellow countrymen. He was a builder of stone and brick and not a soldier of war. He found himself on Ethiopian soil with an old rifle in his hands fighting for his life in the 7,000 foot rampart of the great rift valley which formed and protected the Eastern frontier of the country. He fought in some of the bloodiest of the battles but one day found himself so sickened with the carnage he threw his rifle away and turned his back on the campaign. He was not alone in his decision to retreat as many others joined him on his trek to the coast and freedom.

Two weeks after Carlo lay down his rifle, Italy was soundly defeated in the Battle of Aduwa (1896) by Emperor Menelik. The Italians that survived the carnage retreated hastily to the Eritrean Coast or Somaliland.

Many former soldiers concerned about the methods of recruitment by their government and by the instability of the African political climate crossed the Atlantic to establish new homes in Canada. Carlo was one of those men.

CHRISTMAS DAY 1897

Carlo sat by the fire and pondered the events which had taken place in the past four months. He had returned to Italy to confess his desertion and had been proclaimed a hero instead because he had been one of the very few to escape the battle of Aduwa alive. He even had a paper declaring that he fought in the African campaign! He turned from the fire to watch his sister working by the window in the kitchen.

'Assunta, I will freeze to death! I should better have died in Ethiopia. I was warm there. You will find me one morning, frozen solid in my bed. God chose I should freeze to death in Canada!'

Assunta turned from her meal preparations to look at her brother. He certainly was a pitiful sight huddled next to the kitchen stove with her shawl around his shoulders.

'God chose that you should come to Canada to make a new life for yourself Carlo. Think of your bridges and your dreams! You'll learn to live with the cold. It is not like Italy but when spring comes you will enjoy the country. You dress appropriately and learn not to venture out in a blizzard.'

'There is a blizzard everytime I look out. Always white flakes coming down and wind howling. This plain is at the end of the world.'

'You are not on a plain. You are in the middle of Ontario, Canada and you have a dream. That's why you are here, remember that always. Wait until you see the rivers Carlo!'

She glanced out the window towards the road.

'Quickly Carlo, give me my shawl. Faustino, Carolina and Marie are here Don't look like a woman in front of Marie. She will laugh.'

Assunta changed to the fresh apron she kept behind the kitchen door for company and went to greet the trio. She lapsed quickly from Italian to English as she spoke, first with Faus and Carolina and then with Marie.

'Marie, would you go with Carlo while he does the chores?'

Carlo readied himself for the cold by pulling several pair of socks over his feet.

"The Italian Connection"

(Top Row) Johnny Mattaini, Landoni, Romeo Landoni, Tom Landoni, Louie Landoni (Don's father).
(Front Row) Charles Mattaini, Luigi Landoni, Faustino Landoni, Mario Landoni Sr., Tony Mattaini.

'Is this enough Faustino?'

'No, at least three pair Carlo and two scarves or your toes will turn blue.' He winked at Assunta over the bent form of Carlo.

Marie led the way to the barn with Carlo walking precisely in her footsteps.

'Your legs are uncovered Marie! Are you not cold?'

Marie turned to him, eyes flashing, teeth as white as the snow. She spoke Italian to him, one of the few times she spoke her mother tongue.

'I have been here eleven years, Mr. Mattaini. I do not feel the cold. I remember little of Vergiate. I was only two when Mama brought me out.'

'It is Carlo, Maria.'

'It is Marie, Charlie.'

'Charlie!' He liked the sound of his new English name.

The two spent the next half hour collecting eggs and feeding the pigs. The cows had been milked earlier. Charlie repeated the English words for everything after Marie. Like the Canadian winters, the words sounded harsh to his ears. Someday he would master both the language and the winters. He lead the way back to the house, breaking a path for Marie through the fresh blown drifts. The smells that greeted them as the kitchen door was opened were intoxicating. Such customs the Canadians had of gift giving, decorated trees and feasting on the Christ Child's birthday, but such weather!

Clara had been up since 5:00 am preparing for dinner. The dining room was decorated with cedar boughs and oranges. The table was set with the best dishes. The goose was in the oven and the pudding steamed gently on the stove. All that was needed now was Sootie and his fiddle. He'd been away from the village for several weeks but promised before he left that he would return to 'Stonehome' for Christmas.

Yesterday she and Georgina decorated the living room with cedar boughs and a small tree on a parlour table. The parlour hadn't been opened in some time so it took them most of the morning to dust and arrange the room. She went to the coal yard to arrange for a small bag of coal and some wood for the fireplace. The room had no other source of heat. As they carefully unwrapped the blown glass ornaments both Georgina and she remembered the Christmasses on St. George Street when mother was still alive and small children, including themselves, were around. It took fourteen years for Christmas to finally reach 'Stonehome' for Thomas in his old age would not allow 'the pagan celebration' of the church feast.

The wind was howling when they set off for church and both hoped that wouldn't keep Sootie from keeping his promise. The service was held in the new English Church at the corner of Tower and St. Patrick Streets and it was quite a walk for the sisters. Once at the church they sat in the family pew.

'Father would have been proud of this church. He was such a staunch Anglican!'

'He didn't mind the old church at the end of St. Patrick Street. That was where Rev. Smithurst spoke for the first time in Fergus when both Fergus and

Elora shared him as their minister. I recall father telling of the first time the Rev. came. He was incensed that so many people, most of them not Anglicans, went to church that day and when he got into the church proper, some Methodist had taken the family pew!'

'Father and Rev. Smithurst were close friends, Clara. It had something to do with their devotion to one woman for so long in their lives. Father waited ten years to marry mother and Rev. Smithurst became a minister because of his love for his first cousin, Florence Nightingale. I understand their parents would not allow the marriage and she became a nurse.'

'Posh, Georgina! She had another first cousin who lives in the United States. She gave a communion set to both with an inscription on each. The news of the other cousin was in the paper not long ago.'

'Clara, I do not believe that story and we'll talk no more about it.'

Georgina ended all discussions she didn't particularly like with that statement and it irked Clara. Georgina might not talk to her for a week now about anything!

The service was well attended with the congregation enjoying the festive music of Christmas. Afterward the minister shook hands with everyone at the doors of the church, wishing them the blessings of the season.

'The Miss Youngs. May I offer you a ride to your door?' Dr. Groves pulled up in his six seater sleigh. It was not often that he personally drove the team, leaving the job up to Sootie or some other worthy person but today being Christmas was an exception.

'Delighted, Doctor. Did you enjoy the service? I noticed you sitting to the right of us.' Georgina was suddenly talking again and very cheerful.

The passengers moved to make room for the sisters and the horses pulled their way along St. Patrick Street to the Owen Sound Road. A fast drive with bells jingling on the harness, up the main road and the sisters were deposited at their door.

'Girls, I see you have company. Good day to you Sootie, my friend. Sootie would never accompany the sisters to church and it was very much like him to be at the door awaiting their return. He assisted each of the ladies out of the sleigh while talking to Dr. Groves. Clara, quite suddenly, realized that Sootie had not come alone to 'Stonehome' for standing just inside the double doors was the figure of a small woman. Clara was somewhat surprised but tried not to show any outward sign of it. She approached the young woman cheerfully.

'Come in, come in both of you. Georgina see to the wraps. I'll help Miss . . Sootie put a protective arm out to the woman.

"Misses Clara, Georgina, before we say too much more I must explain. I would like to formally introduce you to Annalee . . . my wife!' He watched Clara closely. She took an involuntary step backwards. She didn't startle easily but this time Sootie had certainly presented her with quite a surprise! Georgina showed both shock and frustration as she had no idea how to handle such a situation. Both exclaimed together.

'Your wife!'

'Yes. Wife.' He spoke gently watching Clara all the while.

'This is Annalee, my wife.'

Annalee offered her hand to Clara then Georgina.

'Annalee knows no one in the village and I was hoping you will be friends, close friends.'

Clara moved first to soften the awkward situation.

'We'd best talk in the parlour. Come in where its warmer. We've a fire laid in the grate ready to light. Please everyone have a seat.'

Sootie took a match and lit the dry kindling under the coal in the hearth basket and the fire sprang to life immediately.

Conversation was strained but cordial. Annalee answered all the questions put to her carefully, as though she had been rehearsed. Was this one of Sootie's practical jokes?

Clara scrutinized both people closely while talking to them and decided not. A twinge of jealousy suddenly stabbed her! Imagine, a man his age marrying such an innocent child! He never ceased to amaze her. Another twinge of jealousy tickled at her and she excused herself to the kitchen to see to dinner. How strange of Sootie not to have confided in her about his marriage. What would she have done if he had? She had never felt jealousy before but as she scurried around the kitchen she felt jealous and threatened. Why? 'Stonehome' wasn't threatened, only her relationship with Sootie. Annalee would now be Sootie's confidante because of her position as his wife. Clara and he could still be friends. Friends is all they really were, wasn't it? Once, she thought, when I was very young I saw myself as Sootie's wife, but he never gave me any encouragement. As a matter of fact, after he came back in '82, from wherever he had been, he grew distinctly cool in his relationship if she even hinted at any intimacy.

'Clara?' Annalee had come into the kitchen.

'Clara, I'm so sorry to have been brought here on such short notice. Sootie wanted it this way. It was a shock to you. I understand. I'm an intruder in your life and in your home. Sootie has told me everything, Clara. We must be friends! Sootie is very much a stranger to me also. You must help me understand him. This was all so . . . sudden.'

Annalee looked so young and so unprotected standing in her kitchen with tears brimming in her dark eyes that Clara dropped the strainer and went to her immediately.

'Annalee, child! You are Sootie's wife and my friend. Of course, it was a shock to me. Sootie said not a word about you but that doesn't make us enemies!'

The two women, one a mere child, the other a mature woman of fortyone, stood in the middle of the Christmas dinner preparations, embracing each other, tears flowing freely.

'Go and make yourself presentable to Sootie. My room is to the front of the house on the left.'

Just before dinner Clara excused herself and went to her room. The trousseau chest stood at the foot of her bed, full but never used. She opened the chest and carefully chose a beautifully handmade nightgown, which she wrapped in tissue, enclosing a small note for Annalee wishing her happiness with Sootie. In the season of love and giving no one deserved to be left out of the festivities. She managed to slip the package under the tree while no one was looking and proclaimed Christmas dinner ready to be served.

When all four were seated at the dining room table Sootie raised his glass in toast.

'To all three of my loves.' He tipped his glass in each of the lady's direction.

They graciously acknowledged the toast and settled in to the bountiful meal.

'What happened while I was out of the village? Anything I might be interested in?'

Clara was careful about the way she broached the information she wanted to relay to Sootie.

'There is a new Italian man in the community above Dracon, Carlo Mattaini. He is a friend of Louis Landoni's and a brother to Louis's wife. I believe Carolina said he came from Vergiate in Northern Italy. Actually she was more specific than that. She said it was three miles from Sesto Galende and 60 miles from Bellinzona in Switzerland.'

She watched Sootie closely for a reaction to the mention of Bellinzona. He hesitated momentarily as he placed his glass of wine on the table. No one else in the dining room knew the significance of the word.

'Bellinzona, Sesto Galende. I have some recollection of reading or hearing of those two places. Is this Carlo an interesting man? Do you think I should strike up an acquaintance with him?'

Sootie looked directly at Clara, returning her gaze so intensely that she had to lower her eyes.

'I'm sure you'll find him an interesting man and it certainly wouldn't hurt to introduce yourself to him. He is a stranger in our community and might just appreciate your interest in him.'

'And you say his name is Carlo?'

'Carlo Mattaini.'

St. David Street North looking south towards St. Andrews Street. Taken from above St. George Street.

St. Andrews Street and Templin Carriage Works.

CHICKENS AND WHEELBARROWS

Clara, dressed in her old bodice and skirt with hair pinned loosely on the nape of her neck, went back to the small barn to retrieve her shovel and wheelbarrow. It was just a perfect day for her walk, warm and sunny, but as soon as she saw 'Ramrod' coming across her yard she knew it had just been spoiled. The woman looked as though a stick had been shoved up her corset from bottom to top and pranced along like a horse with both front feet in a washbucket. Trouble was brewing again. The woman was never happy unless she was complaining and Clara had long ago resigned herself to the fact that 'Ramord's' chief aim in life was to aggravate her at least once a day.

'Miss Young!'

'Yes Ma'am.' That usually got Ramord's' goat immediately as both women were the same age.

'Your chickens were in my garden again this morning.'

'If your dog wouldn't dig holes under the fence to get at my chickens, they wouldn't be able to get under the fence to peck at your garden.'

'It's not fair Miss Young. There are even signs that tell you there's no trespassing on my property. Can't you read.'

'I'm not trespassing personally on your property.'

'But you chickens are and you'll just have to do something about them.'

'I will if you'll give me some help.'

'And what might I have to do Miss Young?'

'Obviously we'll have to teach the animals how to read the signs won't we but I'll bet you my chickens will learn faster than your hound just what no trespassing means.'

'Ramrod' fumed.

'Incorrigible! That's the word my husband used to describe you.'

'It's nice to know your husband thinks of me occasionally as I find him an interesting specimen also.'

'Ramrod' changed her tactics. Her normally shrill voice now purred like a kitten near a bowl of milk.

'Are you going somewhere Miss Young? I see you've got your shovel and wheelbarrow out.'

You know exactly what I'm up to you old bat, Clara thought. She looked 'Ramrod' directly in the eye.

'Horse shit, best thing there is for an asparagus bed and free for the taking on the road. There's plenty for both of us. Get a wheelbarrow and come along.'

A speechless 'Ramrod' wheeled on her heels and pranced back to her house, slamming the door behind her. Clara put the shovel in the barrow and let herself out the gate. By tomorrow swearing would be added to her long list of 'unladylike behaviour' but she really didn't give a damn. The day was warm and there had been plenty of horses down the Owen Sound Road in the past several days leaving their offerings for her asparagus bed.

St. David Street South looking north towards St. Andrews Street. Taken from Union Street.

St. Andrews Street and townhall.

MARIE — AUGUST 1900

Marie saw the buggy coming from her loft window. He said he'd come but she didn't believe him. A teacher visiting her home was akin the Pope visiting in Italy. She hadn't told her mother! She had been afraid to for fear he didn't arrive.

'Mama, there is a buggy coming in the lane.' Carolina drew the curtains aside on the kitchen window.

'Is it a stranger?'

'It is the Insegnante Mama, Mr. Greenaway, my teacher.'

'Insegnante! Marie go . . . 'the Faustino' . . . in the granario . . . bring him.' Marie ran for the barn while Carolina changed her apron and replaced lids on crocks. She covered the pies she was baking with a clean piece of cotton cloth. She closed the kitchen door and went to the parlour. Her loom had been moved from the loft where it shared space with Marie's bed, to the coolness of the parlour for the summer. Her lace cushion lay on a small table. Such a mess for the insegnante to see! She had been busy with meals for the harvesters and worked on the loom by lamplight in the evening. She threw her hands in the air. There was nothing she could do now but greet the man at the door.

Mr. Greenaway had tethered the horse to a fencepost and came across the yard, hat in hand.

'Mrs. Landoni. I'm Mr. Greenaway, Marie's teacher.' He offered his hand and she accepted it, but hesitantly. For a teacher to visit a home there had to be a grave problem or a cause for celebration. She wasn't sure what he wanted.

'We've met . . . sculoa . . . Natale.'

'Yes. You were at all the Christmas concerts the students presented.'

'Please come.' She indicated he should enter the house. He was well prepared for the visit. Marie had informed him on everything which might come up in conversation with her parents. The Landoni's were proud of Marie's progress in public school because they had never gone to school in Italy themselves.

'Scusa . . . it is a busy time.'

She ushered him to the parlour and indicated he should sit on the best piece of furniture she owned, the horsehair sofa. He sat uncomfortably, hat still in hand. Carolina sat directly opposite him on a small chair, obviously waiting for him to speak. He was waiting for some sign of Marie who had promised to be at the house. So they sat in complete silence. The door from the kitchen opened. Marie and 'the Faustino' entered, 'the Faustino' in his work clothes, heavy with sweat and dust of the harvest.

'Mr. Landoni, I'm Mr. Greenaway, Marie's teacher.' He rose and offered his hand. Faustino crossed the floor and shook it, then sat facing the teacher beside Carolina. This visit was not going to be easy. The Landonis seemed content to have him just sit there. He cleared his throat and began.

'Marie is finished her schooling. To progress further she must go to finishing school in Owen Sound. She has done well in school and should further her education.'

'Yes.'

'If she continues in school she will become a teacher, like myself.'

'Yes.'

'It is an honourable occupation for a woman as well as a man. You will, I am sure allow her to continue her education.'

'No.'

He'd been doing so well! He decided to try a different approach. 'Canada is a great country. It has been generous to all those who have come to live here. It has given them hope and security.'

'Yes, oh yes, Insegnante.'

'It has been good to you. You have a home, a farm, good crops but you work hard for it.'

'Yes.'

'If Marie attended finishing school she wouldn't have to work so hard to achieve what you have. She could ask more money for teaching than you could make in farming.'

'Yes.'

'You will consider letting her attend the Owen Sound School then?'

'No.'

He was beginning to get a little annoyed with the one sided conversation. 'But she'll learn so much about the world. She'll know so much more than you. She is rather an intelligent young woman. She'd do well in school, do you not agree?'

'Yes, of course.'

'She'd meet people, travel, perhaps make friends with Canadian men and women her age. Would that not be good for her?'

'No.'

'You do not want her to travel? She could teach in the area. There are country schools right around the area who would consider hiring her.'

'She can travel. It is the Canadian friends. They are not Catholic. They are not Italian.'

'Does it matter to Marie? She is a young woman with ideas of her own. Cannot she pick her friends?'

'Yes. They come . . . We meet . . . We approve . . . No men come. She is an obedient daughter.'

'Perhaps I should put it differently. If she were to attend Finishing School she would be educated. She would not have to put in hours of hard physical labour. For example,' he pointed to Carolina's loom, 'She could use her mind to accomplish the work you use your hands to do.'

'There is nothing wrong with using hands. I spin and make lace in Vergiate long before I read or write. It is honourable work for a woman. It gives money now for Marie's dowry. You read but you would go . . . naked. You cannot wear books.'

'There are machines to do the work. They have freed people to use their minds, to advance their education.'

'Marie will learn a trade, as I. The books can be read at night.'

'Mr. Landoni, you haven't said a thing. Do you not think Marie should further her education? Is it not right that she should have the opportunities I have had?'

Faustino spoke quietly in hesitant English. 'Inesgnante. Have you seen Roma, the statues by Michael Angelo, the Eiffel, the great England, New York, as I?'

'No, I haven't.'

'Then what has the education gotten you? I, a labourer who work with my hands, and Carolina have seen the beauties of the world. You, who think with your head, have not; yet you teach of them. Hard work is not . . . cattivo. These hands,' Faustino held out his dirty, stained hands, ' God made to work. But because I use these hands, does not mean I do not think.' He pointed at his head. 'They work together. Maria, my daughter will travel. She will read but she will work . . . with her hands, before her head.'

'And Marie. Have you asked her what she wants to do? Does it matter nothing to you what she wants?'

Again Faustino spoke quietly. 'We spoke. This . . . domanda, it has caused words between us. Never before she has questioned us. It was . . . as . . . forbici . . . the scissors, were cutting us apart. Maria is obedient, the woman of two . . . cultures. She is born d'Italia and raised of Canada. Carolina and I have only Maria. There could not be more. She is . . . la vita . . . la luce . . . You ask us to put out the light! If she goes away to the school, the light will go out. Do you understand?'

'I think I am beginning to. I have insulted you unintentionally. I did not mean to imply you were stupid because you labour with your hands. This country would not prosper if it weren't for people such as yourself who till its soil and reap its harvests. I am not that different from you. I reap a harvest of young minds.'

'You must forgive if I have insulted you. To be a teacher is a great honour.'

'Why then don't you consider letting Marie become a teacher?'

'She is a woman.'

'I am afraid I do not understand your reasoning. What is Marie going to do with her life?' Carolina turned to Marie who had been sitting quietly by the loom.

'Marie, you speak to Mr. Greenaway of the plans. It is better that you explain.' Marie looked toward her parents then turned to the visitor.

'Mr. Greenaway, we discussed it again. They do not wish me to leave home. They have conceded that after I learn a trade, I can pursue my education but I must learn a trade.'

'You'll learn quickly. There is hope. Perhaps in two years you will be able to attend finishing school.'

'There is no hope or chance of that. You don't seem to understand customs of the old country. They will immediately begin looking for a suitable marriage for me.'

'They'll arrange a marriage!' Mr. Greenaway was incredulous. 'You can't stand for that. You are Canadian now. You are a free woman. This is not Italy!'

'They are my parents and I am their child. I am also a product of two diverse cultures as papa said. I will handle each situation as it comes. I would no nothing to hurt them. They have devoted their lives to me. Mama works hours at the loom, making linen to sell. The money she earns goes back into the farm, and is also set aside as a dowry. Papa doesn't make much in the brickyards and this fifty acres does not support a large farm. Even if they agreed to me continuing my education they could not afford it.'

'I would pay. I have done it for other students.'

'They would be too proud to accept your offer.'

Carolina interrupted the conversation.

'I will please the guest . . . tè . . . caffè?'

'I would appreciate a cup of tea, thank you.'

Carolina disappeared quickly into the kitchen. Faustino remained in the parlour although work was pressing outside. A sixteen year old, single woman was never left unchaperoned with a man.

Mr. Greenaway sensed the discussion regarding Maria was closed and turned his attention to Faustino, speaking about crops and farming. Marie left to help her mother serve the tea.

Not two weeks later Marie stepped inside the small frame building housing the Miss' McGladrey's Dressmaking Shop in Fergus. She came here so often before she could close her eyes and tell exactly how the shop was arranged. Today she wasn't on any errand for her mother. She was beginning her apprenticeship as a dressmaker. She had come into the village, handling the horse and buggy like an expert, with a box of clothing and a box of books behind the seat. Her boarding house was close to the Catholic church in a home totally inspected and approved by her mother. It had been a concession on their part to allow her to board in Fergus. The presence of the Catholic church put her mother's fears to rest that she was entering a 'heathen community'.

'Miss McGladrey. I've come.'

'Marie. Come in. We are busy with fall alterations and there are a number of experienced dressmakers hired for several months work. I'll introduce you.' She walked to the back of the shop where several women sat sewing.

'Clara.' A small freckle faced woman looked up from the hem of a gown she was concentrating on.

'Marie, this is Miss Young. You'll be working closely with her. I could recommend no better woman for you to begin your apprenticeship with as Miss Young is an excellent seamstress.'

Clara smiled at the young woman and thought 'such a striking beauty to be working in the confines of a dreary dressmaking shop'.

'It's Clara. Have you any sewing experience? If I ask you to insert triangular gussets under the arms of the English Cheviot Serge suit jacket on the table, could you do it?'

'Yes, Miss Young.'

'It's Clara! That's an advanced dressmaking alteration. You have had some training?'

'My mother is an excellent dressmaker but she has allowed me the freedom of apprenticing in Fergus.'

That's a freedom?'

'For you perhaps not . . . for me it's a battle won.' Clara liked this young woman.

When Marie drove the ancient mare 'Scarafaggio' into the lane at the farm several weeks later to visit her parents for the first time since she began her apprenticeship, she was surprised to see Charles Mattaini come quickly from the small frame house to help her alight. Her parents were wasting no time in finding a suitable husband for her.

Faustino and Carolina in front of their house — Fourth Line of West Garafraxa, 1900.

THE INVITATION — SEPTEMBER 1902

All the small villages and towns have their share of men's and women's secret societies, all organized for the betterment of the community. Fergus was no exception. Some of the most refined and influential women in the village were said to belong to the 'Women's Benevolent Society' which met several times a month in absolute secrecy. All Clara knew about the organization was that occasionally some poor destitute woman in the village would receive a contribution of money said to have come from the Society. No one knew exactly who belonged, where they met or what rules they lived up to. The invitation that she attend their next meeting was therefore a complete and unexpected surprise for Clara was not the type to be a candidate for admission to the Society. Georgina immediately took charge.

'You've got to wear a hat and make sure your black silk skirt is pressed and clean. This is important Clara!'

'Why? I can't imagine why I'd be selected to join. They must have made a mistake.'

'There's been no mistake. The envelope is addressed clearly to you.'

'I might possibly decide not to attend.'

'Clara! You must attend. They will expect you to be there. Other women in the community would envy you if they knew you were chosen.'

'I have not been chosen!'

Clara had mulled the invitation over in her mind and decided she would go. Her curiosity was getting the better of her. She really wanted to know who belonged and what the Society did do. She couldn't imagine why she had been summoned to the meeting but she was standing on the doorstep on Union Street about to find out. Clara made sure she would be neither too early nor too late. At exactly 1:58 pm she timidly knocked on the door which brought the lady of the house immediately.

'Miss Young; Clara do come in. We've been waiting for you.'

Once in the hall she was left standing while the hostess took her cape and disappeared into one of the side rooms. Clara glanced at herself in a full length mirror to the side of the hall. Her skirt and bodice were stylish and neat and the confounded hat was still on her head. She felt satisfied that she could join the group, dressed appropriately.

'This way. We're in the parlour today.' Clara followed the hostess through the double doors and was shown to a comfortable chair at the back of the room.

'Nice you could come Miss Young.' A woman with a gigantic red feather in her hat leaned toward her chair. Clara smiled and was about to reply when the rapping of a gavel interrupted the conversation.

'Ladies. We've all assembled I see. Perhaps we should begin. Miss Jones, could we have the pledge?' A small woman in a square blue hat stood up and opened her mouth to speak . . . 'but before we repeat the pledge I must stress something.' The Chairman gave Clara a withering look. 'Nothing . . . but NOTHING goes beyond this room . . . beyond these four walls . . . The pledge Miss Jones.'

'We pledge total alliance to the Monarch.'

'I pledge,' intoned the gathering. Red feather glanced at Clara.

'I pledge,' Clara hastily replied.

'We pledge total alliance to the rules by which the Woman's Benevolent Society governs itself.'

'I pledge.' Again the room answered. Clara abstained. She didn't know the rules.

'We pledge to provide a lunch and meeting hall when asked by the Benevolent Committee.'

'I pledge.'

'We pledge that by personal financial donation we will assist our less fortunate sisters.'

'I pledge,' answered half the room which brought a severe look from the Chairman. The gavel came down again.

'Our assembly is open. There are several accounts which need to be renewed. Secretary, are you ready to record?'

'Ready, Grand Mistress.'

'That we continue our $10.00 donation to Widow Moore.' Two hands went up . . . one holding up one finger and the other holding up two. The secretary wrote furiously.

'That our donation to the Farmer's Mechanics Institute this month be "Animals Before Man in North America . . . Frederic Lucas".'

A clap interrupted the proceedings. A massive woman in a huge black hat stood up. 'Wouldn't Shaler's "Sea and Land" be a better donation?'

'Published in 1894. It's 1902 my dear! We are trying to upgrade our library.'

Black hat sat down. Two hands went up.

'That we continue our efforts to purge the village of those despicable persons saturating the community with alcohol.' Two hands went up.

'That being the end of our continuous business, the assembly is open to discussion on our two new interests. Could we have the report from Miss Smith on "the woman".

A buxom woman in a green velvet hat stood. 'She has decided to leave the community. I get that information from most reliable sources.'

'The sooner the better.' A small brown hat quipped from the front row.

'The problem being "she" has no immediate funds to look for accomodation elsewhere, possibly Guelph.'

'With the amount of business "she" does you would expect there would be no lack of funds.' Red feather interjected.

'It's the rumor! Nobody would dare go for fear . . .' The sentence trailed off. Clara touched the arm of the woman next to her.

'Who are we discussing?'

'The "Woman" my dear. You know the . . . the PROSTITUTE!'

'Oh, that woman.'

'I move we donate $10.00 towards the moving expenses of the . . . lady.' The room erupted in giggles.

'Lady is the wrong word to use, Miss Jones. We are ladies. "She" falls in an entirely different category.'

'If we want to rid ourselves of her we should be willing to contribute a little towards her moving expenses.'

Clara coughed.

'Miss Young. I'm sorry. Did you have a comment?' Clara couldn't resist.

'Perhaps you should offer her 'severence pay'. After all it might take awhile for her to establish her "business" in another community.'

'From one who knows?' A snide remark from Clara's left was barely audible.

'Now ladies, Miss Young has "tongue in cheek", I'm sure. It was meant as a joke.'

'Of course.' Clara demured. 'But perhaps you should consider $15.00. That might remove her to Waterloo.' Clara knew "she" was moving to Waterloo anyway.

'Miss Young does have a point.' Green Hat allowed. 'The further away the better.'

'Wouldn't Jack drive that far?' That from a small square purple hat on the far side of the room.

'How dare . . . .'

'LADIES, Ladies. Remember the governing rules!'

Whatever the governing rules, the parlour settled down. Dirty glances were exchanged between the green hat and the purple hat.

'Would we please have hands on a $15.00 donation towards moving expenses for "her".' All hands went up.

'I'll deliver it personally,' said the Grand Mistress. 'The donations basket will be passed around during tea. Please be generous.' She paused to look at her notes.

'Mrs. Deal, you'll be responsible for the meeting hall and lunch in two weeks time. A vote on that please.'

Two hands went up quickly. The secretary lifted her eyes momentarily from her writing to check on fingers; one indicating proposed and two indicating a seconder. Obviously she took down every word uttered although the minutes of the last meeting were never read before the assembly.

'Miss Young.' The Grand Mistress addressed Clara directly. 'You are perhaps wondering why you were invited to this meeting?'

'The question had crossed my mind in the past twenty minutes, I will admit.' A snicker went through the room.

'You've a quick sense of humour. We,' she indicated the gathering in the parlour, 'are concerned about one of our sisters. You are perhaps closest to her and could give us some details on the situation.'

Clara remained silent.

'It has been drawn to our attention that one of our sisters is living in degrading conditions and in poverty. We are therefore concerned. No woman should be subjected to such treatment. We have heard that Mrs. . . . Annalee . . . the wife of Sootie . . . is living in a filthy shanty with no conveniences and in absolute destitution.'

'Who would tell you such a thing?'

'It is in our governing rules that we divulge no sources of information.'

'Have you visited Annalee? Have you spoken with her?'

'Of course not! We prefer anonyminity. If she is in need we will consider financial support but we do not ask directly. We do our own detective work.'

I'll bet you do, thought Clara. She rose from her seat. 'Grand Mistress, your sources are far from the truth. If you visit Annalee you will find her truly happy in a spotless home; surrounded by good books and love. There is no filth, no squalor and no poverty. Sootie has been successful with financial endeavours and is most generous with his wife. She has all the comforts we enjoy.'

'But it's a shanty!'

'It's a home. You seem to forget your parents and grandparents lived in far worse with only the clothes on their backs and a bake kettle on the hearth. And they were content, weren't they. They didn't need grand houses and lavish furnishings. That came later.'

'But this is the 20th century, Miss Young.'

'The century has nothing to do with happiness. If you put Annalee in a tent in the middle of the bush, she would be happy. It depends entirely on your outlook in life. She does not need your assistance and would be embarassed if you approached her.'

The Grand Mistress seemed at a loss as to what to say next. Annalee was obviously going to be her personal crusade.

Clara continued. 'If you are looking for people living in filth and squalor I suggest you turn your attentions to the Irish and Scottish families living in the tenement houses in the village, being paid a pittance by their employers and being taken advantage of by some pompous landlords. They are right under your noses ' She knew she had lit home because some of the wives of those 'pompous landlords' squirmed in their seats. Clara was treading on thin ground not covered in the governing rules.

The Grand Mistress interjected quickly. 'I believe in the case of Mrs. . . . Annalee, we have been misinformed and thank Miss Young for correcting us. We will give some thought to her comments on slum tenements. Shall we have lunch?' The gavel came down on the table for a last time.

'Be it moved that the Women's Benevolent Society Assembly adjourn until the 2nd of the next month.'

Two hands went up.

The hostess and two young maids appeared with tea trays and plates of sandwiches.

'She always serves chopped egg sandwiches, so peasant!' Red feather whispered into Clara's ear.

'I'm plebian enough to thoroughly enjoy a chopped egg sandwich.' Clara helped herself to a cup of tea offered and added a thin slice of lemon. She glanced around the parlour. The women were all busy passing around the latest gossip. The donations basket made its rounds. When it reached Clara, she rummaged into her bag and retrieved a button which she dropped in with the coinage resting in the bottom of the basket. She quietly put basket and tea cup on a window ledge and excused herself from the room. The hostess hurried after her.

'You're leaving us so soon, Miss Young.'

'Yes. I felt a little chill.' She hated to lie.

'Did you find it cool in the parlour?'

'No. Actually it seemed to be quite warm, a lot of hot air in there I think . . . Could I have my cape? The fresh air will revive me.'

Once out in the crisp air she walked quickly along Union Street putting as many blocks as she could between the Women's Benevolent Society and herself. Eventually she stopped in at Ross the Tailors, as she promised Georgina she would.

Georgina sat at the back of the shop by a sewing machine. The dim light did nothing healthy for her eyes.

'You're back Clara. Was it exciting? You've been accepted!'

'Thank God I was never asked!'

BELLINZONA — 1904

The two men sat huddled in the hunting blind. They'd been there for several hours. Occasionally they heard the retort of the guns of their companions.

'You're not paying too much attention to the livestock out there Charlie. You haven't raised your gun yet or bothered to look. You could have missed a good doe.'

'I don't kill anything. I don't hunt. I come with the men. They hunt. I pretend. I supply the good whiskey. They supply the venison. You don't hunt either. Five minutes ago a buck went through. You didn't shoot.'

'I don't kill needlessly. They are a beautiful animal. Have you seen the eyes of a doe when she's startled?'

'Yes. They haunt you.' Charlie wasn't thinking so much about a deer as a man in Africa. 'I killed a man . . . Ethiopia . . . not good. It is difficult . . . to kill a human . . . is it not, Sootie?'

Sootie didn't answer and Charlie knew enough not to pursue the issue.

'You ask me once, long time ago, about Bellinzona. I look at you then and think . . . Italiana! The nose . . . is roman, I think. You ask me about gypsies and I think . . . Ah, he is gypsy! But they do not travel in Canada in 1840's.'

Sootie smiled to himself. Charlie was definitely not stupid! 'They indeed were not in Canada when I was born and I am not Italian. I . . . read once about a gypsy band of Bellinzona. Is the country there beautiful, as I read?'

'Bella, Bellissimo! It is mountains and rivers . . . maybe sixty miles from my valley in Italia.'

'There are gypsies around Bellinzona, I read.'

'Yes once, but no more I think. They went to the four winds when the Prince died . . . the gypsy Prince d'Bellinzona. Four sons of two wives lived. But there were children of the gypsy blood around the whole of Europe from him. He claimed lands of the ancient Castello d'el Monte belonged to his family. They lived around Bellinzona but travelled very much. Two sons became "thieves of the night" and two generous men.'

'You mean two carried on the traditional gypsy image and two settled in Switzerland to lead a somewhat normal life?'

'No. They all wander but two learned from their father the ways of trickery and stealing and two are welcome in the villages with their caravans to trade.'

'I . . . read of the Prince. He travelled throughout Europe, didn't he.'

'The English, the French, Italia, Espana . . . He travelled. He was . . .

attractive . . . dark. The women . . . they were under his influence . . . My grandmother, a young woman told me of him. She went to find her goat . . . it went to the pasture . . . she found a man was leading it . . . She run up and say . . . It is my goat! . . . The man say . . . Perhaps my Bella Madonna but I see it first . . . he smiles and she let go of the goat. He scurry down the pasture with it and before she realize . . . it's gone. It was the Prince. He leave, for my grandmother, a bouquet of flowers, on the doorstep the next day.'

'And the flowers were stolen?'

'From the garden of the priest! He travelled through the country of Lago Maggiore to Abbiategrasso each year because he had family there . . . they were noble and not of the gypsy way. Perhaps he was the prince of the Castello del Monte. Who knows?'

'Was there no record kept of the families of noble blood?'

'Records for families of noble blood but the Prince's grandfather, was I think, the bastard bambino of the woman of the Castello . . . her only son . . . her only child. Who was there to say?'

Shots rang out and a voice shouted from the brush.

'A buck! Charlie it's coming past your blind. Shoot!'

Both men flattened themselves against the ground and peered from the blind.

'Shoot Charlie,' Sootie whispered.

'No, your buck,' Charlie hissed back. There was no need for either to shoot. The buck leapt past the blind followed by a volley of bullets from the brush. The animal didn't stand a chance and his magnificent head went down as he was hit.

'Is much safer on the floor of the blind, Sootie, when whiskey and guns hunt together.' Sootie nodded his head in complete agreement.

Hunting camp with Fergus group including Charles Mattaini and Sootie (apparently).

Royal Alexandra Hospital. Early 1900's.

Dr. Abraham Groves and the Royal Alexandra Hospital 1920's.

GEORGINA — JULY 1905

The verandah was lined with patients getting a taste of the prescribed fresh air and sunshine Dr. Groves believed in. Some were taking light refreshments being served by the nurses in training. Georgina stood waiting for Abraham who'd invited her for a 'walk around' but her attention was taken up by a workcrew laying sidewalk in front of the old Mitchie house, now the Royal Alexandra Hospital. They worked quickly, some pouring concrete, others on their haunches smoothing it with trowels and boards.

'Georgina, I hope I've not kept you waiting long.' Abraham stepped from the large doors towards her.

'Not at all. My attention was held by the workmen. Tell me . . . which one is "the Latin"?'

'The Latin? . . . oh . . . Charlie! The little fellow on his knees with the trowel; the one wearing the gray shirt.' He led her into the entry hall of the hospital.

'I'm surprised you've not come before. I expected you as soon as I opened the doors.'

'You're a busy man and I would have been imposing on your time.' That was like Georgina, so quiet and retiring.

'I opened the hospital too late for you didn't I.'

'You opened it when you had the funds to do so.'

'I could have waited. My first mistake was buying this building. All hospitals should be on one floor but the place was cheap and I overlooked some of the problems. If I had the money now I'd take it down and cover the land with a low, one storey affair. Everyone has the right to a private room, a window and fresh air.'

'You just opened three years ago and you had an architect help you plan this!' Georgina was not prepared for Dr. Groves comments!

'That was my second mistake, hiring the architect!'

'The hospital concept itself wasn't a mistake surely.'

'Definitely not. Bring the patient to the doctor, I say. A house call out of the village costs $20.00 and the same call to the doctor at the hospital or house costs $1.00. I made $60.00 one day for three calls in the country. If they'd come here I'd have made $3.00. I got paid $57.00 for being a liveryman! That day I worked 14 hours but taking off the time for driving it was one and one half hours practising medicine, the one thing I want to do. I can spend far more productive time here at the hospital than travelling the roads.'

With each door that Abraham opened in the building Georgina felt her interest drawn again towards medicine, as it had been years before when Abraham went to the University of Toronto to learn medicine and she went home to tend children. They had gone to school together, one as intelligent as the other. They both enjoyed those subjects in school directly related to the humanitarian fields. She wanted desperately to go to medical school but Thomas refused to allow her to even think about it. Even if he had been more understanding she would never have been accepted. Women did not pursue professional careers. Abraham spoke to her now as an equal, as though she'd spent years in the profession. He knew she read every book and article on medical history and technique and even passed his journals on to her occasionally.

'You could have been a good doctor, Georgina. You're sensitive to human suffering and you have the hands to operate.'

'It's ironic that you went on to sewing humans and I learned the trade of sewing the clothing they wear on their backs.'

'It's ironic that I didn't learn at the University to "sew humans", as you say. I never saw an operation performed! I never saw an abdomen opened until I came to Fergus and operated for an Ovarian tumor in July 1973 and I graduated in 1871! There was no practical work at the University only theory from books!'

'You had some pretty vicious critics. I followed your career in the newspapers. You raised a few eyebrows when you stated "it was far better to go to a man who knows something rather than to a specialist" when asked about country doctors and their knowledge, or lack of it.'

'Do you remember the fellow who stood up after I'd given a paper at the Ontario Medical Association on the Appendectomy and said, "If such doctrines as this become the practice, the death rate will be appalling!" Well, I proved him wrong!'

The two had been walking through the lower and upper corridors of the former home. Some of the rooms were operating theatres, others, bed chambers. Georgina recalled there had been a large drawing room in the house but noticed it had been divided into smaller rooms holding one patient. She never noticed more than two patients to any room.

'You don't believe in wards?'

'I walked into the old drawing room one day when there were eight beds in the room and the smell was so offensive I demanded the room be divided immediately. No patient need to stand a smell not of his own making. The same holds true for kitchen smells. You notice the kitchen is on the top floor of the hospital. That is so the cooking smells won't nauseate the patients. If it was in the basement the smells would travel through the entire building.'

Georgina envied the nurses-in-training scurrying about. How desperately she wanted to be one of them! They were so young. Their whole lives were ahead of them. She was fifty-nine and far too old to join their forces.

'I won't even ask if you have a place for me here. You'd say "in bed" rather than helping out. I feel my whole life has been a waste seeing the accomplishments you achieved and knowing what I've done over the same number of years.'

'You've done the best you could given the circumstances. You were born too early and of the wrong sex.' He was voicing Georgina's sentiments, only the bitterness she felt wasn't in his voice. They'd come back downstairs to the front doors.

'These doors are open to all doctors and any patients except those suffering from infectious diseases. No one is turned away. I ask no grants and receive none. I have no women's society working for the hospital. I set the rules. It is my hospital!'

Georgina was duly impressed. One of the nurses hurried to the doctor's side and had quiet words with him.

'I'll have to say good-bye. Something's come along that needs my attention. Please feel free to come anytime to visit.'

'Thank you, it's been enjoyable,' she stood again on the verandah. The difference between a good doctor and a great doctor had just been pointed out to her . . . personality. Dr. Groves had personality and authority. He never said 'perhaps it might be . . .' but always 'I say it is . . .' and he knew how to handle people. She had just been very skilfully handled! Georgina knew she would never have been a great doctor and possibly not even a good doctor. She would have been too timid and too retiring to take a stand on any issue. She felt bitter, resentful and lonely. It was a short distance between the verandah and the workmen and she walked it boldly and with determination.

'Mr. Mattaini?' The short fellow kept on working, never looking up, pulling the trowel across the concrete.

'Mr. Mattaini?' He glanced at her legs so she knew she'd gotten his attention.

'I am interested in . . . spirits.' There was a pregnant pause.

'If you want spirits, you see a priest. If you want whiskey, you see the livery boy at the hotel.'

'Which hotel?'

'Any hotel in the village. They all know me.' The man never lifted his eyes to her face.

'Do I pay him?' She began fidgeting with her purse.

'You pay when you get . . . only when you get.'

Georgina turned from him and walked down Queen Street. Charlie sat back on his heels. He often wondered what drove middle aged women to drink. They came in all shapes and sizes, rich and poor. There were sure enough of them around providing him with a living. He went back to his work, the July sun beating hard on his back. They provided him with a living but construction was his first priority in life. They were driven by some compulsion to drink and he was possessed by a driving force to build.

Charles Mattaini 1910.

CHARLIE — SEPTEMBER 1908

Business had only gotten better for Charlie since Georgina spoke to him outside the Royal Alexandra Hospital. He stood now at the doors of 'Stonehome', a bill in hand.

Augus 1908

Mis Yongs
Cmenta Poch an sidwak
2 bag cmenta an san $3.00
Men an tim 9.00
————
$12.00

He did not like presenting bills. It wasn't that his work didn't match the money he asked for the job. He knew his work was excellent and that he wasn't overcharging. It was his English! His bills made no sense to anyone but himself! His ledgers could only be read by someone with an Italian accent. No one else could possibly understand his written pidgen English. He learned quickly in the construction business however that he must always present a bill as soon as the work was done; that he couldn't expect money in payment in every case because people simply didn't have it and that he take any job, no matter how small, in order to get established in a community. In the first two years of his fledgling company he was glad to have extra work in Louis's brickyards. When he went looking for work in Fergus he found out quickly it helped to be a Scotsman and a stone mason. He was an excellent stone mason. When he went looking for work in Arthur he found it helped to be Irish and Catholic. He was Catholic. That gave him a foot in both villages but didn't help his business. He'd spoken to Faustino about his problems.

'There is a key that unlocks the doors, Carlo. Find the key!'

Charlie spent a good deal of time looking for the illusive key and it turned out to be right before his eyes. Both communities, in fact all the small villages around had one common bond, the love of a good drink of whiskey! Charlie bought, or manufactured the best, proffered it freely and the jobs rolled in. His company built barn foundations, flumeways, sidewalks, houses and stone houses. No job proved too small or large for them. The quality of his work was excellent and he would tackle any job with zeal except the task of collecting the money and presenting the bills.

He knocked on the screen door and could see one of the women coming down the hall. It had been a warm day. Windows in the house were opened and screened and the smell of chili sauce permeated the air.

'Mr. Mattaini, come in.' It was Georgina. She led him to the kitchen where Clara was busy mixing a pitcher of Raspberry Vinegar.

'You drink that?'

'It's nothing more than raspberry juice, vinegar, sugar and water . . . Very refreshing. I'm sure you've tasted worse! Would you like a glass?' After a remark like that there was nothing he could do but accept.

'Yes, Miss Clara.' He would have preferred something far stronger. He knew there was some in the house but didn't think Clara was the one to ask.

'You've brought the bill. How much do we owe you?'

He produced the bill, sheepishly putting it on the table. $12.00 cement, sand and men's time. He put his hand over the piece of paper so they wouldn't see the writing. Georgina rose and disappeared into the parlour of the home. She reappeared shortly with $12.00 in bills which she handed him.

'Could we have a receipt, Mr. Mattaini?'

'You want me to write a paper saying you paid me?'

'That's right.'

Charlie did some quick thinking. 'You write the paper. I sign it. It's better that way. I can't write the English.'

'I'll do it Georgina. You pour Mr. Mattaini another raspberry drink.'

When Clara left to get pen and paper, Georgina quickly got up, opened a tea tin and quickly poured a shot into Charlie's glass, following it with a dash of raspberry drink. She did the same for herself.

'You hide it there? She doesn't know?' He pointed down the hall. 'You keep it secret?'

'She doesn't approve.'

Clara reappeared with the paper. 'You sign there Charlie. The stoops and front steps look good. There'll be some work in the basement in the spring if you are interested.'

'Just tell Marie.'

"How is Marie and the little one?' Charlie smiled at the thoughts of his wife and children. Since their marriage in April 1903 she had given him four children, the first two dying shortly after birth. Now there was Carlo Sylvestro, a robust two year old and Joseph Francis, a golden haired boy of six months.

'Have you seen Jimmy, the bambino? Marie is tired. Her mother is with her. She did not recover so quickly from this birth.'

'And how is Carolina? We purchase linen from her. She is the only woman in this part of the County still weaving the very fine linen people ask us for. It makes lovely wedding gowns. She is a clever woman but so tiny, almost birdlike.'

'Carolina? Is fine.' Charlie had a good deal of respect for his mother-in-law. Birdlike described her well. Dressed in black from head to toe and in one of her tempers she resembled a vulture!'

'I haven't seen Faustino in the village. He is well?'

'The Faustino is busy . . . the farm . . . the brickyard. They move into the village perhaps. Marie is here now.' Charlie really didn't like too many questions. He appraised these two women as he finished his drink. In their youth they would have been considered pretty and the Miss Clara must have been beautiful. She retained a quality of beauty about her even now. Strange they never married. He knew Georgina, on more or less a business level, through supplying her alcoholic needs. Strange that one should drink and the other shouldn't. He broke the silence.

'You have seen the Sootie lately?'

'He was here last week but left for Goderich on Thursday. He'll be back Monday. I'll tell him you were asking for him.'

'Looking for him please. He leaves his wife alone?'

'He leaves Annalee occasionally. She doesn't seem to mind.'

Charlie's eyebrows raised. It was a trusting husband indeed who would leave a woman like Annalee alone!

'You've left Marie alone. When you were in Yorkton, Saskatchewan she was alone for months and it didn't seem to bother her.'

'True, Miss Clara, but she had her mother nearby to chaperone.'

'More raspberry drink, Mr. Mattaini?'

'No thank you Misses. I have other bills to deliver. They take much time. I must explain them.'

'Why don't you ask Marie to do your books? She's quite capable.'

Charlie pulled himself up to his full 5' 8" height. Obviously these women did not know Italian men. 'Is not a woman's job to know the business of her husband. Marie is to raise my children and keep my house. Business is a man's work.' He retrieved his hat and bowed slightly to the women.

Clara ushered him to the front door. 'Do you see Georgina . . . often, Mr. Mattaini?'

'I do not see Georgina. She does not walk like you.' He gave Clara a flashing smile, bowed slightly again and turned to the open door.

'Good evening Miss Clara.'

Clara shut the door and scuttled back to the kitchen.

'That was a strange question you asked Mr. Mattaini. "Did he see me often?" Georgina's voice had an icy edge to it.

'You have to purchase it somewhere Georgina. I could smell it tonight. Where have you hidden it now?'

'I don't drink much Clara. I use it for medicinal purposes only. Why can't you leave me be?'

'You might not drink much now Georgina, but you will. It's a disease. It's in the pantry somewhere, isn't it? That's where you put it this time.' Clara went to the pantry and began rummaging around the supplies for the elusive bottle.

Georgina sat enjoying the last of her drink. She eyed the large collection of bright tea tins Clara kept on top of the cabinet. In a brilliant red tin under the guise of 'Imperial Blend Tea—Selected India and Ceylon' was her 'comfort'. It had been there for the past two weeks, right under Clara's nose.

THREE WOMEN — APRIL 1910

The warm spring weather was good for business and Clara was tending counter at Steele's store during the spring rush. The job wouldn't last long but Clara enjoyed meeting people.

'May I help you?'

She was looking directly at a small woman standing by the sewing supplies with three children. The woman was a stranger to the area as Clara hadn't seen her before, and if Clara did say so herself, Clara knew everybody!

'I'm interested in cotton yardage for children's clothing. You seem to have a good selection and a low price.'

'You're a new arrival in the area? I've not seen you or your children before.'

Clara busied herself putting bolts of cloth on the counter. The stranger smiled to herself. Each village has one, someone who has to know everything!

'Elizabeth Scott from Eramosa Township. George Scott is my husband. His father is John Scott of Eramosa. The eldest child is Lillias, then Alice and this is Edith the baby of our family.' There she told all. No more questions hopefully.

'Your aunt and uncle ran a store in Mimosa and I know your in-laws. Nice people, the Scotts.'

Elizabeth busied herself with the selection of fabric.

'Do you come to Fergus often?'

'Rarely,' Elizabeth looked up from the material, her attention distracted. 'George had business at the mills and mentioned a week ago we would be coming. I saved my best butter and eggs for barter at the grocer's. It's a good butter. I usually barter in Eramosa or Orton. My firkins are of the best quality and much in demand.'

'One woman, here in the village, had a habit of larding her butter! Another kept an untidy dairy and a mouse once fell into her cream. She churned the cream anyway and took it to the grocer, explaining the situation. She asked if he would buy the butter or trade even for another's churning. "Certainly," he said. He took the firkin down to his cold room, spent a few moments there, and brought back her firkin full of butter. "Thank you", the woman gushed. "I'll never tell a soul." "Neither will I," said the grocer. He'd actually given her back her own butter and she was none the wiser thinking he'd been a good fellow and switched it for some other in the cool room.'

Both women laughed at the story.

'I've just been to the butcher, the middle shop. He seemed quite strange!

Could I have five yards of this print cotton?'

'He drinks, poor fellow. Once someone put sausage links in his apron pocket while he was working. He always kept some loose change in that pocket to give customers. He was quite tipsy that particular day and when he put his hand in his pocket and began pulling out sausage links he thought he was losing his innards. Another time Sootie, a friend of mine, filled his overshoe with pig's blood and the poor fellow, when he slid his foot into the boot at closing time, raced up and down the street screaming he had cut his foot off. I personally make sure I see both of his hands when he is weighing meat for me. A thumb can weigh a pound, I've heard.'

Elizabeth had to admit this woman had a sense of humour!

'I don't believe you've told me your name.'

'Clara Isabella Young, Miss; of "Stonehome".'

'I must really complete my shopping Clara. George will be expecting me.'

'Is there anything else I can help you with?'

'I don't think so. Money is scarce and possibly George needs the cash for machinery parts.'

'Come back soon then. It was nice meeting you. Allan will help you to your wagon with the parcel.'

Elizabeth turned and came face to face with a handsome woman who had just come in the door with two small boys. The women sidestepped to avoid each other, apologizing profusely.

'Mrs. Mattaini, may I help you today?'

'It's Marie, Clara. I'm looking for you actually. I have some information you might be interested in hearing. With you clerking in the store you haven't been able to visit much this spring.'

Elizabeth glanced back toward the woman. She was strikingly handsome, extremely well dressed and was definitely not 'Canadian'. She had heard the name 'Mattaini' before but it was in connection with barn foundations which were being built near the farm. She hurried the children out the door and along to the wagon as she didn't want to keep George waiting too long. Allan came along behind carrying the bundle of cloth. He knew there was not a penny to be made in tips from this trip. Farm women were notorious for their penny pinching ways and his mother had told him it was because they tended to keep all their money in an old sock under their mattress for a rainy day. Miss Young had put him straight by telling him farming was a hard, backbreaking, low paying job and he shouldn't expect tips anyway. He was being paid enough by the store for the little he did.

KING BILLY — 1911

Faustino finally found Charlie working in the coal shed.

'Charlie, I have sinned!' Charlie looked up from his work and appraised the situation.

'You are not alone Faus, only the first man to admit to it.'

'Charlie, don't joke.'

Charlie leaned against his shovel and got himself into a comfortable position. 'What do you talk about?'

'It was because the King, William, needed Pino. I allowed 'Dad' Hayden to borrow the animal. I say sure but she is not a work horse. "Dad" Hayden says he does need a work horse. The priest says I have sinned.'

'Faus. Start at the beginning and speak slowly. You cannot speak English when you hurry.' Not that either of them could speak good English at any time, mind you.

'The priest came to me in the field at the farm and say "Faustino, you are a traitor to the church. You help our enemy. That means a rosary for penance." To get a rosary in Italy you commit adultery! It is serious for me.'

'You tell me you loaned "Dad" Hayden the old white horse, Pino. The priest came to your farm and told you it was wrong to do such a thing. He gave you a penance as in confesion?'

'Yes.'

'Why did "Dad" want Pino?'

'For the King, the parade . . . to ride.'

'The King?'

'King William. He is coming to the village July 12th, in two days time.'

'You talk of the Orange parade. "Dad" Hayden is playing King Billy. He will ride Pino down the streets.'

'Why the priest and the penance? I have done nothing!'

'The parade is because of a battle long ago, fought between Catholics and Protestants. They never forget. "King Billy" rode a white horse in the battle. "Dad" rides one now, your horse . . . Pino.'

'I must do something?'

'You must do nothing!' Charlie thought for a moment. 'Come to the village to enjoy the parade. It is O.K. Faus. Bring Carolina to visit Marie.'

Faustino was apprehensive. He felt reassured but there was still the penance. He turned to leave the shed. Charlie called after him.

'Faus. Don't worry about the penance. The priest should thank you.'
Faustino was more confused than ever.

On the morning of the 12th, he and Carolina left the farm early. The road was already black with vehicles, all heading in the direction of Fergus. He skirted the main area by coming in Union Street to Marie's.

'There are hundreds of people Marie!'

'The organizers of the event expect 3,000 to arrive. There are special trains running to bring all the orangemen.' Faustino felt more a traitor than ever when he heard the figure 3,000!

'Charlie said you should walk down to the construction site behind the main area. He's waiting for you!' She kissed the old man on the cheek. 'And smile, Papa.'

Faustino walked quickly along Tower Street, past the new Post Office building and angled off at Provost Lane to the back of the butcher shops where Charlie was enclosing the stream with concrete culverts. If the parade was so important why hadn't Charlie gotten the area of the creek, which runs directly across St. Andrews Street, enclosed? The sidewalks in front of the News Record building and the new Post Office were still torn up and dust was flying from people scuffling through the dirt.

'Charlie. There is an open ditch across the main street yet.'

'The Orangemen can "straddle the creek" same as everyone else. The least they will do is get a wet foot.' He handed Faus a chair. 'You take this and sit . . . there . . . on St. Andrews Street . . . by the creek. You sit . . . watch . . . listen!'

Faus took the chair and placed it at the edge of the sidewalk right by the creek. One thing he could do well was sit! The crowd was gathering quickly and Faus gave all the ladies who passed him by a practised appraisal. Some people he greeted by name but most he had never seen before.

'Are you not in the enemy camp today Faustino?'

I did not know we were fighting? Where is the parade?'

'It starts on St. David Street, walks north to Garafraxa, over to Tower Street, south to St. Andrews Street, east on St. Andrews to St. David and south on St. David to the park.'

'It makes a big circle.'

' "Dad" Hayden is King Billy, did you know?'

'I understood such.'

'He's marched in Orange Parades for the last 55 years, travelling miles to get to them. This Lodge was formed last year so they are hosting the parade this year. "Dad's" riding a grand white stallion.'

'Pino?' Perhaps he'd decided not to ride Pino. No grand stallion was she!

'Why do they march each year? Can they not forget the battle, ever?'

'It was quite a fight, Faustino, and your side was soundly beaten. But, I agree they should not make an issue of it now.'

The sound of fife and drum was heard down by the Post Office. Charlie's men walked down the creekbed and stood by Faus's chair.

'Where is Charlie?'

'Up the creek. He said he would be along shortly. Look Piper McDonald is leading the parade!'

Faus craned his neck to see. There he was . . . 'Dad King Billy' Hayden . . . plain as day . . . on the back of Pino. Was it Pino? The animal had been scrubbed and chalk rubbed into her coat. She looked marvellous. Marie would be proud to see her. She was a light work horse used to being ridden rather than worked and was high stepping along the street more gracefully than she had moved in years! "Dad" Hayden sat high in the saddle, sword at ready.

Faus heard a faint muffled sound originating up the creekbed.

'Damn Charlie! Dynamite!'

Pino reared, terror in her eyes. She lit out as though the devil was on her tail, helter skelter down St. Andrews Street. "Dad" Hayden clung gamely to the reins with one hand the other holding the sword. His legs flung around in the stirrups beating the sides of the horse. Pino, figuring her rider wanted more speed, lengthened her stride. Dad's sword flailed her side. "King Billy" was on the rampage! Right past the St. David street turn he sailed, scattering people in all directions.

Faus was mesmerized. Didn't Charlie remember Pino shied and bolted at the faintest sound of a dynamite blast? That's why she was retired as a work horse. Even a blast one quarter mile away and barely audible to the human ear would turn her into an uncontrollable animal. She had wrapped more wagons around fences than any other horse he had ever owned!

'Charlie's dynamiting?' He asked the workman beside him.

'No. There's no dynamite at the site. No need for it because we're into a gravel bed. Bedrock starts on the south side of the street. Look, the Orange from Rothsay!'

After the initial shock of seeing 'King Billy' careen down the street the marchers carried on. Bands from Damascus, Cedarville, Metz and Guelph . . . banners . . . fife and drum, they all passed Faus who sat deep in thought. "The priest will thank you," Charlie had said. The realization of the situation struck. Charlie did it on purpose! He rigged a small dynamite charge and exploded it at the exact moment 'Dad' Hayden was crossing the creek. The blast had been so minute only the practised ear could hear it . . . Charlie, Pino and he! Charlie was an expert with dynamite. People said he could blast a flea off an elephant's back and the elephant wouldn't feel a thing! He settled back in his chair to watch the rest of the parade. Wave after wave of orangemen waded through the shallow creek which suddenly seemed to reduce itself to a trickle. He figured seven hundred people in all crossed the creek, all loyal to an ancient battle they never fought but kept alive by hatred.

'Cave-in!' Charlie's men ran back up the creekbed. Faus came along behind them carrying the chair. Charlie was too smart to get himself caught in a cave-in of his own making.

'It'll take us a week to clear out the debris and get those sides shored again.'

'Someone could have been hurt if we hadn't been down at the parade.'

Are you okay Charlie?'

'Fine, fine. I take Faustino home to Marie. You begin the clean up.' Once out of earshot of the men he spoke to Faus. 'You enjoy the parade, Faustino?'

'Yes. You dynamite the creek?' Charlie laughed.

'If you don't know anything, you cannot be blamed.'

Instead of heading to Marie's they took the dray to the entry at Victoria Park and patiently waited the arrival of 'King Billy'. Nearly one half hour after they arrived a bedraggled 'Dad' Hayden appeared, flattened hat in hand, walking beside the horse.

'You are alright?'

'Crazy horse! I must have ridden her wrong. She ran me clear out to Blackburn before she suddenly stopped dead in her tracks, docile as could be. I went right over her head. I didn't take any chances. We,' he indicated the horse, 'walked back into the village by the back route so no one would see us. She kept nudging my back, all the way in.'

'The horse is usually placid and does not run away.'

'Something probably frightened her, maybe the crowd. I am not an expert rider either.'

'You want to ride into the park proudly "King Billy"? I hold the horse. You mount.'

'You take the horse and I'll walk in to my loyal followers.'

Charlie tied Pino to the back of the dray and drove around the corner to his home.

'The women need not know about the cave-in. They would worry.'

'I cannot remember a cave-in.'

'Did you say your penance, the rosary, Faus?'

'I said two, one for me . . . one for your soul.'

Construction equipment on the Tower Street bridge 1920's.

STORMS AND STORIES — NOVEMBER 1911

One night, four months after the Orange Parade, a storm blew up over the Great Lakes and wreaked havoc with the ships on the lakes, causing the loss of many lives. It eventually whipped its way across the highlands between the lakes and vented the last of its anger on the villages of Southern Ontario.

People were standing in the road on St. Patrick Street below the Catholic Church. MacGregor and Sootie were closest to the wreckage that once had been the church steeple and MacGregor could hardly control his glee at the sight.

'Served the Catholics right, it did. After what they did to King Billy!'

MacGregor's disdain of Catholics went right back to the beginnings of the village when in the 50's Fergusson had given them some ground on which to build a house of worship, on the same hill as his St. Andrews Presbyterian Church! The Catholics even had the audacity to put a tower on their church as tall as the tower on St. Andrew's! In MacGregor's mind that was almost a declaration of war.

'They had nothing to do with the Orange Parade, MacGregor.'

'Sure they did. It just can't be proven they did anything with the horse. Storm took the steeple down alright. Look at that. The cross is buried right into St. Patrick's Street and the top is right off the tower. It's just as if King Billy himself took his sword and sliced it off!'

Sootie was glad MacGregor got off the subject of the Orange Parade for he knew full well what Charlie had done but wasn't about to discuss it with such an avowed Orangeman.

'Look! Charlie's over there surveying the damage. You can't turn around now that you don't come face to face with the Italian, or an Irishman. They're coming out of the long grass, Sootie.'

'He's as much right to be here as anyone else MacGregor. It is his house of worship.'

'A person can't find a decent drink anymore either without going through Charlie. He has a hold on the bootleg market! Used to be it was everywhere, d'you mind Sootie. There were seven or eight taverns in the village and someone was always buying a drink. Wasn't the Scots that bought them though.' He chuckled at the thoughts of the free drinks he had managed to cajole from unsuspecting teamsters who stopped for a round or two after coming down the hot, dry Owen Sound Road from Arthur.

'Ah! The Irish were a soft touch for a drink if you used a little flattery. Sootie.

We're a dying breed, you and I. The last of the true Scots. We're being taken over, you know. The village will never be the same again. It used to be you could knock on anyone's door and expect hospitality as long as you brought along a pudding or goose or loaf with you. You don't find that kind of welcome anymore. Just the other day I went to collect the rent and wasn't even offered a cup of tea. If the door hadn't been off its hinges, I'd 've had it slammed in my face.'

'Come on MacGregor. It's not a bad idea to introduce new blood into the village. We've had our day. The world's for younger people and new ideas. We built the village. Let them care for it. It's my village, my home but I'm willing to hand the reins over to the younger generation and the newcomers. I trust them.'

The dusky skinned Sootie clapped the fair skinned man on the shoulder and the two turned toward Breadalbane and 'Mapleshade'.

'Do you remember George D.? He was a generous man to put up with a Catholic Church at his back door!'

Sootie well remembered George Fergusson. Generous he was not! 'Generous with his words, MacGregor. His pocket didn't open freely when money was wanted. After John Thompson died he sent a letter to the widow sending his regrets but reminding her the mortgage was due in two days time.'

'The children in the family didn't fair well either. He thought the sight of children on a man's knee didn't befit the masculine image. That's why he had an addition built on "Mapleshade". He housed the children and their nannies separately and they were only allowed the run of the main house after they were two years old.'

'For not wanting children around him he had enough of them, MacGregor, seven living. He was so tight fisted with his money he told the youngest daughter, the delicate one, she'd have to gain a lot of weight in order to wear her sister's wedding dress for he wasn't going to pay for another. Remember when the girls rolled up the old hall rug and threw it into the river to get rid of it before one of their parties and he made them retrieve it and lay it back on the floor again.'

'I remember his hats, big broad-brimmed warmers brought in from Hamilton . . . white hats for the summer, black for the winter. His brother, David Blair, used to draw cartoons of the local people and hang them on posts and buildings all along St. Andrews Street. He loved picking on George D. He'd draw a big hat, large bulbiferous nose and long clay pipe on a small head, big torso and stubby feet. He'd sneak down from "Westwood" late at night and pin the cartoon on a post right in front of the doors of "Mapleshade". Pity the man died so young. He died at 38 and George died at 53.'

'They both smoked clay pipes. When Blair went over the river bank after the St. Andrews Banquet they found him on his back down on the rocks, leg broken, pipe clenched tight in his teeth, still burning. Dr. Mutch set the leg but Blair insisted on having the cast removed too soon and he always walked with a limp because the leg hadn't healed properly.'

The two were down by the Temperance Hall, walking with coat collars up around their ears to keep out the raw November wind.

'Some piece of architecture, Sootie, and some white elephant. The tea totallers built it before you arrived. Up there on the stone it says 1852. It's sitting pretty solid and square. Didn't harm it a bit to have holes knocked out for Beatty's foundry in the 70's. Wasn't used for temperance purposes long as no one, except the ladies could stay off the bottle. Most entertainments were held at the hotels. No self respecting man would be seen walking through the Hall's doors. You were branded immediately as "One of the doesn'ts" and everyone pretty near did!'

'Seems to me MacGregor that someone should have told the temperance group they were fighting a losing battle.'

'Gibbie Todd tried to. You wouldn't remember Gibbie. He was a school teacher in the early years of the settlement and used to live with George Clephane He took a friend home one night to have a drink with him and then walked him up the road apiece. When he got back to the cabin he found he'd forgotten to turn off the tap on the barrel of whiskey and the whiskey had run all over the floor. He thought it was a shame to waste all that good liquor so he got down on his hands and knees and lapped it up. Clephane came in later and found him lying on the floor dead drunk with whiskey all around him.'

'I don't remember Gibbie but I do remember Baker Walker telling me about James Edwards. He used to live in a log cabin at the corner of Provost and St. George Street and was the gravedigger. All the children used to follow him around to watch him dig the graves. He lived right up the hill from Walkers and came home one night dead drunk. He began to pump water from his well. He pumped and pumped and it all ran down into the baker's cabin and nearly flooded them out.'

They had by this time made their way to the Town Hall, the old Drill Shed.

'Married life has slowed you down Sootie. You've not been up to your tricks recently. Remember the time you caught Constable Lingwood sleeping in his own cells under the Hall here. You locked him in with his own keys and made him recite the "duties he was to perform as Constable as set out by the village council". He bellowed them at the top of his voice and you made him repeat them until he got them right. I, to this day, can recite them from hearing him. He had to attend to all professional business, to take charge of the drill shed, fireman's hall and engine house, to see that the fire engine was at all times in thorough working order, to take care of all apparatus, clothing and property belonging to the fire brigade, to take charge of and look after all corporation tools and implements, to prepare and cut the wood required in the drill shed and fireman's hall and engine house, to repair all sidewalks, to clean and look after ditches and to work upon the street as required, to take charge of Belsyde Cemetery and keep it in order, to collect young men's taxes and finally to perform such other duties as the Council may have from time to time seen fit!'

'You've a good memory MacGregor. You must know then that I'm not as young as I used to be. I can't think or run as fast as I used to, so I keep myself out of trouble.'

The pair crossed the street to the post Office where the locals were waiting for the mail coming by stage from the train station. Sootie left the group and struck off up Tower Street at a brisk gait.

Annalee was at 'Stonehome' helping Clara and Georgina with fall alterations to their customer's clothing. The cold November wind swept the last of the leaves along the road with him. He was deep in thought and never felt the cold. It pleased him to think he'd been in Fergus long enough that MacGregor would take for granted he was a Scotsman and that the blood of the Highlanders ran in his veins. It bothered him that he didn't know what he was, nor who his mother was. Was she part Scottish? He had asked himself that very question many times in the past little while and he had almost gone back to England several times to see if he could find his roots. Now he couldn't. He had Annalee.

Curlers and Pipe band 1920's. Charlie's (Mattaini) house and lumberyard in the background.

CHARLIE'S WOODPILE — JUNE 1913

Doc had given the horse its head and it ended up exactly where he wanted it to go, the Old Melville Church building on Union Street. Any horse Doc owned when given its head, would make a beeline for home and a warm stable and this horse was no exception. Only, it wasn't Doc's home or stable it went to. He'd purchased the beast a year before from Charlie Mattaini and Charlie's stable was where the darn animal would end up! It was like a homing pigeon. Charlie'd bought the old Church lock, stock and barrel after the congregation suffered a division in its rank. Marie had packed away the hymn books and bible which had been left in the building and Charlie fitted it out as a stable —the building being handy to the lumberyards and his house. His use of the building raised the ire of a few villagers but the remarks ran off him like water off a duck's back. Charlie didn't give a damn and Marie hadn't much say in the matter. She was in the building now climbing around the loft after hen's eggs. Doc eased himself out of the buggy. He wasn't getting any younger and he had been up all night.

'Marie, are the men in the woodpiles?' Marie came to the side of the loft, egg basket in hand.

'You'll find them over by Albert Street, Dr. Groves.' He looked at her approvingly.

'You look healthy these days.'

'Who wouldn't be. Chasing these chickens around the building keeps me fit.'

'Where are the pigs?' Marie descended the ladder trying to balance the egg basket and demurely hold her skirts at the same time. Doc stepped over to help her down the last few steps.

'Don't you start in about pigs too. Darn sanctimonious church women didn't want anything to do with the building and wouldn't even come to get their hymn books but as soon as Charlie runs pigs around the pulpit they get themselves in a sweat. The Good Lord shared his birthplace with an ass. There's no harm in sheltering horses, chickens and pigs here.' She hitched up her skirt to walk across the manure strewn floor. 'Did they expect he'd keep it as a church? I had them slaughtered. It's bad enough being shunned by some of the upstanding village women because I'm Italian and Charlie's wife. I didn't need the talk about pigs in the "temple of God" to boot!'

'Must have been hard on the children. The pigs were pets.'

'It didn't register they were eating their pets until I served sausages one evening and the talk got around to pigs. Charlie grunted into his sausage and the whole table erupted into tears.'

The two walked out into the bright sunshine on Union Street.

'Why are you interested in the men over there?' She pointed in the direction of the lumberyard. 'You don't drink. They've nothing better to do than drink. If it wasn't free Charlie wouldn't see hide nor hair of them. You've better things to do than associate with them.'

'It surprises me Marie just who does hide in Charlie's woodpiles. There're some solid, upstanding members of the community who sit back there.'

'And their wives blame Charlie for luring them to the bottle. They were at it long before Charlie came along. You've always been respected in the village. Have you any idea what it's like to be talked about behind your back?'

'I sympathize with you Marie but you can't change people overnight. They're suspicious of newcomers and people of different nationality. I figure if I'd come to the village fifteen years ago as a stranger with my ideas and views, I'd not have been accepted either.'

'They're a narrowminded and shortsighted lot.'

'Some are Marie, I'll agree. The men are down by Albert Street are they?'

'Last I saw of them.'

'You didn't find the whiskey today then?'

'I didn't have time.'

The two parted ways, Marie to tend to the house and Doc to look for Sootie. The woodpiles were a favourite haunt for the 'locals' of the village. Charlie always kept an ample supply of free booze on hand. The supply hopscotched all over the lumberyard. Charlie kept one step ahead of Marie who could sniff it out better than a hound after a hare. Doc followed the voices to a pile of framing planks, where they were all sitting in the sun enjoying the community bottle. Sootie was sitting to the back of the group. He, like Doc, didn't drink but liked the company. The men shifted to make room for another body. They knew enough not to offer the bottle or they'd be in for a lecture. Sootie looked obviously relieved to see him and came immediately to his side.

'Any news Doc?' J.R. always had to know the latest gossip.

'As a matter of fact yes, J.R. Sootie here is now the father of a healthy baby boy. I just came from the house.'

A hoot went up from the men and a toast was proposed. Doc spoke quietly to Sootie.

'You may as well go home now. She's waiting for you and she's had an easy time. The boy's O.K. She did say one thing that's got me puzzled though. Just after the birth she said ... a grandson ... not a son ... a grandson?' Doc's eyes narrowed. 'Women say funny things while in pain but she was quite lucid.'

Sootie answered quietly. 'I wouldn't put much stock in what she said Doc. I don't know what she'd be thinking of.'

'Well, you'd better be off to her. Take the horse and buggy. It's in Charlie's barn. Bring it back to my barn as soon as you can. It's got my bag in it.'

'Thanks Doc.' Sootie hurried away dodging among the piles of wood.

'Hey Doc! Who'd have thought after sixteen years, he'd become a father?'

'Doesn't surprise me at all Howie. Whiskey'll quench the fires of youth long before old age and Sootie doesn't drink!' He waved to the group and set off along Albert Street. He had some time on his hands and wanted to walk through the cemetery where he could do some heavy thinking. This 'grandson' question had really gotten his attention. The baby had carried another questionable mark also which he hadn't questioned Sootie about. Maybe it meant nothing. He never thought Sootie would marry in the first place . . . and picking such a young woman, a sixteen year old . . . and her a lovely lass indeed! Now he was a father. It crossed his mind that no wedding had ever taken place. There was never a last name . . . only Annalee and Sootie. The man had gone out of the village to marry but where? No one knew. Yet . . . they were a devoted couple and the baby was the spitting image of Sootie. Doc had a nose for a mystery. Two and two didn't always add up to four. They never did as far as he was concerned. He strolled along with his hands behind his back . . . his thinking position. And there was Marie. She was quite a woman, direct, right to the point. She and Sootie were alike, both radicals going against the system but Marie was more outspoken than Sootie. Doc figured himself a radical both in thought and action and he admired Marie. He had to admit there was a faction of people in the village violently opposed to 'newcomers' and change. They'd set up a double standard. If one of them got drunk he'd be hidden under the table until he sobered up and no one would talk about it but if an Irishman got drunk they'd put him on the table to dance so everyone could see and talk about it for weeks.

Doc sat on one of the benches in the cemetery. It was quiet here and he liked visiting 'old friends'. It had taken him some time to convince the Village Council that benches were needed in the cemetery and one wag asked if Doc might figure the 'residents' would 'like a bit of a rest' on their midnight wanderings?

He didn't like what he saw for the near future of the village; a class conscious, tight knit, closed community. He'd even been approached by several of the 'ladies' and asked if he didn't think he should change his policy of 'charity cases' being admitted to the hospital! The one large industry had certain criteria for hiring. No one would come outright and talk about it but everyone knew. There were precious few people like Marie who spoke up if a situation demanded attention. But she could afford to, as she didn't need to worry about the next pay envelope. Charlie'd built up his own company and hired the people who couldn't get work at the plant. He had a work force of hardworking Irish Catholics and Italian immigrants.

Ah, life is so complicated but could be so simple if only people wouldn't put themselves in a 'class above others'. He'd dealt with rich and poor and there was no difference once the clothes were off.

He breathed deeply of the good fresh air. It too was free to anyone who cared to 'clear their lungs and cleanse the mind.'

OUTHOUSES AND ANTS — JULY 1915

'You get away from that building!' Georgina came out the back door swinging a broom in the air. 'You get on home and stop hiding in my outhouse. Get along or I'll get you with the broom.' She swooped off the stoop flailing the air with her broom. The children left the outhouse and dove through the bushes to the neighbour's yard.

'Witch, witch! Miss Young's a witch!'

'Are they bothering you Georgina?' That was the neighbour.

'It's embarassing to have to shoo them from the outhouse. How would you like it if you found me in your outhouse when you wanted to use it?'

'I'll speak to them. It won't do any good but I'll try.'

'You do that.' Georgina was always suspicious of the neighbours. There were always rumours flying around the village about she and Clara and they had to come from somewhere. Father's favourite statement was 'Rumours always travel back to those they hurt the most' and he was right.

Where was that Clara? Probably down at the bridge. Georgina set the broom down and began to ready herself for work. She looked at the kitchen. Her breakfast dishes were on the table. Clara could do them. If she had time for a walk she had time for dishes. It was strange how two people living in the same house could learn how to live 'around' each other. She could go for days without talking to Clara and seeing her at the supper meal only. A year ago Clara had made her so mad she had gone for three weeks without speaking. Clara had finally invented some strange illness that put her into bed for several days and she felt obliged to ask how she was, only after the second day, mind you.

A crown sealer sat on the table amidst the dirty dishes. Georgina lifted the screened lid and dropped some sugar crystals into the jar.

'You're slow this morning, boys. You don't want to dance today?' Ants scurried around the sealer and Georgina quickly replaced the screen and zinc ring then took the bottle and placed it on the window sill with Clara's geraniums.

'After I've put in my day at the tailor shop, you'll feel like dancing.' The ants ... wood beetles in the winter ... were her gauge as to alcohol consumed. She kept one eye on the jar of ants and the other on a bottle of brandy. When the ants jumped up and danced around the sealer she put the bottle aside for the day; she'd drunk enough.

Glancing out the kitchen window she noticed the children were back in the outhouse. Well, she'd fix them this time by borrowing a trick from Clara. Taking her broom she went out the front door of the house, out the picket gate at the sidewalk to the lane leading to the field behind 'Stonehome'. Keeping well hidden she made her way down the lane, across the fence row and came up behind the small building, all done very quietly.

'Get out of there, you scoundrels.' She whomped the outhouse with the broom continuously. The door burst open and children scattered in the direction of the street. Georgina carried up the rear, hair flying, laughing at the sight of the children on the run. When she made it to the back door of the house she was thoroughly exhausted but had to admit it had been satisfying. They wouldn't be back for awhile.

Back in the house she got her large cloth bag and checked to see if all her supplies were there . . . a bottle, of course . . . knitting . . . Where did she put her knitting? The boys in the trenches didn't know a 'queer' old spinster was knitting socks to keep their feet warm. It was permissible for her to knit on the job. Mr. Ross was a lenient man. Georgina was an expert tailoress but was in her 60's. Ross allowed she could spend a few minutes a day knitting for the boys. The parlour and dining room were closed so obviously she'd left it in her room. She pulled herself up the steps. Cursed house! Why didn't Clara want to sell it for a one storey cottage? These steps were hard on a woman. She habitually checked to see if the door at the head of the stairs was locked as she went by. All father's and mother's belongings were in the room.

The huge spruce overhung the roof outside her bedroom window never allowing the sun to enter, except for one hour in the late morning. She retrieved her knitting, pulled her blind to the bottom of the side window and shut the door firmly on her way out. If the door was shut, Clara would figure the bottle was in the room and would search for it all morning. She would be as mad as hops when she didn't find it. She checked the old record cabinet in the hall for her supply.

'Safe, she's not found it yet!' Clara was getting clever! It was hard to find good hiding places in the house these days. This drinking was a problem. It was expensive for one thing. She'd tried to stop. Dr. Groves did not advocate drinking, not even for medicinal purposes. He was one of the first doctors in the country to refuse to give alcohol as a stimulant to patients. It was akin to flogging a dead horse, he'd said and he sure lectured her last time he saw her.

'Georgina,' he'd said. 'You're killing yourself. Give it up now. It can do you no good.'

'I can't. My system seems to need it.'

'Of course it does. You've trained it to the bottle. It starts with one of these "patent medicines" and eventually you crave the poison.'

'I read it could be your system lacking an essential element.'

'I read it was inherited also . . . that it's a social inheritance. Like father . . . like son. There was no social drinking in your family, no heavy drinking either. You've got to be strong enough to give it up. Strength and determination are the keys that open the door.'

'Then I may as well give up the battle now, I've neither, only a craving for the drink.'

She shook her head when she thought of the doctor. He was right but so was she. There were other women, and men, like herself who all lacked strength and determination. She wasn't sure she wanted to face the world on a sober level anyway. It had nothing to offer her but a nine hour day in a tailor shop.

Once downstairs, she gathered herself up and went out the front door, locking it behind her. The back door was locked already. People figured they were definitely 'unneighbourly' to lock their doors but 'Stonehome' was on a busy highway and complete strangers passed its doors. She checked the doors to the glassed-in porches and tapped on the windows at the canaries. Clara had already fed the birds. The two porches were full of the small feathered creatures. When they all sang, it was the only bright light in her life. Did she lock the back door? She went around the outside of the house checking doors and windows. This was a habit she'd gotten into. The back door was firmly secured.

At the front of the house again she went out and shut the gate in the picket fence securely.

'Miss Young.' It was one of the Black girls. 'Can I walk with you to the corner.'

'I'm going that way.'

'Did you ever have to do long division? I can't. It's impossible to understand. I like English much better.'

'Why do you worry about that now?'

'Mother and father are paying a tutor to help me before school begins in September.'

'Why don't you bring your books to the house after supper. I'll try to help you. Clara's clever with math. We'll have milk and cookies.'

'I'd like that. You won't mind?'

'I don't mind. Grown children are welcome.'

'Did you like school? I do, except for the inspector. He frightens everyone, including the teacher.'

'I remember an inspector at the log school. I was so young . . . it was probably my early years in school Adam Fergusson used to come. The teacher would drill us for days in our reading and Mr. Fergusson would listen to us. After we had all finished he would pull a sack of alleys from his pocket, turn his back and dump them over his shoulder. They would drop all over the floor and the boys would scramble on the floor for them. The girls would sit primly and he would come down the aisles giving us candies. We didn't want alleys anyway.

'They don't do that now. He sits at the back of the room, eyeing the teacher. We're all so frightened we can't answer her properly, even questions we know and if he asks me a question, I'm tongue tied.'

'Don't ever let the man bother you girl! You look him straight in the eye next term and think "you were young once too . . . you just forgot". Once people get a little authority in their hands they tend to use it to berate people. Don't you forget now . . . after supper tonight.'

The girl skipped down the street while Georgina stood watching her. She and Clara craved company so much they often stood at the gate and invited the young people coming up the street in for a treat and a talk. No one paid much attention to them, except Sootie. Since his son was born he didn't come around much either. Annalee came with the child and Georgina's heart melted at the sight of the small creature. Children were alright if they knew their place. Those young hellions at the outhouse were uncontrollable. She looked at the tailorshop. For two cents she would turn and go back up the street but the money came in handy. That Clara, wherever she was, only worked part time when needed at the shops and did dressmaking at home. More and more women were sewing their own clothes or buying them 'off the rack'. So Clara wasn't busy.

Patting the cloth bag containing the bottle, she entered the door at the shop for the day's work.

The swinging bridge spanning the river from "Westwood" to "Craigshead" looking towards the village and the Blair Street Quarry.

Clara had come straight to the swing bridge today. She usually sat on the church steps watching the sun come up over the village but she was anxious to see the quarrying. They had dynamited yesterday and were going to pry the loose rock to the river bed today.

The haze was slow in lifting from the river but once the sun reached above the tree line the men on the river bank took on a more human form. She stood on the suspension bridge watching them closely. It was unusual for men to quarry in the summer. The Blair Street Quarry provided the stone for many of the old buildings but hadn't been used in some time. This summer Charlie had his men hauling stone for a house in the village. It was hot, strenuous work reserved for the strongest men in Charlie's employment. He usually liked to quarry in the winter to keep his men busy, otherwise they would be out of work until spring and the cooler temperatures in the winter made quarrying stone far less a chore. The men strained at the crowbars now, sweat staining their clothing. Clara could see Charlie in the midst of them, taking personal charge when they seemed in trouble. She knew that he personally set all the dynamite charges which loosened the rock. Wagons stood on the flat waiting to be loaded; the horses, oblivious to the noise around them, were browsing on the grass growing up between the cracks.

She'd spoken to Charlie once about the cave and the stone bridge on the edge of the quarry and he had assured her that he would try his best not to ruin them. She could see that he certainly was avoiding the area. She waved to him from the suspension bridge when he looked her way.

'Dammit, she's on the bridge again.'

'Watch your tongues! The woman is present again.'

He looked up at the figure on the bridge. Charlie didn't mind her standing there but he couldn't understand what fascination would bring her day after day to watch the work. Marie had told him that the stone for 'Stonehome' had been quarried at Blair Street. But how a woman could be that fascinated with stone bothered him.

'Miss Clara! Sootie is looking for you. Do you hear me?'

Clara nodded her head from the bridge above.

'He was on Tower Street when the men came down this morning. He didn't say what he wanted.'

She nodded again and waved to let Charlie know she had heard him. She watched now for Sootie as she looked up and down the river at the scenery. It was beautiful here since the trees started to grow again. At one time the banks of the river had been completely stripped of every vestige of green by the settlers in their rush to clear land. Thomas used to say "anything green and vaguely resembling a tree or bush was hacked to death like an enemy." She noticed Sootie long before he acknowledged her presence. He had aged since his son was born and he walked more slowly but the bounce was still in his step. His hair was streaked with white but the skin on his face was still taut and wrinkle free. She didn't mind Sootie's looks in old age. She thought he had just become much more distinguished. She didn't try to disillusion herself either. She knew she was aging rapidly.

Sootie came onto the bridge causing it to sway as he walked. 'Clara, I thought I'd find you here watching the quarrying. You must have come early. I looked for you at the church before I came down here. You made an old man walk quite a distance just to talk.'

Clara patted Sootie's hand mockingly. 'Not so old Sootie, just out of practise. You haven't been walking much recently have you?'

'I've not had the time. A young child in the house keeps a man busy.'

They both laughed and walked off the bridge to the ruins of 'Westwood'. Sootie cleared a patch of ground next to a wall and they sat down to enjoy the sun. They looked across the river to 'Craigshead' and the fields beyond. The wall they were leaning against was all that remained of David Blair Fergusson's house.

'You want to talk to me Sootie. Is that what you said?'

Clara thought Sootie looked upset and he certainly seemed ill at ease now that they were sitting together by the wall.

'Have I done something wrong that you would leave word all over the village that you were looking for me?'

Sootie turned to her. 'I've a lot on my mind concerning Annalee and Tommy . . . and you. I'll not stall with you for you read my mind too well for me to try to deceive you. I'm leaving the village Clara.'

'Sootie! I don't hear you correctly! You're taking your wife and child and leaving the village!'

'You aren't hearing me correctly Clara. Annalee and Tommy are staying in Fergus but I'm leaving.'

'Why Sootie. Has someone found out about your past? I haven't spoken to anyone of it.'

'The reason has to do with my past . . . But it's nothing you've done or said. Do you recall our talk on the St. Andrews Church steps when I told you of my past life?'

'I remember. I'd never forget that night.'

'Look at me and listen Clara. It is most important to me that you understand what I am telling you. That night I said to you I had actually found true love.' Clara nodded. 'You also will recall my absence from the village for nearly 2½ years?' Again she nodded. 'I went west and worked for a time. While I was in Manitoba I met a woman and I lived with her . . . as man and "wife". Marriage was impossible because there were circumstances she and I couldn't overcome.' He looked away from Clara now. 'We had a child, a daughter. Don't condemn me Clara! I am a human with feelings like any other man.'

Clara shook her head as though she was trying to rid herself of the words she had just heard. Sootie went on. He knew that if he stopped now he would possibly never tell Clara the truth.

'The child's name is Annalee.' He looked at her again. 'I had to come back to my roots, to Fergus but Annalee's mother refused to come so I left my child, just as my father left me and came back alone to Ontario. I sent money for their upkeep regularly and I wrote.'

His words finally evoked some response from Clara. "Annalee is your daughter Sootie, not your wife! Is that what you are telling me!'

He nodded an affirmative. 'When her mother died Annalee came to live with me, not as my bride but as my daughter.'

'Why if you loved the woman did you not stay with her?'

Sootie had no answer for that question. He lowered his head so that Clara couldn't see his true feelings.

'Tommy is your grandchild, Sootie!' Clara now had a look of absolute disbelief on her face. 'Why the deceit Sootie? Why didn't you tell me?'

'It was too difficult to explain Clara. There still are circumstances that can't be explained.'

'The child, who is the father?'

Sootie looked across the river, his face hardening with the thoughts of the man. 'A prominent member of the community suspected something was amiss. He had an eye for Annalee and was very astute with his observations. He faced me up with the truth and I confessed thinking of Annalee's happiness. If the man loved her I could easily have walked out of her life.'

Clara felt a wrench in her bosom. 'No Sootie! You couldn't have left the village, not forever!'

'Yes, I would have done it for my child, but he didn't have marriage in his plans. He wooed Annalee discreetly and privately and she, in a weak moment, gave in to him. A child was conceived. The man was annoyed and accused her of tricking him and threatened to tell all. We reached a compromise. I accepted responsibility for the child and the man swore secrecy of the situation.'

'But now Sootie, what about now? Why are you leaving if everything's alright? Won't he still talk once you've left? Won't he bother Annalee again?'

'He didn't have so much luck the next time around. He was forced to marry the girl and there'll be no more trouble from him. I'm personally going to England to find some link with my past, for the boy's sake. Isn't it the logical thing to do? I realize a war is on but I must try to find my relatives, for my sake also Clara. Do you understand?'

Clara couldn't think of an intelligent answer for him. She sat facing Sootie looking completely lost and uncertain of what to do next.

Sootie had to turn away from her. He hated to injure his beloved Clara, his only true love, his reason for going West in the first place. She would never know that thirty-five years ago he had asked for her hand in marriage. Thomas' hatred and ill feeling for him surely surfaced that night! She would never know the woman in Manitoba accepted him knowing that he loved another and gave him emotional and physical support when he needed it most. As he looked now at the delicate woman he loved so much, Sootie knew he should have approached her directly and openly confessed his love for her. He had wronged her by allowing her to live in spinsterhood. Damn Victorian customs! Damn Thomas for his narrowmindedness and his hold on Clara! He realized he had kept his devotion so well veiled that he had never held or kissed the woman he loved. She would never see him again as he had no intentions of returning to Fergus. In time Annalee would receive word her 'husband' was dead and possibly she would find happiness in a true marriage. Sootie took Clara gently by the shoulders.

'We've been through a lot, you and I. There've been good times between us. You must see the bright side of this situation Clara. Look at me.'

She lifted her eyes to him and he kissed her full on the lips.

Was this the feeling of love, this surge of warmth which swept through Clara? She felt completely drained of all physical strength. Her emotions ran wildly from elation to desperation. She reached for Sootie's hands. The kiss was tender and gentle. They clasped hands for a moment searching each other's eyes, then Sootie let go and rose. He too was visibly shaken with emotion. Neither spoke. He turned and walked toward the swing bridge and for the second time in his life he was crying.

Clara leaned against the ruin and watched as Sootie walked out of her life over the bridge.

'I love you Sootie.' Clara whispered the words. She spoke to the air around her. 'I've never said those words before. I love you.' She said it louder now but he had disappeared into the cedar on the opposite side of the river. He never looked back. He never said good-bye.

Scott Homestead early 1900's.

THE SCOTTS — SEPTEMBER 1916

T he young child let herself out the pasture gate and turned to wave to her mother and father standing on the side porch.

'She's still too young to be walking that distance to school.'

'Elizabeth. She is seven. We have kept her home an extra year because of the distance.'

'But she's so small!'

'She'll meet other children at the fifth line. She knows the road. You fret too much. Look at her swinging her lunch pail with not a care in the world. I'll walk to meet her tonight. I promised her I would. She'll be alright.'

'But in the winter! The snow builds so much on the Shiloh road.'

'We'll cross those bridges when we come to them. Alice and Lillias managed. Edith will too. If you've got the butter ready I'll hitch the team and get it down to Orton. Do you want to come?'

'I'll change my skirt and get Margaret. By the time you have hitched the team we'll be ready.' She entered the house and busied herself with getting the butter ready to travel to Toronto. A crock in the kitchen held all the cash they had and she tipped it onto the table. With Alice in Normal School, money was scarce. The butter would be sold by Alice in Toronto to pay her board. She would meet the train and had certain customers waiting in the city. The coinage in the crock wouldn't buy her staples in Orton so she checked the back kitchen for eggs to trade. They would at least get her some flour and sugar.

The baby was ready by the time George pulled up and while he loaded eggs and firkins Elizabeth changed into a better skirt.

The lane was a long one as the house had been built in the middle of one hundred acres. After the disastrous fire in 1903 when they lost everything, Elizabeth thought they would never move back to Eramosa. She looked at George handling the reins of the team. He had farming in his blood and town life was not for him. He couldn't take working in the tannery. They had saved and finally in 1908 replaced the burned out log cabin with a two storey frame and concrete home. She wished it had been built closer to either road as the property was on a corner but a tributary of the Speed River ran diagonally across the corner ten acres and the land was low, wet and swampy. The lane passed close to the wet ground and all activity ceased in the rushes as the wagon passed.

'You're glad to be back, aren't you George?'

'I've known little else than farming. My grandfather before me was the same. The five years in Acton and Guelph did me no good. These hills are where I belong.' The gravel hills of north Eramosa surrounded the Scott property.

'It's a harsh master George. It takes much but gives little. We have built the land up until it gives a crop but it's going to be the death of us.'

'There's no place else I'd rather die. You'd be happier in Fergus or Eramosa wouldn't you?.'

'I'm not saying I don't agree. It's a hard existence for a woman; you on the land all day and me helping when I can between the housework, baking and laundry. And we don't have much to show for our labours.'

'We have the farm and four healthy daughters. You couldn't ask for more, except maybe some money to keep it going.'

The conversation was one which was repeated a good many times when the crock was empty.

'Do you think Edith is alright?'

'She'll be at school now. You're worrying needlessly. She can take care of herself.' He slapped the rumps of the horses with the reins and pulled across the seventh line.

If he'd seen Edith he wouldn't have been so sure of his statements. She walked down the cowpath which led to the spring then angled off the path to the back lane which took her to the concession road. She'd been down this lane countless times before to explore or fish but now that her parents had alerted her to the dangers of walking to school alone, everything appeared as a threat. The cedars overhanging the lane harboured monsters ready to reach out and grab her. Every noise or movement in the swamp sent her scurrying faster along the road. When she walked faster the handle on the lunch pail rattled making her increase her speed even more. When she ran the shadows of the trees seemed to be moving and she thought they were chasing her. Why did she have to go to school anyway? She was perfectly happy at home with her mother and father. She was breathless when she arrived at the corner of the fifth line.

"Hello. Are you a new kid?'

'Yep.' She looked up at a very tall youth.

'Where'd you come from?'

Edith pointed down the concession road.

'Are you a Scott?'

'Yes.'

'Your farm's on the corner. You're scared aren't you?'

"No I am not!'

'Sure you are. Come on. I'll walk with you. We'd better hurry or we'll be late.'

Edith scurried along taking three steps for his one large stride. She actually breathed a sigh of relief. For the last mile to school she didn't have to walk alone. It must be awful to be alone all the time.

While the young girl was embarking on the most important phase in her life, an old man was ending his. Three thousand and five hundred miles across the

Atlantic ocean, an old man lay in a small garret room. The garret was clean but sparsely furnished with only bed, table and chair. But the derelict was not alone. A stranger sat beside the bed where the frail body lay, sometimes lucid but most of the time in a semi-conscious state. A knock roused him from a light sleep. The stranger went to the door and opened it just enough to accept a tray of food from the landlady.

'Everything alright in there?'

'We're doing nicely.'

'The money's run out. This is the last meal I'm providing. I'm not liking having to serve meals in the room. Rules are . . . no meals in the rooms.' The stranger drew some bills from his belt and handed them through the crack.

'You'll do exactly what I say won't you. There's more money where this came from but you'll follow instructions won't you?'

'If you pay me I will.' She tucked the money down her dress front.

'You'll continue to provide meals as long as I request them.'

'Yes sir.' He shut the door and carried the tray to the bedside. He lifted the old man and gently propped him up with cushions, adjusting the cover around the lower part of his body.

'You'll take a little drink Sir?' The white head nodded agreement. Gently the cup was held to the lips. The tea, laced with sugar, seemed to revive the man and he was anxious to talk.

'You've taken much of your time to be kind to me.'

'My time is worth nothing. I was in the gutter once myself.'

'I'm not worth bothering with.'

'Any human being is worth saving, although I admit I do not usually make a habit of plucking them from the gutters of London, England often.'

'You will not tell me your name.'

'My name, like yours, is of no importance to anyone.'

The old man sighed heavily. 'You are not much younger than I.'

'Life has been generous with me and given me time.'

'It has been unkind to me. I haven't much time do I?'

'No you don't.'

Again the old man sighed. His strength was sapped by merely talking. 'Is everything acceptable to us . . . the letter . . . the money?'

'I think we understand each other. I've arranged the details.' He held the wrinkled hand. 'Do not worry. You will not die alone. I will be here.'

The fingers tightened slightly but the strain of talking caused the frail body to shudder. The stranger slid the cushions aside and made him comfortable in the bed again. He picked at the food on the tray and began another patient vigil. It was not unusual for him to be here with the derelict. He believed no man should face death alone.

Gradually the old man lapsed into complete unconsciousness and one chill, damp day just before noon the pathetic human breathed his last. The stranger gently pulled the cover over the body and placed a letter on the table addressed to 'Miss Clara Young, Fergus, Ontario.' Beside it he left another sealed envelope addressed to the local police. Inside the second was a sum of money and instructions for burial of the body. He erased all signs that he had been in the garret room, shut the door firmly behind him, and walked down the four floors to the landlady's flat.

'It's you. You've decided to come out of hiding.'

'There seems to be a problem upstairs with the old man. You'd better summon the local constabulary.'

'It's that serious?'

'Yes. I'll return to the room and await the police.' He turned from the door but instead of retracing his steps up the stairs, he let himself quietly out the side door. An alleyway across the courtyard gave him shelter from the rain while he waited to satisfy himself the police had been called.

As soon as the first bobbies appeared he turned away from the alley and disappeared into the streets of London, his tall figure gradually being consumed by the fog. He was no stranger to these streets. He had done what he could for the old man but preferred no questions asked of him.

THE PICNIC — SUMMER 1919

It is said that in the drama called 'Life', all characters in the production meet together once in their lifetimes, if even for a single moment. It was not divine providence which brought the Youngs, Scotts and Mattainis together on a sunny afternoon in the summer of 1919. It was a mistake no one would admit to. Every summer the various churches held a picnic, each on their own day, in their own bush. Never before had the picnics been held on the same day and in the same area. The Catholics were holding their picnic in McCann's bush right down the road from Shiloh and the 'others' who were holding their picnic at S.S. #5, Shiloh. There was not ¼ mile between the two. The Speed river ran through both properties.

Charlie was loading the car with hampers of food and his family.

'Run, get your Uncle Johnny. We are ready to go. Tell him . . . no bottles today. It is a church picnic. The hampers are ready for loading.'

'There is food for 100 Marie. We are feeding the congregation?'

'It won't last long when the relatives find it. Landoni's will meet us at the bush.'

As a courtesy by the organizers, church members from all the surrounding congregations were invited. Belwood, Ostic, Speedside, Metz, Dracon, Elora and all the small country churches received notices of the picnics. By the time Charlie arrived at Shiloh with his load, cars had lined both sides of the road for a mile. All horses and buggies were tethered in a riverside field on McCann's property.

'Hey! Horses don't have any sense when it comes to religion!'

'Charlie, we'll never find a space to park.'

'I've arranged it.' He eased the car up to the barricade at the bridge construction site.

'Johnny. Move the barrier.' Johnny jumped over the door of the car and shifted the wooden gate. Charlie parked among the piles of sand and cement mixers.

'The garage. Everyone out. You children, help with the hampers.' The children scrambled over the closed doors also and dashed into the bush following the sounds of their friends already arrived.

'Marie! They don't listen anymore to their father.'

'They don't pay much attention to me either. You gentlemen will have to carry the hampers.' Marie moved in the direction of the noise also.

'Johnny, be careful . . . the square hamper . . . don't rattle!'

The picnic, 1919.

Long makeshift tables were set up in an open flat area of McCann's bush. The ladies were setting out a noon meal of every conceivable food that could be packed. As soon as Charlie and Johnny arrived with the hampers, Marie set out platters of fried chicken, potato salad and cakes.

The 'others' set their food on plank tables under the maples at the school. Women, being naturally curious, began sauntering to opposite sides of the 'fence' to see who had the better meal. All religious conviction was set aside when the ladies began exchanging recipes. It wasn't long before husbands went looking for wives and the children went looking for food!

'Johnny look! There's a Methodist eating with the Browns!'

'Hush, the Youngs, good Anglicans are right down the table from you!'

'Where is Jimmy?'

'I told him he could eat with Harold at the school.'

'Harold's Presbyterian!'

Charlie had his fill of food and leaned back against a tree surveying the picnic. There hadn't been so much fraternization between churches before that he could remember. They all seemed to stand at arm's length from each other. Even today, the pastors were so busy running back and forth from bush to school keeping an eye on each other for fear one would make a convert, they didn't have time to eat!

The children were running from bush to bush getting in on all the races and contests. Each group had candies and favours as prizes and after the noon meal, ice cream was dished out in cones. The flavours in McCanns bush were equal to those at the school. The young boys started a game of scrub in the field at Leslie's. Those people who believed there should be no 'fooling' on the Lord's Day chose to ignore the activity.

'Charlie. Do you want to walk over to the millpond? The men are swimming. It's just around the bend.'

'A walk, I need.' He dipped into the square hamper and put a bottle in his pocket. The two set off along the riverbank.

'Can I ask my brother a serious question? Did you ever desire to return to Vergiate? Like Tony . . . Madre?'

Johnny glanced cautiously at his brother.

'At the beginning . . . It was difficult adjusting to the weather . . . the people. I am Canadian now. I will not return to Italy. Madre was old when she came. She went back to Vergiate to die. She knew we had a new country. She saw the space . . the opportunity. You have thought of returning?'

'To visit. I risk much. I have the discharge certificate from the Italian Government but I did not earn it. The Government gave it innocently.'

'Charlie. You came out alive. You were welcomed in Italy. Forget the past. Many acted as you. It was an unnecessary war. Our government should not have been in Africa. You were not a coward. You did not submit to slaughter. You took a stand and held to it.'

'I want to go . . . in 21. I cannot leave before then. But I must see the homeland again . . . regardless of risk. The dreams of the death in Ethiopia haunt me. I cannot forget easily. Look! People are inspecting my bridge. They do not see an arch bridge before.'

The Shiloh bridge was still passable but was flanked on either side by the iron reinforcement rods of the new arches. This was not the first concrete reinforced arch span Charlie was building and it wouldn't be the last. The two men diverted from the riverbank to the roadway.

'They ask questions because they do not understand my bridges. They say bridges should be flat . . . square . . . ugly.' Charlie was looking forward to the questions. He was in his glory defending his bridges.

'They say the bridges look "artistic".'

'In Ethiopia I dreamed of these bridges. They kept me alive. They are my addition . . . the Italian contribution to Canada. The stone buildings are Scottish and Irish contributions. We all leave a little of our . . . culture . . . in an adopted country. Those bridges . . . they will stand long after I die.'

While Charlie and Johnny were at the bridge site, Clara and Marie was walking up the road to Shiloh.

'Look at Charlie. His hands are moving continually. He must be explaining his bridge. Who is that woman standing with Georgina?'

'It is Elizabeth Scott. Come I'll introduce you.'

The introductions over, the four ladies settled on a thick rug under a maple tree to relax. Around them children played and young men, just back from the war, courted their girls. The bush provided cosy little nooks for serious courting but children were everywhere and there was no privacy. George Scott brought ice cream cones for all four ladies then went off to join the older men relaxing by the fence rows. Elizabeth's youngest child was at her side.

'It's been a grand picnic! This should happen more often.'

'I don't think there'll be a chance of it occurring again. I can't imagine the organizers making the same mistake next year.'

'If a picnic were put on by the village everyone would attend but as soon as it is supported by a church, the crowds get smaller. You couldn't possibly get all the churches co-operating but it didn't used to be that way. I remember the stories of Rev. Smellie. He took his flock and left the Auld Kirk on the hill in Fergus. But he had nowhere to worship with his followers except back in the Auld Kirk so he shared the church with the Presbyterians with the full permission of those he left!'

'This picnic proves to me there's no difference in people only in what they have been lead to believe. There's such bitterness over religious differences. It's the same God, no matter where you worship. Everyone just goes about praying a different way.'

'Hush Clara! Don't you let a Methodist hear you say that!'

'Or a Catholic either!'

'Well look here, on this rug. We have Marie, a Catholic; Elizabeth a Methodist; Georgina, an Anglican and myself.'

'What are you, Clara?'

'I've been in every church in the village, but was baptized an Anglican.'

'We could discuss this for hours but it's such a nice day, perhaps we should change the subject. Religion is always so volatile a subject! It is such a personal thing for most people that it is a breech of good manners to question them on it.' The ladies went on to discuss the current fashions, a less controversial topic.

Down by the river an ancient cedar exposed its gnarled roots to the sun. Sitting on one of its roots facing the river were two young children. One threw stones and the other contemplated the ripples on the surface of the water. They had been sitting there for the past thirty minutes, the girl finding the pebbles for the boy.

'What's your name?'

'Joseph Francis Mattaini. What's yours?'

'Edith Alberta Scott.'

'Where d'you live?'

'In a house.'

'So do I.'

'Do you have animals?'

'We did. Now we only have a dog and some horses. Do you?'

'Yep. We have chickens and pigs and cows and horses.'

'Do you go to school?'

'See that building up there on the hill? I walk to it to go to school. It's a long way from my home.'

'I walk across the bridge in Fergus and go to a school on a hill too.'

'Is a village nice to live in with people and cars and stores?'

'I'd rather live in the country with animals. Does your mother know you are getting dirty?'

'No.' Edith tidied her dress. Mother had spent quite a number of hours sewing dresses for the picnic. 'I'm not as dirty as you. Does your mother know you were wading in the river?'

J.F. looked down at his filthy wet knickers. 'She'll never be able to tell.'

'You're dirty and wet!'

'I look like this all the time. Hey! Do you want a piece of chicken. Let's go see if there's any left in mom's lunch basket.'

'No thank you.'

'Well, I'm going to look.' J.F. jumped up and ran off in the direction of McCann's bush. Edith stood up and straightened her dress, watching the retreating figure of the boy.

'I'm nine years old,' she shouted after him. He turned and yelled back. 'I'm eleven.'

'Are you coming back here?' He was now out of earshot. She waited a few moments then went off looking for her sister at the school. It was no fun throwing pebbles alone.

STALEMATE — SEPTEMBER 1921

D r. Groves' living room was pleasantly arranged but far too austere for Clara's tastes. Even now at sixty-five her preferences ran to bright colours and odd furniture arrangements. She stood by the large windows which overlooked Queen Street, the horse pasture and the river. Across the river the huge stack of the old Groves Hydro Plant dominated the scene with the turrets of the Royal Bank and Marshall Block visible behind it. The sun, full on the river, made it difficult to watch the fast flowing water, but, at the angle it was in the sky, the brown colour of the river was turned into a beautiful blue as it reflected the sky above it. How the village had grown in the last thirty years! It was now 'the Town Hall', 'the Town Council' and 'the Town Waterworks' but to her it was still a village and would never be anything different. She wondered if so much growth had been part of Fergusson's dream and what Webster would think of the village in the 20th century. He was all for its growth in the 1850's but he liked the open fields and woods so close to home also.

When Abraham Groves invited her to his home for a chat, Clara knew exactly what he was after. Everytime their paths crossed in the village he questioned her on the mysterious disappearance of Sootie. He hadn't given her any peace in the past six years but since the letter arrived five and one-half years ago he became very persistent indeed. The fact that he knew about the letter in the first place proved to Clara the village possessed some of the most 'meddlesome' people alive. Every village had one or two people who minded everybody's business but their own and Clara was quite capable of gossip herself. Her very early morning and late evening walks divulged some strange facts! She knew plenty but she never talked.

She could have said no to his invitation but she wanted information from Abraham also because Georgina was ill and wasn't telling her anything. Georgina was like a clam whenever the subject of her health came up.

She wanted information on Georgina but it wasn't going to be a trade-off. No indeed! She'd never divulge Sootie's secret and she knew for sure Annalee wouldn't either. Only harm could come from the information. Annalee and Tommy were living in Fergus and their integrity would be upheld. She owed that debt to Sootie. Abraham didn't know just what he was dealing with as he'd never come up against Clara's stubborness. She could be as tight lipped as a safe with three combinations and Abraham knew none of the three!

Abraham walked down the hall to the living room. He was beside himself to find out the true story about Sootie. It had become an obsession with him in the past few year. He could piece nothing together from the bits of information he had. Sootie told him nothing. Annalee told him nothing and Tommy had a birthmark, the position of which he shared mysteriously with a well known member of the community. He decided the best way to solve his mystery was to approach the subject directly. He'd face her up with his views and watch her closely for her reaction to his information. He knew Georgina well but Clara was as much a mystery to him as Sootie as she never needed his medical attentions. Georgina was so open about her emotions that he assumed Clara would be the same.

She turned from the window when she heard the door to the livingroom open.

'Clara. It's good of you to have come.'

'Why wouldn't I if I promised. I'm rather anxious to hear what you have to say. I gather you want to question me about your former driver Sootie.' Her face was a mask, revealing nothing. Abraham was taken completely off guard. He'd been caught at his own game!

'Have a seat Clara.' He motioned to a comfortable side chair and once she was seated, sat himself in another directly opposite her.

'I must admit that crossed my mind . . . to question you about Sootie but I wanted to speak to you about Georgina.' Two could play the game and he had lots of time today.

'I wanted to talk to you also . . . about Georgina. She's very ill isn't she? She won't tell me a thing.'

'She's dying Clara, of consumption.'

'I thought so. How long does she have? What can I do? I'm no nurse, mind you.'

'There's nothing much anyone can do for her. Don't bother her about her drinking any more. It won't hurt now. Later she'll be in constant pain and she'll need medication. If I give it to her too soon she will develop a tolerance for it and when she needs it most, it won't be effective. Did Sootie die of consumption or was it his heart?' He looked Clara directly in the eyes.

'I haven't heard recently that he died, Abraham. Do you perhaps know something I don't? The last time I saw him, he looked perfectly healthy.' Her eyes revealed not a thing!

'Getting back to Georgina. Darn woman reads too many medical books. She first drew the symptoms to my attention and she also decided to report all her physical and mental changes to me, just in case it might assist me in treating others with the same type of disease.'

'An operation wouldn't help? Is it that far advanced?'

'An operation would be useless and would only prolong her death. Her drinking didn't help her condition. It actually caused part of it. Her heart isn't strong either so you see, it's a combination of illnesses, Clara.'

'Strange! Drink caused her illness and drink will ultimately comfort her in her final months. I'll not harp on her habit again.'

'You knew Sootie well didn't you?' Again he watched her.

'Why do you ask?' Ah . . . a flicker of interest.

'I liked the man. He simply went off the England with no explanation.'

'Did you ask him for one before he left?'

'No.'

'Perhaps you should have. He'd have told you he was going to find some long forgotten relatives.'

'He had relatives in England? I didn't realize . . . I just assumed he was alone, that he had no one.'

'You should know that assumptions are often wrong, Abraham. Is Georgina able to work or should she be resting? You've gotten off the subject we were discussing.' Clara felt the conversation needed redirection quickly.

'We'll let her work as long as she is able. She's not one to sit at home or lay in bed. Toward the end she'll need much attention and the hospital would be the best place for her. You might find her a burden.'

'She's my sister and "Stonehome" is her home as much as mine. It will be her decision as to where she wants to die and I'll bide by it. If it means nursing her, I'll manage.'

'Clara. I'm going to be truthful. She won't be easy!'

'I'm up to it. You don't need to worry about me. I've never been a good "nurse" but I'll learn if need be.'

'You've cared for Tommy a good deal and certainly noticed his birthmark. I've always wondered if he inherited it from his father.'

'You've a nerve, Abraham! Thinking that I would know if Sootie had the same birthmark! That implies to me you think we had an illicit relationship.' Clara's nostrils flared.

'No my dear lady. I wouldn't suggest such a thing!'

'How else would you suspect I'd see the birthmark unless he was naked? Let me assure you our relationship was always purely platonic. I never had a brother until Sootie arrived.'

Clever woman! Abraham had to admit she was an extremely tough old bird.

'Do you know if Annalee . . . if possibly there was any . . . difficulty between Annalee and Sootie that she might possibly turn to another man?'

'You're implying now that Annalee was unfaithful to Sootie. They were devoted to each other! Has she seen another man since he left?'

'Well . . . not that I know of . . .'

'Doesn't that indicate her devotion to him then. Surely, if she'd been seeing another man she'd have done it quite openly after he left.'

'What happened to him? Why hasn't he written? Why did he leave a wife and child in Fergus? If he's dead why doesn't Annalee remarry?'

'Why don't you ask Annalee, Abraham? She's the logical one to ask, not me. I must go. Georgina will wonder where I've gotten to. I appreciated the information on Georgina but it was what I suspected.'

Clara rose and walked to the living room door. She turned when she reached the door.

'If you were meant to have all the answers about Sootie, he'd have told you himself. He admired you very much. It doesn't pay to press too hard for the answers now. Good day to you Doctor.'

Abraham stood for awhile after Clara left, his fingers stroking his chin.

'I'm going for a walk,' he called down the empty hall for someone to hear. He clamped a hat on his head and went out into the sun. His path took him right past the cottage Sootie had bought in the village for Annalee and himself when Tommy was born. He wasn't looking for Annalee but kept his eye out for Tommy who would be coming home from school. Sure enough, the slender youth was at the end of the street, walking quickly home.

'Hello my boy. How're you today?'

'Fine Dr. Groves. Did you come to see mom? Is anything wrong?'

'Not at all lad. I was out walking and just happened to see you. How's your ankle been since we patched it up?'

'Great. I can run and kick the ball like anyone else again. Mom says I must have sprained it when I fell off my bicycle.'

'Have you a moment to sit down and talk while I rest?'

'Sure. There's a great stump over there. You can sit on it.' The old man and the young boy sat together on the rotting wood.

'I've been meaning to ask you Tommy. Do you remember your father?'

'No, but Mom told me about him. He was a nice person, kind, loving. Mom said he was a very well known man in the community.' Doc bristled with anticipation . . . from the mouths of babes comes the truth . . .

'She said he always was careful in case the community found out about him. He had a reputation to keep, whatever that means.'

'And his name Tommy. Did she ever tell you his name?'

'Yes. Sootie — S O O T I E, I can even spell it.'

Doc patted Tommy on the head and resigned himself to the fact he'd never solve his mystery.

SPRING — 1922

Six months after Clara's talk with Dr. Groves, Georgina announced she was leaving for Lindsay to live with the Barrs.

'Are you sure they want you Georgina? Louise is not well and they will have enough to do without taking care of you also.'

'There's nothing visibly wrong with me. I can take care of myself.'

'Have you written them? Did they agree?'

'I wrote I was coming to visit Louise. I'll speak to them about my staying on when I get there.'

'You don't have to leave "Stonehome" Georgina. No one's forcing you to leave the house or the village.'

'I'm not staying here to have people stare at me in my last . . ." she stopped suddenly.

'Say it Georgina!'

'I'm not having people stare at me dying. I'm dying of consumption Clara. I won't be back.'

'I know about your illness but you will be back . . . and long before you die. You won't be able to live in Lindsay as you have in "Stonehome".'

'You are talking nonsense Clara. They're sensible people.'

'They have been exceptionally good to Louise especially after Elizabeth's death. But we are almost strangers to them.'

'They are all the family you and I have Clara. It's time we got to know them better. You'll need them when your time comes. I'll take the train. You arrange tickets and a car to the station. I won't discuss this further. Enough's been said.'

On the day of departure Clara asked the driver to come a little early so that they could sit on the rise of land at the station looking out over the village. He left them alone and walked down to Blair Street to watch the ice as spring breakup had come early this year. Huge chunks of ice built up at Monklands covering low land and road but once the chunks began to move they sped dizzily over the two dams and shot the narrows at Blair Street, careening out into the flats below the old Harvey place.

'They say the main street's empty. Everyone's watching the ice at the bridges.'

'They've probably nothing better to do.'

'It's fascinating Georgina. The power of nature is so awesome. You can't help but be impressed when you see those huge pieces of ice. If the sun shines on them it's beautiful. They become multi-coloured gems.'

'They are full of the filth and pollution of the river. You see everything with such a strange perspective Clara. You can never see the bad side of a situation, always the good.'

'You can't go around being a grouch all you life either Georgina. There is good in every situation. You might have to dig a little harder in some cases but you'll always find a bit of good news.'

'What's so good about ice backing up in a river and carrying everything in its path downstream. That's destruction.'

'After the spring breakup come the tulips, daffodils, lilacs and apple blossoms!'

'You try telling that to the people who've lost buildings and livestock in a flood.'

Clara changed the subject. 'Are you sure this is what you want to do?' How can you leave this?' Clara indicated the village spread before them.

'Look, the Post Office building . . . father's store stood there. And the old English church used to stand right down there on Breadalbane. And the schools. Your whole life has been spent here. You can't just pick up and leave your roots.'

'Our parents did.'

'You're surely not comparing your situation with that of our parents!'

'Of course not. I just have no love for this place or I have not found it yet if it's in me. Elizabeth and Louise left the village early in their lives and seem to have found happiness. I have never been happy here.'

'It isn't the village that makes you unhappy. It has every ingredient for happiness within the confines of its streets; good schools, churches, entertainments, park land, music groups, dance groups. Look inside yourself Georgina. Your answer lies within yourself.'

'You're being vindictive and cruel!'

'I'm being truthful and hope you take my advice.'

The sound of the train whistle brought their argument to a close. It was arriving from the north, rounding the large curves before Garafraxa Street. Mr. Wilson helped the women assemble the baggage on the platform.

'You've got your ticket?'

'Yes, in my bag.'

'And you haven't forgotten the lilac branches? Put them in a vase of water as soon as you arrive. The buds will be forced to open in the heat of the house. Louise will be pleased to see them.'

'They're in my luggage.'

'Give my love to Louise, the Barrs and all the nieces and nephews. Write to me Georgina. I'll wait to hear from you.'

'You should be making the trip with me.'

'I can't afford to leave "Stonehome" at the moment. There are things that have to be done this spring.'

The train pulled to a stop with a grinding and squealing of metal against metal. Steam rose in the cold spring air.

'Look Clara. I've lived in Fergus all my life and no one could take the time to come to the station to say good bye. There are people who know I am leaving. Doesn't that tell you something?'

Gerogina turned to the steps and was helped into the coach by the conductor where she took a seat near a window. The train did not linger long in the station. Steam was released again as it began its journey towards Elora and Guelph. Georgina waved from the dirty coach window, her hat primly pinned on her severely drawn back hair. Clara turned from the platform and walked across the tracks heading for "Stonehome".

Jimmy heard the whistle down by the stagnant pond below the railyard where he and Frank had been poking around in the oozing mess with sticks. The pond never froze and always gave forth bubbles, belches and obnoxious smells.

'You're going to be late Jimmy. You'd better run.' Jimmy lit out up the embankment but by the time his legs got him to the station, the caboose was at the Alardice Road and a lone figure of a woman was walking over by the Beatty Plant. Frank puffed up behind him.

'You're in trouble now!' Jimmy looked at the small package and letter he had pulled from his pocket.

'You don't have to tell me. She's my mom! She said make sure these were delivered to Miss Young or else!'

'She threatened to wash my mouth out with soap if I didn't apologize for calling them "the crazy Youngs".'

'You apologized didn't you. You were scared not to! Lucky you did. She told Willy the same thing when he called me a "dago". He wouldn't and she grabbed him and gave him a mouthful of Sunlight suds. He went home bawling his face off and his mother came back like a rhinoceros pawing the ground.

' "You apologize to my son you filthy *dago*", she yelled. Mom picked up her soap and a mop and said. "Apologize woman or I'll use my mop to wash out yours."

'They stood glaring at each other. Mom took a step towards her and the woman said, "Well don't do it again!" Mom said, "Apologize now!" She began moving the mop.

' "Sorry" the woman mumbled.

' "Say it louder!"

' "SORRY."

' "Now get out of my yard." The woman hightailed it.'

'You'd better have a good excuse for missing this train or we'll both be in serious trouble.'

'What did we do that took so much time?'

'We watched the ice from the Tower Street bridge and we watched the blacksmith.'

'Let's go to the clubhouse. I've got to think of something.'

They set off down the Colquhoun Street shortcut to the old stave factory and down a lane which ran along the river behind the houses on St. Andrew's Street. Between the Temperance Hall and the Town Hall Jimmy moved a large flat rock at the base of a lilac bush. They lowered themselves through a narrow cleft which had been exposed by the removal of the stone, into an eerie grey hole. Water dripped from the roof and a small riverlet covered their shoes.

'Frank. You got matches? Let's get this lantern lit so I can stand out of the water. It's cold.' Jimmy felt on a rock ledge for a lantern. Once the lantern was lit the outlines of a fairly large cave began to take shape. The opening onto the river was practically covered with an icefall and light coming through the ice gave the cave its eerie grey colouring. Only a portion of Gow's kiln could be seen clearly from the entrance. They sidestepped the riverlet and sat on wet rock ledges. A stock of 'borrowed' goods lay at the back of the cave: C.P.R. lanterns, apple crates, cigarettes.

'Geez. I hate getting in here that way. It's better when the ice melts and we can climb to the entrance from the river.'

'Only way you can see the entrance is from the top of the kiln. The trees hide it from the "washing green". Carl nearly fell in there once. He was two and onehalf years old and climbed almost to the top of the kiln before a workman spotted him and hauled him down. All Dad said when told was "Sylvester" is living up to his namesake! What am I going to do Frank?'

'Maybe she wouldn't be that mad?'

'She will! Almost as mad as the day the priest was visiting and all dad's wine bottles started to blow their corks. They were hitting the floor of the living room like bullets. You'd hear a whop and then the worst cussing I've ever heard. Dad was in the basement running from bottle to bottle swearing like a trooper. The priest was upstairs drinking tea and trying to keep a straight face. What bottles didn't explode were no good anyway. Mom went downstairs after the priest left and smashed every one of them.'

'I remember the day she came home and found us all helping with "the crushing of the grape". Your dad gave us an old vat and several boxes of his grapes. We all took off our shoes and socks and stomped around in the vat having the time of our lives. She said Charlie was polluting our minds and he said he didn't care as long as that's all we were polluting. She hauled us out and made us scrub our legs with lye soap. I still haven't any hair on them!'

'That's not from the lye soap stupid! That's from shaving them with a straight razor so you could dress up as a girl for the party. You looked good too mincing around in your sister's dress. You won the dollar but didn't keep it long. Fred beat you at holding his breath and you had to pay up.'

'It's getting late. What are you going to do?'

'I've got three choices. I can go directly home to mom. She'll kill me. I can hide in the lumberyard until Dad comes for supper and tell him. If he takes my side there'll be war for a week.'

'And your third choice. You can run away from home!'

'I can go to Grampa Faustino's. They are only a block from home. Grandma might understand. She can talk to her daughter. But I'll probably have to chop a week's supply of wood for them. Grandpa believes the punishment should suit the crime. Once I killed a sparrow. He saw me and said "You eat what you kill and you kill only to eat." He took the bird, wrapped it in wet clay and baked it over the fire. When he peeled away the baked clay the feathers came too but I had to eat what was left! I'll never kill another bird.'

'So what will it be?'

'Grandpa Faustino's.'

They blew out the lantern and pulled themselves through the cleft in the rock. Jimmy pulled the stone over the entry.

'We're lucky it's quiet back here. Otherwise everyone would know about the cave.'

'Someday we'll be down there and the roof will give way or there'll be a tremor. We'd better find a new hideout.'

'Spike told me about the ruins of an old kiln out by Monklands. We should go take a look. It's close to the sawmill so there'd be plenty of wood.'

'Creeps Jimmy! A man got sawed in half out there last fall. They had to bury him in two coffins! And you want to play around there?'

'Well, we can take a look anyway. Come on.'

'What about your grandpa's?'

'It's still early. Let's go. You chicken or something?' Jimmy led the way. Frank followed close at his heels. Parents and problems were forgotten as they explored their world as only children can do well.

EARTHQUAKE — SEPTEMBER 1922

Steam rose from the canning kettle when Annalee lifted the lid. She eased the rack into the water, replaced the lid and checked the time . . . 10:25 am. Stepping over Tommy who was busily stacking zinc jar rings and box tops to make a pyramid, completely oblivious to the heat in the kitchen, Annalee mopped her brow with the apron she had around her waist. The kitchen range hadn't been moved to the summer kitchen and the small main kitchen of 'Stonehome' felt like a steam house. Why Clara didn't purchase an electric stove was beyond Annalee. She often came to help Clara with housework. The two women shared a common link, the memories of the man both learned to love.

'Why are you doing this canning, Clara? You're alone and can buy tomatoes and other vegetables by the tin for the winter months.'

The older woman, hair limp with the steam threaded her way through the obstacle course Tommy had created on the floor to the table where she sat down and wiped her face with a tea towel she carried over her shoulder.

'She'll be back! Georgina will be back. She's not happy in Lindsay. She'll expect canned tomatoes because we've always had them.'

'She won't be back Clara. She's far too ill and you mustn't get your hopes up.'

'I didn't say I wanted her back. I don't need the responsibity of her care day and night but this is her home as much as mine. She has a right to die here. I understand her well.'

'She's written to you to let you know she's coming?'

'No. She's coming. I know. She doesn't have to write.'

Glass began to chatter softly in the windows of the building. Dishes rattled in the flatback beside Clara. Her head went up. She glanced quickly around the room and put her hand down to silence Tommy.

'What is it Clara? The pictures are shaking against the walls!'

'Quickly! Don't alarm Tommy but we must go outside immediately.'

Annalee grabbed Tommy's arm firmly and all three went through the summer kitchen to stand in the garden. Leaves rustled gently on the apple trees as some unseen breeze seemed to pass through them.

Not a bird was singing and the ground was vibrating very gently under their feet.

'Clara, what is it?' Annalee was quite alarmed by now. She had a hold on Tommy and was gripping Clara's arm.

'It's an earth tremor. It won't last long.'

Sure enough, as soon as she said it the rustling stopped and the ground stopped vibrating. They waited several more minutes and then walked slowly toward 'Stonehome'.

'It's not the first tremor around here. There was one in 1903, I call it a "settling"; and a large quake struck in 1870. I remember both very well. After the small tremor in 1903 which was just like this one, geologists came and told us this hill which "Stonehome" is situated on is a gravel bank 20 to 30 feet deep and below that yet, many, many feet below is an underground river. It runs in a wide circle around the village coming in from the north, right under this area and crosses the Grand River at a 90^0 angle somewhere out by the House of Industry and Refuge.'

'How did they ascertain that Clara?'

'Heavens, I don't know. They just went by the lay of the land and the depth of the wells and they had a water witcher with them. He was a clever man. We watched him witch the whole area from the field across the road, back and forth, right through the property and over to T.J. Hamilton's.'

She waved in the direction of the Beaver Meadow. 'Sootie used to say the springs in the Beaver Meadow came directly from a river. There's an area over on the other side of the village between the old Smellie residence and the Landoni property where the water drains down from the hills and fields directly into a natural hole in the ground maybe ten feet below the natural terrain. Sootie said it ran directly into an underground river but he could never find the exit for the waters along the river. He tramped the bank between Fergus and the flats below Elora and figured that's where the water must have been going, right into the underground river. The tremor just now and the one in 1903 was just on account of the earth layers settling because of changes in the river and its flow washing away layers of sand and gravel above it. I don't imagine many people would feel this tremor, only those with properties along the underground river course. The earthquake of 1870 was felt as far away as the Eastern Seaboard of Canada and the United States.

Once in the house Clara went through the kitchen to the second floor.

'You check the stove Annalee, especially the pipes. The shaking could have loosened them. I'm going to check the second floor and the attic.'

The kettle was on when Clara came downstairs again.

'There's no more cracks than usual. You see the big rough spot up on the stairwell? That came down in 1903. Didn't Sootie ever tell you about the big quake?'

'He said not a word about it to me.'

'It was a strange phenomenon which started on September 20th, 1870. Doors would shake open and balls bounced gently up and down off the floor for hours. Window glass rattled in its frame and dishes clattered on their shelves. The ground wasn't visibly moving but there seemed to be subtle movement everywhere. Animals became quite nervous and snappish and had to be well penned. Our old dog ran around constantly, always uneasy and growling at the slightest noise. Some people blamed the train because it had made its first official run to Fergus seven days before the shaking began. But it wasn't the train. Of course, there were those people who said, "It's the end of the world!" but no one believed them either. No one knew what to believe. Even Sootie couldn't understand why the earth that he was so attuned to would shake relentlessly for so many days without a let up. He knew it must be a tremor but usually they last only a short time and never for weeks on end. After the first week everyone seemed to settle down to await whatever fate was in store for them. They were even able to joke about "the moving village".

'Mother was ill and the constant rattling made her quite distraught only adding to the load on her heart. She died on October 18, a beautiful autumn day when the tremoring seemed to cease for awhile. Father shut himself in his office to be alone with his grief and immediately the rattling began again. Even in his darkest hour of grief he could have no silence and peace from the incessant movement and noise. Father simply refused to leave the office and only went to the parlour where mother was laid out after Sootie spoke to him. But even in the solemn atmosphere of the black crepe draped parlour the rattling would not cease. Sometimes it shook sporadically and other times it was a constant tremble with the movement showing in the curtains and draping around the coffin.

The day of the funeral, October 20, the large horse drawn hearse arrived for the casket as the service was held at the Anglican Church on Breadalbane Street. The horses were all covered with black flynets and all were skittish and nervous on the way to the church. Sootie spoke not a word to anyone but he noticed that the horses were more agitated than ever. During the service the rattling continued relentlessly and the glass in the windows began singing, like crystal vibrating to a high pitched noise. Everyone seemed so used to the rattling that they no longer bothered to be disturbed by its changes and variations. Only father who had tolerated the relentless and unwanted intrusion on his grief, sensed a definite change in the noise and he also detected slight but pronounced motion. Sootie, who was in the back seat of the church, was fully aware of the definite aggression in the pattern. He managed to catch father's eye once and concern showed on both faces.

When the service was over and the hearse brought to the door to receive the casket again the horses were uncontrollable with nostrils flaring and heads up. The drive through the main area to the burial ground was difficult as a tight rein had to be maintained on all the teams. People along the route stopped work and doffed their hats out of respect for mother but you could tell that they too were now beginning to sense the change in the tremor activity.

Once at the grave site Reverend Cooper read a short commital passage and the casket was lowered into the ground. Father took a shovelful of earth and threw it onto the coffin to signify he accepted mother's death. It was an old family custom or tradition which he brought with him from Scotland. Just as the shovelful of earth struck the coffin a violent shock rumbled through the earth. The sides of the grave collapsed nearly covering the coffin completely in a matter of seconds. Trees swayed dizzily overhead and everyone at the graveside felt as though a rug had been pulled from underneath their feet. The ensuing rumble was deafening and a peculiar smell pervaded the air. Suddenly, everything was absolutely quiet! The trees stood without a leaf moving and, I'm sure we were all holding our breath also. Not a beast moved and the air seemed to be taken from us. We all stood absolutely terrified of what would happen next.

'Sootie finally moved. "The earth is finally at peace with itself," he said. "Come Thomas I will take you home now." We were all greatly affected but father was quite incoherent and accepted Sootie's arm.

'There was complete and absolute quiet in the village. The rattlings and movement had indeed ceased after a full month in which we were never without them. Father locked himself in his office again where he could at last have absolute quiet and be alone in his grief.'

'Your father didn't recover from Mary's death did he?'

'Never. He was never the same again. Georgina raised Louise and me. One year after mother's death Elizabeth married and moved to Lindsay where her husband owned the newspaper. Charles Desroche Barr was an influential man and Elizabeth had her hands full with children and entertaining so Louise eventually left for Lindsay also. Father rarely spoke to me of mother. He seemed some days to be quite normal but often he would be despondent and I relied on Sootie a great deal for company. We seemed to be always together after mother's death and always in trouble according to father.'

'Sootie told me some of your "exploits". Your father maybe had reason to be angry with you on occasion. No woman should have taken part in some of those pranks.'

'If I had to live my life over again I would not change a day in my early years. If Sootie walked in this very minute and asked me to tie the grocer's apron strings to the doorknob again I would. This time I'd make sure he didn't see me behind him.'

Annalee watched Clara as she scurried around putting tea on the table. Although the woman was sixty-six years of age she had the agility of a much younger woman. Her hair was literally standing untamed on her head and to talk to her you would never suspect the woman held to her peculiar habit of midnight walks and strange behaviour. Who else but Clara would race to the street, shovel in hand, as soon as a horse went by? What on earth would she ever do when there were no more horses. Cars do not leave droppings!'

'Clara. When Georgina dies I expect you will sell "Stonehome". You know you are welcome to stay with Tommy and me. This house is much too large for one person and you will need someone to take care of you in your old age.'

Clara looked at Annalee in absolute disbelief. She had never heard anything so utterly ridiculous.

'I will never leave "Stonehome" Annalee. I will always remain here, always! This is my home and my life. I will stay here forever.'

THE HOMECOMING — 1922

Clara could have said 'I told you so' but she didn't. She went to the station and acted as if Georgina had never been away. A different woman alighted from the north bound train, older and perhaps more mellow.

'Well aren't you going to lecture me and tell me you knew I'd be back?'

'No.'

'Aren't you going to ask me why?'

'No. 'tis none of my business.'

''I'll tell you anyway. They hated ants! Teetotalers all of them! Besides here is where I want to die and, believe it or not I want your company.'

Clara had waited years to hear those words but never let on she was moved almost to tears. 'The car is waiting. I din't think you should take an open cutter.'

The luggage was stowed in the front seat and the two women were assisted into the back seat. 'Could we go by way of main street?' It didn't take much longer to travel from the station to St. Andrews Street, so Clara agreed.

'Look at that Clara. I could walk into any store and buy an assortment of linen, china, jewellery, furniture and clothing. And cars; I was born too late! The street is lined with cars. They've taken the place of the horse.'

'If they haven't they surely will in the future.'

'I want to get behind the wheel of a car and drive. Speed appeals to me now.'

'You've changed Georgina. You're as I remember you when I was a child.'

'I haven't time anymore to feel sorry for myself. I spent a lifetime doing that. With weeks left I want to talk to you. I've not changed that much. I have good days and bad and I still drink Clara.'

'It's for medicinal purposes I would imagine.'

With the baggage unloaded and standing inside the doors of 'Stonehome' Georgina seemed to assume her former role. 'Why are these confounded buttons on the wall?'

'Electricity.'

'I know that. What are they doing on this wall?'

'Push one Georgina.' A push to the mother-of-pearl button produced light in the hall.

'It was senseless not to have the conveniences when the wires were going right past the house.'

'It's an expense!'

'It's a luxury. Push another.' Clara opened the door to the parlour which was now nicely lit up.

' "Stonehome" did not complain. It accepted the wires and fixtures gracefully. You should do the same.' Georgina pushed several more.

'It's still an expense we don't need.'

'I've borne the cost until now without your help. Don't let it concern you. I didn't think it was necessary to write you about the installation because you would have gotten upset.'

'You've probably installed a telephone also?'

'No. It is quite an expense and I don't understand how they work. I haven't gotten rid of the old cookstove either. You look tired. Come up to your room. I haven't changed it in any way.'

Georgina climbed the stairs with difficulty. There wouldn't be many trips up and down those seventeen steps! Clara sensed Georgina's thoughts.

'I would have moved your bedroom to the pantry downstairs but it is such a dingy, small room, you wouldn't be comfortable. I'll be here all the time and you mustn't get out of bed if you feel ill.'

'Not ill so much as pain, constant relentless pain. The violent illness will come later.'

The two settled into a routine. Clara ran up and down the stairs for Georgina on those day the pain was severe enough to keep her in bed and Annalee came often to give support and help.

'How long Clara? Has Doctor Groves said?'

'She might last until after Christmas. He can't be more specific. The woman has been through so much now.'

'We must have a good Christmas.'

A small tree was set up in the parlour with strings of small coloured glass beads in its branches. Old ornaments were unwrapped and parcels were tucked around its base. The village was full of Christmas entertainments at the Town Hall, churches and schools and Carolers came one evening to sing for Georgina. Annalee, Tommy, Clara and Georgina had Christmas dinner together, Georgina in good spirits propped up in an armchair.

'Have you ever been on a sleighride Tommy?'

'Not a big one.'

'There's nothing like it. Dangerous if you drive on ice but when you get two rigs racing each other it is exciting. The horses make the ride. Some take up the challenge of the race! Have you ever owned a horse?'

'Never. We don't have room at the cottage.'

'You'll have to get one to court your girl.'

'I'll probably use a car, Aunt Georgina.'

'A car will take all the fun out of courting.'

'I understand it's put a bit into courting!'

Georgina ignored Clara's remark and continued. 'There wasn't much danger. Occasionally a cutter would tip but the snow was soft in the ditches.'

'I remember Marie telling us of a friend of hers who died as a result of a sleighride. The young lady had gone out for a ride with her beau and was too shy to mention that she needed to use an outhouse. They drove miles and she never said a word, just suffered agonies. When he finally stopped and said "How was that ride Nellie?" she stood up in the cutter and fell over dead!'

'Do you recall two years ago while the Presbyterian Elders were meeting on the hill someone sneaked into the driving shed, switched some of the horses, unhitched others and finally broke or stole all the lamps. When the men came out of session they couldn't see a thing. What confusion! Some just went home with the wrong horse and they sorted the mess out the next day.'

'I recall when we opened our own front door to find a horse in the entrance. He'd bolted with the train up here and ran through the picket fence, right up the steps. The driver was left holding the reins, sitting on the wagon at the picket fence. You said the noise at the door was probably Sootie. But I said "no, what I am seeing isn't Sootie, unless he's changed in the past week!" '

'You're much safer in a car these days.'

'Not so, just last week a horse bolted on the main street and ran right up the front of a new car parked by Steele Bros. There were hoof marks all over the hood and roof of the car and the owner stood there repeating . . . "my new car . . . my new car . . .!' Oscar Day walked by and said "not any more it isn't!" '

'Is everyone ready for the plum pudding?' Clara went to the kitchen and brought back a large molasses and spice enriched pudding. She heated a silver ladle of brandy over a candle, lit it and poured the flaming liquid over the pudding.

'Father tried this once. He tried heating his brandy but it wouldn't light. So he figured he needed more on the pudding. He poured a bottle of the finest brandy over the pudding and tried to light the whole thing. It turned out to be coloured water and the pudding was soggy and ruined. Everyone blamed Sootie! It turned out to be one of the maids who drank!'

At Sootie's name everyone at the table fell silent, each to her own thoughts. Annalee and Clara remembered the good times. Georgina was thinking back fifty years. She had actually envisioned herself Sootie's wife. He was a year or two older than she, but so uneducated and childish. She eventually put the thought out of her mind. It bothered her to this day to think that she had found him physically attractive, for it was his masculinity that drew her to him. She assumed it was a weakness of hers and hardened her attitude to men in general. With the exception of Abraham Groves they all seemed uncouth, uneducated and bawdy.

New Year's day Georgina took to her bed and Clara was now her constant companion and nurse. She sat in the darkened, muted room by the side of the bed. Georgina asked that the curtains be drawn. The light was a reminder of the outside world and an intrusion on her last days.

'You love this house, don't you?'

'I have never loved anything as much.'

'I was jealous of the attention you paid "Stonehome" rather than your family.'

'I didn't ignore you.' Oh how time and pain warp the mind. It was Georgina who ignored her!

'I understand now. In the forty-four years I have shared the house with you it never demanded my loyalty or trust as the humans who shared my outside world did. Everyone around me complained, demanded, lied . . . but this house stood ready to accept me for what I was and it stands now sheltering me from the present. I needn't worry about the future. I wasn't very pleasant was I?'

'You were my sister. You are my Georgina.'

'I learned how to live with people much too late in life.'

'You were an intelligent, brilliant woman who was born too soon. No one understood you properly and you were frustrated by Victorian standards which kept women at home waiting on their male counterparts. I adjusted more readily to that life than you.'

'You've bathed, dressed and fed me and I realize I've kept everything on such an impersonal level I don't know much about you.'

'I'm as complex a woman as you, perhaps more so.'

'We're both beyond redemption!'

'I've accepted that fact. I expect I shall become quite senile. I do things now with no accounting for my behaviour. I shall live up to our reputation of the "mad sisters of that house".'

Even speech became difficult for Georgina as she was under heavy medication for nausea and pain. Clara propped her up on pillows to enable her to breathe more easily. Annalee and she took turns at bedside watch, day and night.

'Clara?'

'Yes, I'm beside you.'

'Your hand, could I hold your hand?' Cold fingers gripped Clara's warm hand.

'What day is it?'

'Wednesday.'

'Have you painted my room? The light is so bright.'

'I have not touched your room. The curtains are drawn.'

'You're wondering where it was, aren't you?'

'Where what was Georgina?'

'The whiskey! It was in a tea tin in the kitchen. You never did find that hiding spot did you?'

'No, I didn't.'

'Clara? I'm sorry . . . I'm sorry . . .' The fingers relaxed their hold.

DIED

In Fergus, Wednesday January 17, 1923,
Georgina Margaret Young in her 77th year
daughter of the late Mr. & Mrs. Thomas A. Young.

Overlooking Fergus from the Beatty Watertower near the train station.

THE NEWSPAPER AND ITS EDITOR — 1926

Hugh Templin was right on time. He pulled into the laneway of 'Stonehome' and Clara was at the door waiting. George Templin, Hugh's uncle, was the Essex dealer in the village, the cars sharing room in the St. Andrews Street Building with the carriages. Of course, Hugh drove an Essex. For some months he had been driving older residents of the village through its streets getting their recollections and memories on paper for use in his columns. It was Clara's turn in the front seat.

'You're the only woman that hasn't kept me waiting while she adjusted her hat.'

'And you've a bit of the silver tongue in your head, Mr. Templin!' She had a lot of respect for this man behind the wheel. He was carrying on a great tradition in the history of the village. Fergus wasn't the first in the area to have a newspaper. Guelph and Elora both claimed that honour but in 1854, August 15, George Pirie of the Guelph Herald ran the first copy of The Fergus Freeholder. In 1856, Clara's birthyear, Thomas Gibbs started a paper called the British Constitution which a year later absorbed the 'Freeholder'. In 1867 the name became 'The News Record'. Other papers were started, the Fergus Express and Wellington Advertizer by Wm. Pemberton, The Advocate in 1885 and 'The Fergus Canadian' in 1903 but the 'News Record' survived all.

'You know your paper is as old as I?'

'A woman telling her age is a rare woman indeed!'

'When you are as old as I you have nothing to hide.'

'Everyone has something to hide.'

Clara mulled that statement over in her mind. 'You're right. Take your "Local News" column. It doesn't tell one quarter of what's really going on in the village.'

'It only tells what people want us to know. You, in my opinion, in your walks round the village at night could probably write me a good gossip column.'

'You'd be sued if you were ever to print what I sometimes see.'

'Is the village that bad?'

'Not having lived anywhere else, I've nothing to compare it to.'

Hugh had driven down to the Town Hall and parked in front of the Miss' McQueen's property. 'Tell me all you know about that house.' He pointed to the stone building on the river bank to the right of the Town Hall.

'It'll take all day.'

'I've the time.' He retrieved pencil and notebook.

'Rev. E.G. Fessenden lived there with his family, four sons, in 1870. Miss Ardaugh was the governess and teacher of the boys and a friend of ours. They left in 1876, went to Niagara. The one son, Reginald became an inventor; still alive and at it actually. The wireless telephone (radio), the heterodyne principle, relay wireless, wireless compass, flexible insulating cloth, the tracer bullet and the Pherescope, a seeing radio that throws a picture on a screen are all his inventions. He broadcast from shore to ship in 1907 and spoke the first words across the Atlantic in 1908.

'Peter Perry just received a letter from him. I'm going to publish it in the newspaper. As a boy he remembered this Parsonage and its russet apples, the "Old Armitage Place" and its plums, the brook back of Dr. Ortons, the mill and sled riding. He especially mentions the Church at Harvest Home and Christmas with its decorations.

'Ah . . . I remember the decorations! People used to bring the bounties of the harvest, sheaves of wheat, corn, apples, pumpkins, squashes and grapes. The sanctuary was beautifully decorated with the harvest produce and sheaves of wheat stood by each pew. Evergreen and cedar boughs and ropes, candles and wild red cranberries decorated the church at Christmas.'

'He wrote that the Grand River or contact with the Scottish pioneers influenced many electrical inventors. Edison lived at its mouth in his early years; Bell, of the telephone, resided at Brantford; himself at Fergus and MacKenzie or Mann of the power transmission was from Guelph.'

'We've been blessed with many great men from Fergus and Elora . . . Charles Clarke of the Insane Asylum in Toronto. Remember his father in Elora always looking for likely candidates for his son's asylum? David Boyle, a blacksmith by trade and teacher by profession whose collection of specimens began as a museum in Elora and eventually formed the basis for an entire department at the Royal Ontario Museum.

'And Frank Mann "Tater" Harris who writes for the Star Weekly.'

'Why the name "Tater"?'

'It's a nickname acquired because when he visited his grandfather he mistook the young potato bugs on the vines for a new species of taste berry!

'There's J. Connon of Elora, J. Black of Blackburn the cattle dealer and Mrs. Fessenden herself who founded The Daughters of the Empire.'

'Don't forget Thayendanegea, Chief Joseph Brant. The Grand River is synonymous with his name and history.' Clara pointed across the street. "Matthew Anderson had a blacksmith shop opposite the Town Hall but in the early part of the century he made it into a home, and Hugh Black owned that corner property.'

'The Town Hall . . .'

'Really the Drill Shed.' Clara interrupted.

'That building has quite a history. Recently it's had its share of political meetings with the elections coming along.'

'Meighen will lose.'

*The House of Industry and refuge — 'The Poor House' — midway between
Fergus and Elora.*

'If he does he'll have been in Ottawa only two and one half months! How do you know so much about politics?'

'I follow them . . . even went to a political meeting once. Rev. Beecher Parkhouse was chairing the meeting, funny little fellow that he is. The hall was full . . . of men. There were maybe a dozen women. I knew I was in trouble as soon as I walked in. A young fellow came up and said, "There's a seat to the left towards the front.' I looked and all the known Conservatives were sitting on the left. Immediately another young man scurried up and said, "I think you'll find an empty seat over there,' and he began steering me to the right. That was the territory of the Liberals!

"No thank you.' I said, 'I'll stand.' I wasn't about to wear my politics on my sleeve!

'It'll be a long meeting and standing will be quite uncomfortable Ma'am.'

'Then get me a chair, young man.' Both of them turned away to get a chair figuring a chair would buy them a vote and they both arrived behind me at the same time, chairs locking legs like bulls locking horns!'

Hugh started the car and drove up St. Andrews Street towards Elora. New houses lined the street but once on top of the hill the land lay flat and open. At Kinettles, a stone farm house on the right, the old Harvey house on the left, the railway trestle and the "Poor House" were visible. They drove until they reached the circular drive of the 'House of Industry and Refuge'.

'My father used to say "Don't ever let me end up in the Poor House". It has quite a reputation.'

'When it was built in 1877 it was considered one of the best in the Province. The concept was right. The County was prepared to take care of its destitute and poor.'

'It wasn't the County that was to blame for its reputation. It was the Keeper and the Matrons they hired. Some were tyrants.'

'We have no idea what they were faced with during their terms.'

They were entrusted with the care of fellow human beings and were to show some compassion for their sufferings.'

'The lives of those inmates would make for a good book.'

'It's such a peaceful setting for a Poor House, on a hill between the two communities always feuding.'

'Sparked by comments from other editors. You probably read the editorial comments of the Arthur Enterprise. He was eulogizing on my comments about a shared high school. I can quote verbatim: "Someday, when the dreams of the Fergus News Record are realized, and the two places have expanded and developed to such an extent that they come together in one big community, a joint high school may be built. In the meantime, this growth will have to go on with the Poor House only, the centre and common goal of these two thriving communities."

'I replied that a poor house was better separating us than thirteen miles of hot air blowing from the Arthur direction.'

'I disagree with your comments that the two communities will eventually be one. That time will never come about. There's too much pride in each village. I can't imagine the day they would share a school.'

'There was pride in Aboyne and Kinnettles too and look what happened to them. You used to be able to see the mills at Aboyne from this driveway and now there is only a ruin to show where the village stood. Back there at Kinettles only two houses stand where a settlement was planned, Lingwood's and Harvey's'

'You can't have four villages within three miles of each other. The strongest survived and they happened to be Fergus and Elora.'

Hugh drove around the circular laneway of 'the Poor House' and turned his car back towards Fergus.

'What do you know about the Harvey Place.' He pointed towards the large stone house situated between the road and the river.

'It was built and lived in by Webster around 1838 shortly after he married. He even had a tunnel built from the cellar to the river where he kept a boat to use for fishing. There was also a good spring down at the end of the tunnel and the housemaids used to fetch water from it. The house had a cellar kitchen and the tunnel was used as a pantry. It had a heavy wooden door at the river end.'

'I heard the tunnel was built in case of Indian attack.'

'That's misinformation and you know it! We never had any trouble with the Indians! I couldn't find the river entry if I tried but I could take you right to where the passage began in the the cellar of the house. There were some fine parties held at that house when Harvey owned it but he had some enemies too. Someone actually tried to burn the building down around his ears one night.'

'Do you remember the gala events at all?'

'I was never allowed to attend so I can't tell you anything about them. I do know Harvey bought the property in 1855 with the intention of founding Kinnettles and he had the entire property surveyed and divided into lots. Webster was the land agent for him.'

The car swung over the Tower Street bridge and turned sharp left on Queen Street. Hugh stopped in front of a frame, rough cast house.

'What about this place?'

'Miss Unsworth's school, between Grindley's old foundry building and White's furniture. Mrs. Tobin's residence is at the top of the angle. After Miss Unsworth, Wm. Murray lived there. He had a shoemaker's shop on top of the little hill on Union Street which employed several men.'

'What about Miss Unsworth?'

'It was a small school and in opposition to the village school but her pupils used to write exams in the village buildings. Because her classroom was too small for all her pupils they used to attend at staggered hours. She was a strict teacher but the students were well drilled. The school was called The Fergus Girls School but some younger boys were accepted. She taught for five years and left in April 1860. The McQueen's and Cattanach's attended her school for a time.'

'Your mind amazes me. Most people have forgotten the school.'

'I've never let my mind idle. It might be fuzzy now and again but most of the early details remain clear as a bell. It's recent events I don't remember.'

'Do you remember Mr. Burgess, the teacher?'

'Only that he had a habit of rocking his chair back and forth on its legs and one day he overbalanced. He fell backwards hitting his head. The pupils saw the humour in it but he didn't and gave them pages to do as punishment for laughing. His classroom was so cold that two women were heard to mutter when they left after a visit "Another minute and my bum would have been frozen to the chair." '

'We've one more place to visit before you'll take me home for a cup of tea and a slice of your famous Molasses cake.' The car turned onto St. David Street and went north to St. George where Hugh made a left turn.

'That old log cabin on the left is in jeopardy if Charlie Mattaini has his way. He wants the Council to put the rink on the land. That cabin and the house next to it will have to come down if the building goes on the hill.'

'I thought someone mentioned it would be moved down Provost Lane. It's the oldest structure in the village built in 1834. The rink will cover the spring!'

'Charlie figured he can tile it right down to the river. No one will know the spring or brewery ever existed. Such is progress.'

'Do you agree with progress, especially in the village?'

'Of course! It's the only way the village can survive. It's not going to be a village long Clara. There's serious talk of incorporating into a town soon.'

They crossed Provost Lane and pulled up in front of an unassuming frame house on the north corner of Tower and St. George Street.

'Ah, you want to know about Alex Fordyce Jr.'

'And his library.'

'The house suited the man, inconspicuous and quiet. He came as a young man in 1835 and shared a cabin with Valentine for the first winter then took land in Nichol next to Valentine. He was a mild mannered, gentle man who sketched for a hobby. His glowing accounts of Fergus and Nichol pursuaded his father Alex Fordyce Sr. to settle near him in Nichol in 1836. From the beginning I think Alex Jr. figured he made a mistake! His father completely overshadowed the man. The elder Fordyce was a stern, aggressive man indeed! In late 1836 this house was built and Alex Jr. with his sister Elizabeth moved in. He took his selection of good books with him and set up one room of his home as a public library. They were both lovely people. Elizabeth died in 1891 and Alex, a close friend of Father's three months before father died. In 1857, a year after I was born, the library became the Farmer's Mechanic's Institute but Alex still ran it from his home with Elizabeth's help. He was also the School Superintendent of North Wellington.'

'Was he a lonely man?'

'I think so. His father when he moved into the village in 1842 took over everything Alex Jr. did so well, except the library. The elder Fordyce died in 1852 at Belsyde. He was the driving force of the Presbyterian Church.'

'Did people frequent the library as much as they do now?'

'Even more because there were few other entertainments in the 50's and 60's that the women could attend. They sat at home and read political histories and travel journals, etiquette books and recipe books.'

Hugh pulled the car around the corner onto Tower and turned right at Garafraxa Street.

'Up here somewhere a man lived by the name of "Sootie", a strange character too, from all reports. Did you know him?'

'I don't readily recall the face.' Clara could be very vague when necessary. 'Are you thinking of the two Frenchmen who worked in the saw mill? They moved to Arthur and settled somewhere up on the Owen Sound Road.'

'No I mean a fellow by the name of Sootie. I vaguely remember the man but paid little attention to the stories I heard about him. In talking to the older people his name keeps cropping up.'

'You can't recall ever hearing the last name of the man?'

'No, come to think of it I haven't.'

'Without a last name I'm lost on details of people. Besides you've asked enough questions of an old woman for one day. Pull around the corner and I'll make you that cup of tea.'

The corner of Tower and Queen Sts. 1920's, not too far from Miss Unsworth's School.

THE DEPARTURE — 1927

The years pass quickly as time has a habit of never standing still. Annalee and Tommy had, in the past several years, found life in Fergus rather difficult and they were leaving to live in England. They sat waiting in the garden for a car to take them to Toronto. Their baggage had gone on before and the household effects had been sold by auction. Annalee kept several personal articles which had belonged to Sootie for herself but gave the rest to Clara, who had walked down to say good-bye. Tommy watched at the gate for the auto.

'You do realize why I must go. Tommy's getting older and the questions are far more pointed than before. Children can be so cruel to each other. How could they be so malicious to a fourteen year old?'

'Easily, if they are encouraged. Does Tommy understand why you are going to England?'

'Once we're settled I'll tell him the truth. It can't be told now, while his father lives in the village. He's part of the reason I'm leaving. In the past year he's not left the boy or myself alone. People are beginning to talk. I've done nothing to encourage him but neither apparently has his wife!'

'If I were younger Annalee, I would go with you, not to live but to see if I could find Sootie's grave. You remember the information in the letter . . . the names . . . the places. Follow his footsteps carefully. Perhaps you can find something he overlooked. Write me often. Your letters will give me something to live for.'

'Clara, don't talk as though you were going to die!'

'Have you looked at me recently? Have you listened to me? I feel old . . . I forget . . . I repeat myself . . . I get confused easily. When you leave I expect my reasons for living will leave with you.'

Annalee patted the time-worn hand. Every word Clara uttered was true. She had watched as the woman who accepted her into home and heart in 1897 matured, then grew old. As the years passed, her eccentricities became quite apparent to everyone and she was known locally as 'the queer Miss Young'. She was still the energetic woman Annalee admired but old age had taken its toll on her.

'Everyone ages to some degree. I am not the youthful girl you welcomed at Christmas twenty-eight years ago. Who would have known then the problems we've surmounted together.'

'Will I ever see you again . . . or Tommy?'

'I won't return to Canada and it will be up to Tommy whether he wants to return when he's of age. By then he'll know the truth but I'll not give up Clara until I find Sootie's family. I have all the pictures and personal documents he left. Somewhere I'll find a clue to his identity.'

'He tried so hard but died without any new clue, Annalee.'

'Did he die? The letter didn't say so. It only said he was "officially dead" but it was in his own handwriting. I have to see a grave before I'll believe him dead. Someone must have seen him die.'

'I've wondered too Annalee. All these years I've asked myself the same question, but it's impossible that he's alive. He'd be an eighty year old man.'

'Your father lived to be 84 and it's not impossible if he set his mind to it to deceive us. He could have posted the letter himself or he could have left it with someone.'

'We're both talking nonsense now. Why would he do such a thing?'

'To uncomplicate my life Clara. He couldn't write you either if he was "officially dead". I'll persist until I find something or someone.'

'There was a war. Records will be obscure. So many people died. Annalee, is there a possibility?'

'I should never have opened the subject Clara. I've gotten you upset. Look now . . . I've closed all my accounts, transferred my monies and all traces of my living in the village will be erased when I leave, except for you, who knows my story. You've kept Sootie's secret and I know you've kept mine. Leaving you is the hardest decision I've ever had to make. Had life dealt you justice, you would have been my mother and Tommy's grandmother.'

'I was a naive woman who mistook love for childish affection and I never took anything seriously until it was too late. I took security from an object rather than a person because . . . I can't explain why. The explanation has never come clear to me. All I know is I had my security, "Stonehome" even after Sootie left and I'll have it now when you go. I'll go home and shut the door and I'll be alright.'

Tommy raced around the side of the house. 'Mom, the car is here.' He was a young man, tall, dark haired with a healthy tan skin. There was an awkard silence as the three realized they had to say good-bye. Annalee rose from the bench and busied herself with her dress. Tommy fidgeted from one foot to the other, then ran to Clara throwing his arms around her. Young men do not cry easily but Tommy cried against Clara's shoulder.

'Hush child.' She stroked his head. 'You'll come back to see me.' 'She kissed the wet salty cheek, her tears mingling with his. 'You'll come back.' He tore himself away and ran to the car.

'Annalee, the poor child!'

'Clara.' Annalee's eyes were full of tears too.

'Don't say anything. I know . . . I know . . .'

Annalee put her arms around Clara and kissed the dear old woman on the cheek.

'Write me. Don't ever forget to write.'

'I won't.' The tear-choked Annalee followed Tommy to the car. They waved and threw kisses as the car pulled away from the curb leaving a sad old lady standing on the sidewalk.

Dr. Groves, a parrot on his shoulder, tapped Archie on the shoulder and waved him on.

'Drive it Arch.'

'Shouldn't we offer Miss Young a ride home, sir?'

'We shouldn't let Miss Young know we were even on this street young man!' He was still no closer to the true story of Tommy than he had been on an April day fourteen years before when he delivered the child into the world.

THE QUILTERS — 1929

The sun, coming through the lace curtains of the dining room windows, spread its soft light over the intricate pattern of the quilt the three women were working on. The colours of the patchwork danced before Clara's eyes as her fingers nimbly drew the needle through the fabric.

The three women were as different to each other as day is to night and hot is to cold. Clara was still impetuous, independent and very eccentric balancing Fanny Tobin who was a no nonsense, methodical woman who relied on her daughter for support and companionship. Marie was the balance between the two. She was a full generation younger than both Clara and Fanny but the trio were the closest and best of friends. The two white-haired women bent to the task of stitching as enthusiastically as the black haired Marie. The quilt frames were set up at Fanny's so that Marie could slip across the road to help and not be far away from home and family. Clara certainly didn't mind the walk across the village.

'Have you counted the number of times we've done this pattern Fanny?'

'I lost track a long time ago and if Clara wasn't so insistent I start another, I'd be putting the frames away. I'm getting far too old for this?'

'There is no such thing as being too old to sew! Quilting is the only thing that takes me away from "Stonehome". Otherwise I'd never leave. I never keep track of time and two or three days might go by before I realize I haven't made myself a decent meal. That's when I walk over to visit and sew.'

'That's a sign of old age, the forgetting to eat proper meals and not caring about the time or day.'

'It's nice to have someplace to come to. If I want a quiet day I quilt and if I want action I visit Marie's.'

'You would never have a quiet hour across the road at my house Clara.'

'I don't mind the young people around but it's too confusing for me to keep track of their comings and goings and their friends. They're all so grown up now with young lady friends and Jimmy's thinking of going to the University of Toronto I'm told.'

'He's a young man now Clara, not the little boy you remember so fondly and he has a young lady friend, Edith Scott. Fanny sits here and watches the young people across the street shaking her head in disgust at some of the carryings on.'

'They're young rippers, all of them! I can't imagine young people smoking and holding hands in broad daylight!'

'Now Fanny. They're a new generation. Friendship is a great asset in life.

The three of us are proof of that.'

'I suppose you're right Clara. Do you remember the first time we met? It was on that hot Sunday in 1862 when both our families were attending the Free Church. Your father was a confirmed Anglican but he had been invited to attend the services dedicating the enlargement and renovation of the interior of the building. Because it was so hot the main doors were left open to allow for a bit of a breeze. Low and behold, in the middle of the service, two good sized pigs sauntered sedately down the centre aisle. My brother said afterward they were "highly respectable Presbyterian pigs". As soon as you saw them you began to giggle and your father tried to hush you. My family was sitting directly behind yours. The louder your father whispered, the more you giggled. He finally took you firmly by the elbow and marched you smartly up the aisle to the doors. As soon as he'd left his seat the pigs turned and began following you out of the church. It was quite a procession and reminded me of "the Pied Piper" so I began to giggle too and was ordered outside by my father.'

'We spent the remainder of the service sitting in the meadow beside the church watching the people cross Tower Bridge. We weren't very old.'

'I never heard this story before! I thought I was the only one that could be accused of running pigs in the Free Church!'

'It was scullduggery of the part of some character in the village. Everyone tried putting the blame on the new lad, Sootie, but he denied he would ever "think" up such a diabolical trick. Clara and I saw him though, herding the pigs back across Tower Street bridge when we were sitting in the meadow.'

'We didn't say a word to anyone about seeing Sootie. Father would have been furious for he was living with us at the time. When I told Sootie I'd seen him, he admitted he'd done it on a bet from a staunch Presbyterian up on the hill.'

'St. Andrew's was rebuilt in 1862 also but no pigs walked down the aisle at their dedication! It was the sound of a key-bugle that disturbed their service. Mr. Perry used to summon the congregation to the 'Auld Kirk' with his bugle before the bell was installed and he blew it at the dedication of the new church. In the middle of the most solemn dedication prayer a small child, who'd sneaked the bugle off the seat beside Mr. Perry, found out how it worked! The reverend figured he'd been called for and his book leaped out of his hands, hitting the floor with such a whack it sounded like a gunshot. Anyone trying to sleep through that service certainly got a rude awakening.'

'We Catholics are a pious lot. There is no such nonsense in our church, except when "wee Bobbie" put his pet toad in his pant's pocket before he had to serve mass. It managed to hop its way out of his cassock right onto the altar. It leaped from one end of the altar to the other with Father and Bobbie after it clutching at mid air all the way across as the toad kept one leap ahead of them. They had the congregation on its feet wondering just what was taking place. They finally cornered it and Bobbie carried it outside. "Wee Bobbie's" a big man now and doesn't like to be reminded of the incident. The boys call him "Toadie".'

'That particular gentleman was at "Stonehome" the other day wanting to know if I'd ever thought seriously of selling the house. He said there was a shortage of housing in the village and he didn't see why I should be keeping such a large house "all to myself". Those were his words exactly. I told him the very idea that he would come and ask me made me angry and then I ordered him out, chasing him all the way to the street with my broom. Why should I sell my house? It's the only thing I have left. It and my memories. Why don't people just let me be in my house. He is the third person to come around and they all receive the same treatment. I always keep a broom handy by the front door.'

'Maybe they consider they are being kind offering to take the house off your hands. Maybe they feel it's too difficult for you to maintain.'

'Posh Fanny! They're in it for the money but they won't buy my home, none of them.'

'What will happen to "Stonehome" when you die Clara? You have no children to inherit the property.'

Clara was silent for a long time, her head down, her fingers rethreading her needle. When she glanced up Marie and Fanny could see they had upset her.

'I don't know. I can't give you an answer because I have never given that question any serious thought before. I suppose I assumed I'd live forever. That's what each of us wishes we could do isn't it?'

Main Street looking west, Fergus, Ontario, Canada 1930.

THE OLD AND THE BEATEN — 1930

Fate has a reputation for altering the destinies of people, bringing the strong to their knees and elevating the weak to positions of authority. as the years unfolded in the village Charlie managed to amass quite a fortune through his various endeavours, both above and below board. It'was fate that eventually brought Charlie and the depression of "29" together at the exact moment in his successful career when he was most vulnerable. He invested in the grain market and lost heavily. He sat now, hands on his head, on the verandah of his home, a broken man, quietly looking at the floor but not really focusing on the boards. He had lost everything . . . his wife . . . his children . . . his business.

'Charlie.' He looked up trying to focus on the man in front of him and groping for his glasses in his pocket at the same time.

'So that's what you are going to do. You're going to sit here and feel sorry for yourself.'

Charlie bent the glasses around his ears and Doc came into view.

'I'm going to sit here with this sore head forever. No one would care.'

'Your head is aching again is it? Aren't you going to invite me to share your step?'

Charlie moved to allow Doc some room and slid his bottle behind the wooden pillar of the verandah so Doc wouldn't see it. Doc noticed the move but didn't say anything. It wasn't drink that was causing Charlie's violent headaches, but something far more serious.

'Why didn't you tell Marie or me about the severity of the headaches when they began? Why did you leave it until it was too late?'

'It wouldn't have made any difference between us. It was my temper that caused her to leave.'

'But the rages are caused in part by the headaches. Whatever happened in the accidents caused a personality change. Don't you remember anything? Think of the accident in "25".'

'I remember rounding the corner back of Beatty Bros, heading for the construction site. The train was coming round the corner too. I remember the train coming at the truck and everything began to crack. The sound of wood and metal breaking began and everything went blank. I don't remember being hit. Next I remember lying in a bed with you leaning over me.'

'All I could find was a mangled foot. Your clothing was torn off you but there was no bump or bruise on your head. They shouldn't have moved you. Perhaps there was something wrong with your neck. You must have hit your head though because the headaches started after that. You didn't do yourself any good when you smashed your head against the roof of the car two years later, on Elgie's hill. You live dangerously Charlie.'

'I always did. It wasn't my fault the second time either. The men washed the cut in the creek water.'

'And you almost died of blood poisoning. Marie nursed you back to health.'

'But the headpains got worse and my eyes are affected now. Today the head hurts like hell!'

'Did you ever really speak to Marie about your problems?'

'Yes. But I am not a man of gentle words and she is a determined woman. She couldn't understand Doc . . . why I drink . . . my nightmares. A friend told me once the memories of Africa would not let me rest and he was right.'

'Maybe if we both tried talking to her.'

'It's too late. Her house is built up there by her mother's and the children are with her. She's only two blocks away but miles away emotionally from me. She doesn't need me now. I'm broke and I've nothing left to give her.'

'Marie didn't ask anything but love and understanding.'

'It's best she went. The children are grown up now and I'm not a good influence on them. There was always shouting and fighting. I couldn't control the anger. They are good children . . . rebels like me but with Marie's blood in them. They'll do alright.'

'You're not a rebel Charlie as much as an eccentric. What are you going to do?'

'I have some property left I can sell. As long as I have a little money to buy whiskey I'll have friends. They'll come like flies. As soon as I run out of whiskey they'll leave. Then I'll go crazy, slowly.'

'You don't need those type of friends. They are leeches!'

'They are all that's left. When you have money, independence, success you command respect and are listened to. People come around because they want to be part of your success. When you lose it, the village considers you a blemish and you are forgotten.'

'You had everything.'

'I even learned to speak the English but not to write it well. You know Marie and I were from the same village in Italy yet are two different cultures. She is Canadian and I am Italian.'

'She is also Italian!'

'But she came at such a young age the traditions and customs of her homeland were forgotten quickly. I expected an obedient homewife. Italian women do not question their husbands! She is different . . . independent, strong, questioning. She will be alright Doc. She has talents and is a business woman. She'll demand respect in the village.'

'Why don't you begin again? Start fresh.'

'I'm too old and have lost the desire. It takes years of hard work to build a company and six months to totally destroy it.'

'I lost thousands speculating in the stocks and grain markets.'

'There were good times for both of us, weren't there? I'm an old man Charlie but I've not regretted a day of my life. When I came back to the village in '71 there was a job to be done. The villagers needed prodding. There was so much potential here all going to waste. They were beginning to rest on their laurels.'

'You pushed Doc. You fought for improvements and even paid for some of them out of your own pocket. I wish I were here in the 80's and early 90's. We would have made a good team. You had a plan for the village.'

'You had a plan also. You pushed as much as I. You cajoled the right people into spending money on improvements. You took a loss on some of the jobs also just to get the job done properly . . . the waterworks . . . the arena. Your methods might have been slightly underhanded but you got action on cheaper homes for the needy, decent sidewalks . . .'

'To get to the roosters you talk to the hens first! It was easy to plant suggestions in this village of gossiping women.'

'Too bad about the high school parked up there on the windy hill. The land should have been left for expansion of the park. They'll regret their decision in thirty years time.'

'You see that Doc but the councillors and school board don't. They bought the land over there by the old church, Craig's house now, for $500.00 from me in '25 for the school . . . Then Beatty Bros. donated land on Colquhoun Street . . . Then the merchants say the school isn't needed. They eventually end up with at least five sites proposed! Such a mess! And they were all mad at me because I received $500.00 and they decided not to use my land!'

'Davie was in to the house last week and asked about you. Do you remember Davie and the "raise" you gave him?'

'Ah Davie! . . . of the Guelph Bridge. Such a temper the man had! He came to me second week of the job on the Friday payday.

' "You paid the young boys as much as me yet I worked twice as hard." he said.

'That's my way. My men are paid equally. A young lad will work just as hard as he can and deserves a man's wage. Because you are stronger does not mean you put more effort into the labour than a weakling who tries his best.'

'He began to argue but I turned my back to him. I don't like fighting. He lost his temper completely and came at me swinging so I picked him up bodily and threw him into the river. He swam out madder than ever, climbed up the bank and began swinging again. I threw him in again . . . back out again . . . in again . . . four times! Finally he dragged himself out of the water and just stood there in front of me.

'I said "You got a raise. You just earned it." He worked twice as hard as he had before. Maybe he was afraid I would rinse him again. Do you remember my concrete boots?'

'You had one as a door stop at the barn. If I recall the men took your boots, set them in the wooden sill forms and poured them full of concrete.'

'After that I waited until they were all asleep at the bridge camp one night and took most of their socks, filled them with wet concrete and hung them on the cook's pan line.'

'You sure had the devil in you Mattaini when you took the Scots up on their own territory . . . curling!'

'Groves, you don't realize curling, like the bagpipes, originated in Italia. It wasn't exactly the same but similar. The Romans introduced both when they conquered Britain.'

'Now Charlie, let's not get into that argument!'

'I'm serious Doc when I say the village has been my home for the last twenty-four years and I wouldn't want to have it any other way. Sure there were insults and insinuations but I never carried a grudge. I learned to tolerate everything. It's been harder on my children. Strange enough it is the members of their own church, the Catholics, who are narrowminded and intolerant of them.'

'It'll be that way well into the next generation Charlie. The English are coming into the village now but they are not as volatile as the Irish and Italians. I know they are a docile people.'

'Better for them that they are. But that's not my worry now. I leave it up to my children. I'm going to try to concentrate on all the good times I remember. Sometimes this head hurts so much it takes all my strength just to think but I've got to remember the good times. Do you understand Doc?'

'Completely Charlie. There is one question I would like to ask you. Did Marie ever mention anything about the child of Sootie's? You know how women are when they get together. Annalee was friendly with her. Did she ever speak to you about . . . the boy . . . the mother?'

'That's a strange question Doc considering the man's been gone for fourteen years and the boy and mother for three.'

'It's important to me Charlie. Think hard.'

'There's no need to think. She told me nothing about either the boy or his mother. I don't listen to idle gossip of women. I know nothing about the family.'

Doc sighed and rose to leave.

'I'll be around the corner if you need me. You don't buy my friendship with whiskey.'

The old doctor made his way back up Union Street. He turned back once and waved but Charlie had already removed his glasses and couldn't see him. There was something wrong with Charlie's head. If Doc were a younger man he would operate. Possibly that would alter Charlie's violent outbursts. There had to be pressure from an old injury! Doc couldn't attempt the operation of so delicate a nature because his eyesight was failing him. He knew for certain Charlie would not allow another doctor near him! Even if he did operate what would he be looking for? The whole spectrum of mental illnesses and injuries associated with the brain was only just beginning to get attention. Doc wished he had another fifty years ahead of him. There was so much more to accomplish in the medical field. Perhaps he had been born too soon.

OCTOBER 1930

Clara stood looking out the front window on the late autumn day. She was stone deaf and couldn't hear a thing, not even the brass bell on the front door. Children were walking home from school, laughing and talking with their playmates. They must be laughing, for all children laugh as they never have a care in the world. Her ability to hear went gradually, the first indication that something was wrong came when she couldn't hear her canary singing.

Clara corresponded immediately with the Barrs in Lindsay. As Georgina predicted she found she needed family ties and the Barrs proved to be gracious relatives with a genuine interest and concern for her. When her deafness became very apparent and a problem the Barrs decided the best course of action would be for her to move to Lindsay. She flatly refused to leave "Stonehome" and a compromise was reached if she found a family to share the home with her. Each autumn she would leave to stay in Lindsay over the winter with her niece. It was not difficult finding a couple to care for her and share her home. It was an arrangement which was upsetting to her but necessary if she wanted to remain in "Stonehome" and she learned to accept it. The hard part was leaving each autumn and she was always overjoyed to return in the spring in plenty of time to see the lilac buds.

She stood by the window knowing she had only several hours of her life left to enjoy her home. 'Stonehome' had been her life for forty years. Memories clung tenaciously to each room and those memories kept her in her own small world of normality. When she left this time for Lindsay she would not return in the spring because she was dying of consumption. She had known for some time she wasn't feeling well but not being one to complain she didn't go to Dr. Groves until the pain she was living with became a nuisance. He offered no hope.

'You know it's consumption, don't you?'

'Of course. I watched Georgina die with it.'

'No one knows for sure who gets it and why it strikes. We only know there is no cure for it.'

'A cure would come too late for many now. It is an insidious disease. They will never find a cure for it. It takes too many forms.'

'We never know Clara. You shouldn't give up hope for the future. You know what you'll go through before it's over don't you'

Yes. I'm not afraid of the next six months. And I won't be alone.'

'You always see the bright side of the situation Clara. Tell me, what's the bright side of this one.'

'I'm thinking of those that went before ... Mother, father, Georgina, Louise. I believe there's something afterwards and they'll all be there.'

'Hold to your beliefs Clara, even during the roughest times.'

Yesterday she opened the room at the head of the stairs and spent the afternoon in her silent world going through its contents lovingly touching everything. Memories flowed through her mind as water might spill over a dam .. . a remembrance of mother when she fingered the delicate lacework on a table cover; and of Georgina when she touched the sewing machine Georgina had used for the last thirty years of her life. In a small leather bound trunk Clara found the letter she received fourteen years before from London, England. She sat for a long time with the letter clenched to her bosom. When she finally locked the door again she had the letter in her hand. She went immediately to the lilac tree in the garden, now a huge gnarled tree showing its age. Under it she dug a small hole, ripped the letter into shreds and buried it. She was determined Sootie's secret would die with her.

When she returned to the house she went from room to room remembering, as best she could, the events which made her life a joy to live ... Christmas, the quiet hours around the kitchen table, the baths in the pantry, Tommy and Annalee. 'Stonehome' surrounded her with warmth and security in her last hours within its walls.

She was still standing at the window when the 'girls' came along the street from the Beatty Plant. Times had certainly changed. The young woman were unescorted, with dresses up to their knees and short bobbed hair tucked into tight fitting caps. They too were laughing, as young women always had when there was something to be happy about. She envied them, not for their youth, but for their mobility. She hadn't the nerve to walk far from 'Stonehome' now with her hearing the way it was.

The scene before her too had changed. Where once there had been a dirt cart track, there was now a decent highway and sidewalks. Houses crowded in on 'Stonehome'. Cars sped by and trucks hauled goods from town to village where the rail lines didn't reach. The scene outside was completely foreign to her way of life. She realized suddenly that she had no place in this day and age. She was the woman of a different time intruding on a lifestyle she didn't understand. Her memories were so real to her and had been for so many years, she had lost all touch with reality. She was a product of the past suddenly out of date with the fast paced present.

She let the curtain fall slowly and wept quietly. Her life was coming to an end but she wept not for herself. She had reconciled herself to the fact she had only months to live. She wept for her beloved Sootie, the gentle, loving man born of the same era as she. The tears fell for the man who wished to remove all vestiges of himself from the village. With her death his wish would almost become a certainty. She had not questioned his request in the letter but followed his instructions carefully, methodically erasing every tangible trace of the man from Fergus.

She had one wish too that she hoped would not be forgotten. Her wish was that 'Stonehome' might be remembered in some small way as Thomas and Mary Young's contribution to the village. She did not wish to be remembered herself but she regretted that she had not left any children to carry on the name of Young. They would have been part of the bustling, foreign world outside her door which was so bewildering to her now. She was leaving nothing of herself except 'Stonehome' in the village. Its timeless edifice had fit in with the changing scenery gracefully . . . as though it was meant to.

'Stonehome' built like a small fortress was meant to last forever. Clara realized she was not.

DIED

At Lindsay, May 25, 1931, of consumption
at the home of her niece, Louise M. Barr,
Clara Isabella Young, age 75

Pat Mestern was born, raised and is presently living in Fergus, with her husband and four children. Although she works in the Wellington County Museum by day, at night she turns her talents to writing.

Anna
A child of the Poor House

The second offering from the pen of novelist Pat Mestern, "ANNA: A Child of the Poorhouse" is a fascinating story of the life of a young woman who was orphaned into a world of poverty, illness and abuse in rural Ontario in late Victorian times.

A traumatic childhood experience in the County poorhouse left Anna, heroine of the story, emotionally scarred and mute. Bound out at an early age to an elderly couple, Anna eventually finds herself in the home of a wealthy industrialist and his family in the Rosedale district of Toronto. Anna's life begins to take a dramatic turn for the better when the industrialist takes a fatherly interest in her. Through therapy her mute condition is eventually corrected. She returns to the Fergus area in 1904, now a wealthy and beautiful young woman seeking out the mystery of her past in the hope that she might achieve some emotional stability.

The fear of ending ones years in a poorhouse haunted the people of rural Victorian Ontario. The stigma of being born into the poorhouse is unparalleled in today's society. Mestern masterfully recaptures its aura and society's attitude towards the people who ended up under its roof. Her in-depth knowledge of local history and folklore has allowed Mestern to set the novel in the placid rural countryside of the Grand River valley and the villages of Fergus, Elora and Drayton. Mestern weaves a tale that blends the supernatural, mystery, wealth, blackmail and romance. However, it would be most accurate to call "Anna" a love story.

The poorhouse in Mestern's novel, a large forbidding stone building in the 1880's still stands today on the road between Fergus and Elora. Recently two eminent psychics found evidence that indeed several of Mestern's characters still roam the building's corridors, perhaps awaiting the return of beautiful Anna.

Cleverly written and beautifully presented "ANNA: A Child of the Poorhouse" can take its place in the ranks of good fiction written in Canada.

ANNA A CHILD OF THE POOR HOUSE:
Large Format 6"x9" soft cover, 328 pages — Historical Photos — $9.95.

Available at your local bookstore
or directly from Back Door Press, P.O. Box 182, Guelph, Ontario.